The Eye of the Seal

Daniel Garber

PAGE PUBLISHING, INC.
New York, NY

First originally published by Page Publishing, Inc. 2018

Illustrations by Sean McGraw

ISBN 978-1-64298-754-6 (Paperback)
ISBN 978-1-64298-755-3 (Digital)

Printed in the United States of America

Contents

CHAPTER ONE

Daniel Peterson, the Immigrant

Daniel Peterson was born in 1892 in Uppsala, Sweden. He married his wife, Olga Swenson, in 1910. Both were eighteen years old. Daniel worked in the woods as a lumberjack for several years, along with his brother, Carl. In 1913 Daniel went to work for his best friend, Ollie Stephenson. Ollie owned and operated several sawmills in Uppsala.

Daniel's wife, Olga, worked on her family's dairy farm until she became pregnant with their first of seven children. Olga was a natural beauty. She had long flowing blond hair, a beautiful smile, perfect teeth, blue eyes, a perfect body, and a personality to go along with it.

The Uppsala area was located in east central Sweden, between Malaren Lake and the Gulf of Bothia. Uppsala was noted for its dairy, potato, and grain farming. Sawmills and lumber were also dominant in the area.

After Daniel had worked for his friend Ollie for a year, Ollie bought two more sawmills. He promoted Daniel to manager of one of his mills and hired Daniel's brother, Carl, to work at one of his new mills. Ollie now had five sawmills and was doing very well financially.

Ollie, Daniel, Carl, and several other friends would attend family functions on Saturday nights. They would eat, drink, and polka every Saturday evening. These events were always held at Ollie's big home in Uppsala. He always put on a big feast and had a three-man band playing polka music.

Daniel was a big man 6 feet, 2 inches, 220 pounds, and very handsome. All the ladies loved to dance with him because he was good-looking and a great dancer. Daniel was a great storyteller and had a tremendous personality. His nickname was Dandy Dan.

Towards the end of the evening, the men would always talk about possibly immigrating to America. Some of their friends and family had already immigrated to America. Correspondence with their old friends was very encouraging as they were all doing well as farmers and lumbermen in the new country. They had all immigrated ten years earlier and ended up in Wisconsin and Minnesota, where the weather and terrain was very similar to Sweden.

Ollie's older brother, Eric, was one of those who had immigrated to America and ended up in a small town in Wisconsin called Rhinelander. He bought some land and started a small farm, had some dairy cows, was growing potatoes, was doing very well, and loved America.

Ollie's five mills were doing very well and employed over ninety people. At the end of 1916, Ollie was made a wonderful offer to buy out his five mills from a big lumber company located in Stockholm, Sweden, by the name of Stockholm Lumber.

The president of Stockholm Lumber, Mr. Peter Johnson, made a trip to Uppsala to meet with Ollie and tour his five mills. Mr. Johnson was very impressed with Ollie and his five mills. After checking Ollie's books and financial statements, he made Ollie an offer of $650,000.

This was about five times what Ollie thought his holdings were worth. Ollie had thirty days to accept or decline the offer. Ollie was excited but nervous. He called for a meeting with his five managers: Daniel, Carl, Phillip Erickson, Nathaniel Grayson, and Bart Sorenson. He explained to his managers that he had thirty days to accept or decline the offer. He was leaning toward selling the mills and immigrating to America, locating near his brother in Rhinelander, Wisconsin.

In prior communications with his brother, Eric, he was informed that he could buy tracts of land in parcels of forty acres for around one hundred dollars per acre. This was timberland with mostly hardwoods, such as oak and maple, but some pine. With hard work, the land could be cleared and the lumber sold for much more than the price of the land. The land could then be sold or kept and turned into farmland.

Ollie had given this a lot of thought and came up with a plan. He would start a sawmill just like he did in Sweden and produce finished lumber. In order to have a successful sawmill, you had to have access to lots of timber.

Ollie told all five of his managers that if he sold the mills to Stockholm Lumber, they would have three options: (1) they could stay with Stockholm Lumber as managers for one year at the same salary they now earned, and at the end of the first year, it was up to Stockholm to determine whether they stayed on or not, but they would be guaranteed their current positions for one year; (2) they could leave the mill after the sale and pursue their own future, and if anyone chose option 1 or 2, they would be given a $2,500 bonus upon the sale of the company; (3) they could immigrate to America in approximately six months and work at the existing mills for two months for Stockholm at existing benefits while training their replacements.

If they chose option 3, they would be given a $5,000 bonus upon the sale of the company. This would give them enough money to immigrate to America and get settled. They would have about six months to sell their possessions and get ready for immigrating to America.

Ollie would arrange boat passage for all the families. Their destination would be somewhere around Rhinelander, Wisconsin.

Upon arrival in Wisconsin, Ollie would loan all of them money to purchase two hundred to four hundred acres of wooded land. They must purchase a minimum of two hundred acres up to a maximum of four hundred acres at approximately one hundred dollars an acre. That would be between $20,000 and $40,000, depending on the cost per acre. Land had to be bought in forty-acre parcels. The going price of land as of last year was between $85 and $125 per acre.

The loan would be paid back by delivering the timber to Ollie's sawmill. Once enough timber was delivered to pay off the original loan, plus 5 percent interest, the rest of the income from the remaining timber would be theirs. Once all the timber was harvested, they at their discretion could pull up stumps and make it into farmland or sell it.

Ollie would sell them whatever finished lumber they needed to build their home and any barns or outbuilding they would need at his cost. They would have to sign an agreement that they would not start up a sawmill to compete with Ollie for a ten-year period.

They had one week to make their decision because Ollie had to get back to Peter Johnson with his decision and any changes. The managers were told to go home and discuss it with their families and give Ollie their decision. Another meeting was scheduled in one week at Ollie's home to discuss the offer and answer any questions.

Of course, there was much to discuss about this proposal with their wives. Daniel and Olga now had three children. All the other employees—including his brother, Carl—had families with children, not to mention brothers, sisters, cousins, and friends that would remain in Sweden. Some still had parents still alive. Most of the women did not want to go and leave their homeland and relatives to go to an unknown life. However, the men made the final decisions and would take responsibility for their decisions. They would listen to their wives' concerns, try to answer them, but would ultimately make a decision on what they thought was best for their family.

One week later, they all met at Ollie's home. Many questions were asked regarding the three options, guaranteed employment, immigration, bonuses, price of lumber in America, length of journey from Sweden to America, temporary housing once in America, compensation, record-keeping with regard to delivered timber once in America, cost of living in America, climate, and so on.

All the questions were answered to the best of Ollie's ability. He let everyone know the only absolute guarantees were the bonuses, passage to America, loan guarantees, and the sale of finished lumber to them to build their homes and outbuilding at Ollie's cost. The guarantees were only valid if they settled in Wisconsin in the Rhinelander area so that Ollie would have access to timber when opening his sawmill.

Four of the five managers wanted to immigrate to America, only Nathaniel Grayson decided to stay in Sweden and continue to work at the mill. Ollie told all of them that they would have another meeting one week from that day and he would have more information for them after speaking to Peter Johnson of Stockholm Lumber.

Ollie had a meeting with Mr. Johnson and agreed to sell the mills with some stipulations: (1) that the sale and transfer of the $650,000 would take place within sixty days; (2) that four of the five managers would stay on for sixty days to help train their replacements and that Stockholm Lumber would pay their wages; (3) that Nathaniel Grayson, the manager of the east mill, would be guaranteed employment at his current wages for a period of one year; (4) that Ollie would stay on for sixty days to help coordinate the takeover and would be compensated $7,500 for his efforts.

Mr. Johnson agreed to all terms with the exception that Ollie and his four managers must stay on for ninety days, not sixty. All would be compensated accordingly. Also Ollie had to sign a not-to-compete clause, which would prevent him from opening any sawmills in Sweden for the next ten years.

Mr. Johnson also informed Ollie that his sister worked in a top position with immigration in Stockholm and that she would help guide all those immigrating to America through all the steps necessary during the immigration process.

Ollie had his next meeting with all the managers and informed them of the changes that had been required by Mr. Johnson in order to complete the sale. All agreed; however, Nathaniel had changed his mind and now wanted to immigrate to America with his friends.

The final meeting with Peter Johnson was held three weeks later on December 1. All the managers were asked to attend this meeting. During this meeting, all agreements were signed and notarized. Peter Johnson's sister also attended this meeting to answer any questions that Ollie and his employees had about immigration to America.

Everything was settled, and all would continue working until March 1, 1917. The $650,000 would change hands on February 1, and all the managers would be given their $5,000 bonuses on February 15. The actual voyage to America would take place mid to late June of 1917. Everyone had at least six months to get their affairs in order and immigrate to America.

All six men had wives and children and owned property and possessions that had been gathered through the course of their lives, so there was much to do over the next six months.

CHAPTER TWO

The Voyage

T he voyage was scheduled to depart from Stockholm on June 20, 1917, on the Swedish ship *Viking Sky*. They would sail from Stockholm to Southampton, England. They would spend three days in Southampton and transfer to the English vessel *New Hope*.

New Hope would sail from Southampton to Ellis Island in New York Harbor, where they would be indoctrinated into America. From there, they would board a train and travel through New York; Philadelphia, Pennsylvania; Cleveland, Ohio; Chicago, Illinois; and on to Rhinelander, Wisconsin. Total travel time, including layovers and indoctrination, would be between thirty and forty days before arriving in Rhinelander.

All families would be allowed five large sea chests to pack clothing, bedding, family heirlooms, etc. No large furniture could be shipped—no animals or perishable foods. Anything else could be shipped as long as it fit in the chests.

All six families had members who spoke good English, some spoke broken English, and a few spoke no English at all. They all had six months to improve or learn the English language. English was the secondary language of Sweden, and most Swedes spoke some English. The Swedes spoke with a strong drawn-out accent.

All six men were stout and muscular. They were all in very good shape from the hard work of the timber business. Daniel and Ollie both had large handlebar mustaches. Carl had a full beard, and the others were all clean-shaven.

On June 20 at 8:00 a.m., all passengers were aboard the *Viking Sky*. By 11:00 a.m. all cargo had been loaded, and the mooring lines were released. The long voyage had begun. The passengers would see Sweden and Norway to the west, Finland to the east, and Denmark to the south. The *Viking Sky* sailed over the Baltic Sea and through the beautiful fjords of Denmark on its way to England.

The fjords were magnificent, and the Baltic Sea and North Sea were very calm. It made for an easy journey to England. As all six families were admiring the beautiful scenes of Scandinavia and the scenic fjords of Denmark, they were all wondering if America had the beauty of their homeland. All the fifteen children ranged in ages of one to fourteen and were enjoying the voyage. They were able to run on the decks and play games in the warm sunshine.

The adults were also enjoying the great weather and calm seas. In the evening, they toasted each other with wine they had brought with them. All but Nathaniel Grayson's wife, Ingrid, were enjoying the wine. Ingrid was seven months pregnant with their fourth child, but she joined in with singing, storytelling, and discussions of their expectations of America.

After arriving in Southampton, England, they stayed in a hotel for three days before transferring to the English vessel *New Hope*. The journey from Stockholm to Southampton took only three days instead of the customary four-day trip because of the calm seas.

The ship *New Hope* left on schedule on June 27 from Southampton en route to Ellis Island in New York Harbor. This voyage was to take between seven or eight days, depending on the seas. They sailed through the English Channel into the Atlantic Ocean. When they entered the Atlantic Ocean, the weather took a turn for the worse.

High seas and winds altered their course, and they tried to find better weather. The weather became very bad. They were stuck in a terrible storm with gale-force winds and seas waves from twenty to thirty feet. Everything on board was battened down, and all passengers were required to wear life vests and stay off the decks. Instructions were given in regard to life boat procedures in case it became necessary. Most aboard became seasick; some became deathly ill. The passengers and the crew were vomiting and told not to eat but drink water.

Nathaniel's wife, Ingrid, became deathly ill and was sent to the infirmary. Ingrid was seven months pregnant and having severe pains. The doctor on board informed Nathaniel and Ingrid that the rough weather had forced Ingrid into premature labor and that it might become necessary to try to deliver a premature baby.

The weather did not let up, and things continued to get worse. The doctor was forced to deliver Ingrid's baby by C-section. The baby was born weighing five pounds but seemed to be healthy, and all things looked positive. It was a baby girl, and they named her Hope, after the ship's name.

They had been at sea for four days but were still at least six days from New York. The weather had improved but still very bad with squalls and high winds. The next day, the weather improved dramatically, and everyone could take off their life vests.

That same day, things turned bad for Ingrid. Complications had set in, including staph infections. Hours later, Ingrid died. Everyone was devastated, and Nathaniel broke down with grief. Daniel's wife, Olga, took over the care of the new baby, Hope.

The captain of the ship tried to comfort Nathaniel and his family as much as he could. It was not uncommon for people to perish at sea on such voyages. All passengers and crew had to sign legal documents consenting to burial at sea. If the ship was more than forty-eight hours from port, a burial must be performed at sea. This was a maritime law to prevent many kinds of possible diseases and for legal entry into port.

Much to the immigrants' dismay, they must prepare for Ingrid's funeral and the burial at sea. The protocol was for the deceased body to be wrapped and secured in some form of blanket or flag, weighted down, and lowered into the sea to sink to the bottom of the ocean.

The ship was still five days from port, and the burial would be the next morning. Nathaniel asked for a gathering of all the Uppsala immigrants that evening for a prayer session and a remembrance of life. Nathaniel had decided to wrap Ingrid's body in a large Swedish flag for the burial at sea.

The next morning, the sun was out, and the seas had calmed. A service was held on deck, and all the ship's passengers and crew attended. Prayers were said, and last rites were given. Nathaniel and all his children kissed their mother goodbye and said their final farewells. The crew then gently lowered Ingrid's body into the Atlantic Ocean, and she slowly sank to the bottom.

The voyage now continued onto New York. There were many thoughts from all the immigrants about what a horrible beginning it was to their new life in America. Nathaniel gathered his friends and family and gave a heartwarming, tearful eulogy, paying their last respects to his beloved wife, Ingrid.

Nathaniel said, "Ingrid would have wanted all of us to continue our journey to America with hopes of new beginnings and successes, to think of her life in America being lived through her new daughter, Hope. What an appropriate name, Hope. Let us continue our journey to a new land, for a new prosperous life and the memory of Ingrid always in our hearts and minds."

The good ship *New Hope* arrived at Ellis Island on July 8, four days behind the original schedule.

CHAPTER THREE

Arrival in America

On July 8, 1917, the immigrants finally arrived at Ellis Island in New York Harbor. Arrangements had been made for berthing quarters for all the families.

On July 10, the immigration and indoctrination procedures would begin for all the immigrants in order to become US citizens. This was a lengthy process and would take approximately ten to fourteen days before they could board the train to Rhinelander, Wisconsin.

Because of the help given to them by Mr. Peter Johnson of Stockholm Lumber and his sister, who worked for Swedish immigration, they had all the necessary paperwork and knew most of the questions that would be asked of them. They could now all speak English. This helped in expediting the process. On July 20, they all finished the immigration and indoctrination requirements.

They were now scheduled to board the North West Railways on July 22 and arrive in Rhinelander, Wisconsin, on July 28, 1917. This was a six-day train ride that would take them through Pennsylvania, Ohio, Illinois, and Wisconsin. They would see the mountains of Pennsylvania; two of the Great Lakes, Erie and Michigan; thousands of acres of farmland; the big city of Chicago; and the many lakes, farms, and woods of central and northern Wisconsin. Once they entered Wisconsin, it reminded them of their homeland, and excitement was dancing in their veins. They were now only hours from the end of their journey to Rhinelander. It had taken them over thirty-five days to reach their destination.

They were all starting to sing some old Swedish songs, anticipation on their faces and goose bumps on their arms. Daniel's brother, Eric, was meeting them at the train station in Rhinelander as well as all the family's hosts, who would take them to their temporary rental property and introduce them to the Rhinelander area, a farming-and-logging community with a population of about five thousand people.

As the train pulled into the station, there was a crowd of about two hundred people awaiting the arrival of the North West.

Looking out the window, Daniel immediately spotted his brother, Eric, with a huge smile on his face shining through his full beard. There were others there who had earlier immigrated to Wisconsin from Uppsala and old friends of the new immigrants.

There were plenty of hugs and kisses and handshakes. Condolences were given to Nathaniel for the loss of his beloved wife, Ingrid. It was one o'clock in the afternoon, and a reception was planned by Eric for 6:00 p.m. that evening after the new immigrants had made their way to their temporary rental homes.

The first thing the children saw was a big mural hanging on the train station's wall; it was of a big green creature with thirteen large horns extending out of his back and traveling down his tail and two big fangs coming out of his mouth that was full of vicious-looking teeth. This mammal was about seven feet long and quite frightful looking. They were told it was called a hodag, and they would be told more about the hodag that evening.

Before their arrival, Daniel's brother, Eric, had been locating temporary housing for the immigrants and putting out the word that his brother and their friends would be looking for acreage to buy and also that one of the immigrants was going to build a sawmill and would be looking for some employees.

A lawyer from Milwaukee, Wisconsin, Mr. Raymond Russell, got wind of these immigrants soon to arrive in Rhinelander. He contacted Eric and informed him that he represented North Woods Lumber Company located outside of Rhinelander, in the Sugar

Camp area. He explained to Eric that North Woods Lumber had recently shut down their milling operations in Wisconsin. They had hired Mr. Russell to sell the mill, machinery, nearly two thousand acres of timberland, and any other assets North Woods had in Sugar Camp.

Mr. Russell asked Eric if he thought the newly arriving immigrants might be interested in buying the whole operation and its assets, and if they had the money or resources to make such a purchase.

Eric informed Mr. Russell that Ollie Stephenson might be interested in such a transaction and that he would be arriving in Rhinelander in less than two weeks and that he had the funds to make such a transaction if he was interested and the price was right.

Mr. Russell told Eric that he was already fielding inquiries about the assets, but no one was interested at this time in buying all the assets in one transaction. If he could set up a meeting with Ollie shortly after his arrival, he would hold off selling the assets piecemeal until after that meeting. Eric agreed to set up a meeting with him and Ollie Stephenson to view the assets and discuss details as soon as possible after Ollie's arrival.

Several hundred people attended the welcoming reception being held at the Rhinelander community center. The food was Swedish style. There was lutfisk, beef brisket, lots of fruit and vegetables, Swedish desserts, and of course, Swedish meatballs. There was an open bar, a five-piece polka band, and games for the children. The reception lasted until midnight, and fun was had by all.

The new immigrants were given a history lesson about the Rhinelander area by the mayor, who was in attendance. Most of the county of Oneida where Rhinelander was located was basically settled by immigrants from Germany, Poland, Sweden, Norway, and Finland.

Most Rhinelander residents were involved in either farming or logging. Two new schools were just built, a grade school and a high school. Many topics were discussed, and many questions answered.

They were all told about the city's emblem and the high school's mascot, which was the hodag. The hodag was green in color, about seven feet long, weighted about two hundred pounds, had thirteen white horns going down his back, two large white fangs coming out of his upper jaw, and a mouth full of razor-sharp teeth. It was said that Paul Bunyan the famous mythical giant lumber jack, found the hodag in a cave. Paul Bunyan tried to capture the unusual creature, and a bloody two-hour battle took place. At the end of the battle, a bloody Paul Bunyan rode the hodag out of the cave and made him his personal pet, along with Babe the Blue Ox.

The children were told that the only thing the hodag would eat was white bulldogs, and that was why today it was very rare to see a white bull dog in the Rhinelander area. The children were told that there were rumors that there was still a hodag roaming in the area's North Woods. All the children were given a T-shirt with a picture of the hodag and an inscription that read, "Rhinelander, Home of the Hodag."

A wonderful time was had by all, and they enjoyed the fun, games, eating, drinking, and dancing. Eric had made all the arrangements, and Ollie paid for everything.

The next day, a meeting was held at Eric's house for Ollie, Daniel, Carl, Phillip, Nathaniel, and Bart. Eric told them about his encounter with Mr. Russell, who represented North Woods Lumber, and all the pertinent information. He told them that Mr. Russell would meet with Ollie if he thought he might be interested.

There was general excitement about this possibility, but all agreed it sounded too good to be true. Ollie agreed to an immediate meeting with Mr. Russell but warned the others that this sounded too easy. The price might be too high, the land might not be good timberland, and the mill was most likely run-down, or a number of other obstacles could come into play.

The meeting took place two days later between Ollie and a gentleman named Clinton Garber, who was an agent for Mr. Russell. Ollie had asked his brother, Eric, and Daniel to attend the meeting with him. Ollie didn't want too many people at the meeting but wanted Daniel and Eric with him as he respected their knowledge and opinions.

They all went to the old sawmill operations and checked the building, warehouses, equipment, and other inventory, including some finished product and a lot of stacked logs. They then went to see the timberland, which took most of the day. At the end of the day,

Ollie thanked Eric and Daniel for their help and told them he would see them later in the evening. Ollie and Mr. Garber then had a meeting to discuss many things but, most importantly, the selling price. Mr. Garber told Ollie the selling price for everything was $270,000.

Ollie asked Mr. Garber how they arrived at that price, as it seemed like a lot of money for a run-down mill and some timberland. Most of the equipment in the mill was in pretty bad shape. Mr. Garber told Ollie he was not in a position to negotiate a price, that it would be Mr. Russell's responsibility, but he could tell Ollie how the price was determined.

North Woods had put a value of the mill, equipment, and the forty acres of land that the mill was located on at $100,000. The eight hundred acres of timberland on the river was valued at $125 per acre or a total of $100,000. The four hundred acres of timberland not on the river was valued at $100 per acre or a total of $40,000, and the four hundred acres of cleared land not on the river was valued at $75 per acre, totaling $30,000. The grand total was $270,000.

Ollie told Mr. Garber that he would be prepared to make Mr. Russell an offer in one week. Ollie wanted time to revisit the mill and the timberland in order to justify such a high price. They set up a meeting one week from Monday at 1:00 p.m. at the sawmill. Mr. Garber said that both he and Mr. Russell would be at the meeting.

Ollie met with Eric and Daniel that evening at Eric's house. They discussed the condition of the mill after being operating for over six years. The equipment was of some value. Most of the saws, planers, and barkers could be refurbished and be good for maybe three more years. Several of the larger saws and two of the barkers were as good as new, but some of the equipment would need to be replaced but could be used for parts in the future. All this would not have to be done right away as the mill would not and could not be run at full capacity for a while. The mill itself sat on forty acres on the Wisconsin River, which gave the land value as well. There was an additional sixteen hundred acres of land that they briefly looked at that day. Eight hundred acres of timberland on the river and four hundred acres of timberland not located on the river and another four hundred acres that had already been logged.

All this land was in fairly close proximity to the mill. They all three agreed the timberland was excellent and consisted mainly of hardwoods, mostly oak and maple, and a small amount of pine. They agreed to get together with Phillip, Nathaniel, Bart, and Carl for the next two days and revisit the mill and the timberland. After all seven had visited the mill and the sixteen hundred acres, they would all meet to discuss the issues of who wanted what and a sale price of the land they each might be interested in. This meeting would take place on Friday, three days before Ollie's next meeting with Mr. Russell and Mr. Garber.

On Friday, the seven of them had their meeting to find out the price of the land. They had all visited the mill and timberland; it was now decision time. Did they want in or out? They all understood that Ollie would loan them the money at five percent interest with the stipulation the timberland must be logged and sold to Ollie at fair market value. The logging operation must begin within the next sixty days.

Ollie told them all the cost of the land was $125 per acre for the eight hundred acres located on the river, $100 per acre for the four hundred acres of timberland not on the river, and $75 per acre for the four hundred acres of already cleared land. The cleared land was mostly full of stumps, which would require a lot of hard work to turn it into productive farmland. That land had to be bought in forty-acre parcels.

Those who wanted to log the land must buy at least two hundred acres, sell Ollie all the timber, and sign an agreement not to start up a sawmill within a 150-mile area for the next 10 years. They would all buy the land from Ollie, which he was financing, and Ollie would hold the mortgage on the property until it was paid off.

Without any guarantees, Ollie estimated the value of the timberland once harvested and delivered to the mill at between $200 and $250 an acre. That would mean they would at least double their money that they paid for the land and then own the land free and clear, which they could sell for a very nice profit or start their own farm. Ollie didn't want any of the six to have any doubts about what they were about to get involved in. He wanted them all to have a complete understanding of their commitment and what it could mean for the future of them and their families.

The river property was more valuable because the river would be used as a less expensive way to deliver timber to the mill. All the men were experienced lumbermen and understood the value of timber and the cost of harvesting and transporting it to the mill. They all had experience in buying and selling timber; after all, they all managed sawmills. Anybody not interested in getting involved could come to work at the mill as an employee. All these men were friends of Ollie's, and he didn't want any of them getting involved for Ollie's benefit. He wanted them to get involved for their own benefit and have an avenue to becoming wealthy and independent and, at the same time, allow Ollie to benefit from their labors.

All but Nathaniel and Eric were interested in buying and logging the timberland. Nathaniel Grayson, because of the loss of his wife on the voyage over here and the need to raise his children without a wife, told Ollie that if he could pay him a good salary, he would manage the new mill and buy forty acres of the already cleared land to build a home on and one day have a small farm. Eric, who already owned a small farm and was doing very well growing potatoes and raising dairy cows, was interested in the remaining cleared land to expand his farm. He was older than the rest and was not sure he could go through the rigors of logging.

The other four were interested in purchasing the remaining twelve hundred acres of timberland but were all interested in buying the timberland located on the Wisconsin River. Phillip and Bart each wanted to buy two hundred acres with river access, as they knew the cost of transporting the timber could be very expensive. Daniel and his brother, Carl, both agreed that they would buy two hundred acres of river access timberland and would each buy two hundred acres of the remaining four hundred acres not located on the river, but at a reduced sale price of $85 per acre.

All were in agreement that they would pay $125 per acre for river timberland, $85 for the timberland not on the river, and $60 per acre for the cleared land.

The math was simple. The four hundred acres that Daniel and Carl wanted to buy totaled $42,000 each or $84,000 total. The two hundred acres that both Phillip and Bart wanted to buy would cost them $25,000 each or a total of $50,000. Eric's cost for the three hundred and sixty acres of cleared land would be $21,000, and Nathaniel's forty acres would cost him $2,400. Ollie was willing to pay the $100,000 North Woods wanted for the mill.

With that, everyone was willing to pay a total of $258,000. North Woods Lumber wanted $270,000.

The meeting took place at the sawmill. Mr. Russell, Mr. Garber, and Ollie were the only people at the meeting. Much was discussed, and negotiations began. Ollie told Mr. Russell that he felt like the existing mill and the machinery was well overpriced and that all the timberland and cleared land was also overpriced. The only land that was close to its real value was the timberland located on the river. Ollie told Mr. Russell that he could build a new mill in a better location for less money and that he could always buy timberland; however, because even though the old mill needed lots of work and some new machinery, it was already there and he could start his new company a lot sooner than normal and that had a value to him.

Ollie made Mr. Russell an offer of $225,000 for everything with an immediate closing and a cash transaction. Ollie was prepared to pay the asking price of $270,000 and had a commitment from his friends of $158,000, and if he paid $112,000 for the mill and equipment, that would total the $270,000 that North Woods was asking.

Mr. Russell flinched and said he didn't think that North Woods would accept an offer of $225,000.

Ollie stood up and said, "I completely understand. I am sure you can get more money by piecemealing the assets. It may take you a lot longer to liquidate all the assets while you're still paying taxes for them, but you may get more money." With that, Ollie shook Mr. Russell's hand and thanked him for his time. He said, "I will pursue some other options."

Mr. Russell said to Ollie, "Let me advise North Woods of your offer. I know they would like a quick sale but not sure they can sell at that price. Give me two days to get you an answer or a counteroffer."

Ollie told Mr. Russell that he didn't think he would entertain a counteroffer but he would wait two days before he made any other commitments. The immediate closing and cash transaction should make their decision fairly easy.

Two days later, Mr. Russell informed Ollie that North Woods had accepted his offer. Ollie was elated. He had been prepared to pay the $270,000. Ollie felt like he just made $45,000. That was a lot of money in 1917.

Ollie was a very good businessman and also very generous. Ollie took some of the savings he made on the purchase and rented a large dance hall. He invited all his friends and relatives and their friends from Sweden and held a big feast and dance. He held nothing back and served the finest food and drink that could be bought. A grand time was had by all. He had also invited the mayor, the police and fire departments, the local hospital staff, and all council members of Rhinelander. Ollie and the other new immigrants from Sweden got an opportunity to meet important people in the community and make new friends.

Nathaniel even met a beautiful Swedish woman about his age who was recently widowed. Her name was Mandy Swenson.

Ollie also bought two big draft horses for each of his friends who immigrated from Sweden with him, plus two for his brother, Eric, as a start to their new logging and farming business. He gave Nathaniel a very handsome salary to manage his mill as well as a $2,000 bonus to help pay for a nanny to help raise his children while he managed the mill.

Ollie had now given all his immigrant friends plus his brother an opportunity for a bright future and wonderful life in America. Now the only thing left was a lot of hard work on their part to secure their future.

The closing was held two weeks later, and money and titles changed hands. The land was divided to everyone's satisfaction, and everyone started with the necessary preparations to begin their logging operations. Ollie's brother, Eric, decided to sell his small farm and move his operation to his newly acquired 360 acres, start pulling stumps, and prepare for next season's potato farming. He would build a new home and outbuildings on his new land.

Ollie named his new company, New Hope Timber Company, after Nathaniel's daughter who was born at sea.

Nathaniel went to work immediately as manager of the New Hope mill. He hired six men to help him get the mill up and running, and if they turned out to be good and reliable workers, he would hire them as permanent employees.

After four years of hard labor, all seven men became financially independent. After the timberland was harvested and all the timber sold to Ollie's mill, they all had quadrupled their investment, owned their own land, and started their own farms. Eric was now the largest potato farmer in Oneida County. Ollie was about to open a second sawmill in Tomahawk Wisconsin, about forty miles from the New Hope Mill.

Nathaniel married Mandy a year after they met. They already had a son, and Mandy was expecting another. Daniel, Carl, Phillip, and Bart had all added more children to their families and were all now farming their land. Ollie was now one of the wealthiest and most influential people in the county. He ran for mayor in 1925 and was elected by more than 80 percent of the vote. He served as mayor for over twelve years.

Daniel Peterson became the most successful farmer of all the immigrants. In 1935 Daniel was the biggest potato farmer in the five-county area of Oneida, Forest, Langlade, Lincoln, and Vilas. He was also involved in politics and was the county commissioner of Oneida County. His best friend Ollie was the mayor of Rhinelander, and it seemed as if these Swedish immigrants were taking over northern Wisconsin. Daniel and Olga Peterson had seven children, the youngest being born in 1930—a son named Ben.

CHAPTER FOUR

Ben and Happy Peterson

B en Peterson was the youngest child of Daniel and Olga Peterson, the original immigrants who came over from Sweden in 1917 via England on the vessel *New Hope*.

Ben was born on February 10, 1930, during a snow blizzard with minus-forty degrees below zero temperatures. His father, Daniel, had to make the delivery as the doctor could not make it through the blizzard. Daniel had delivered many folds and calves but never a human being. His wife, Olga, later stated that Daniel was more nervous than a whore in church. The delivery went well, and the Petersons delivered a healthy baby boy. Ben was the last child born in their family.

Ben married one of Bart Sorenson's daughters, Becky, in 1950. They had two children: a daughter, Brandi, born 1952 and a son, Happy, born in 1954. Happy was born with a big smile on his face and didn't cry his first two weeks of life. He just kept smiling, so they decided to name him Happy—Happy Benjamin Peterson.

Ben's father, Daniel, became seriously ill right after Happy was born. Ben took over all the operations of the farm after his father became ill. Ben's father had incorporated the farm and named it Dandy Dan Farms.

Daniel died six months later in 1955 at sixty-three years of age. Ben inherited the farm and was also looking after his mother, Olga, whose health was also failing her. Ben, Becky, Brandi, Happy, and

Olga were all living in the big farmhouse. Ben was working the farm, and Becky took care of her mother-in-law and the two small children.

For the next twenty-three years, Ben busted his ass at Dandy Dan Farms. The potato farm remained one of the largest and most successful potato farms in northern Wisconsin. Ben did not want his son, Happy, to become a farmer like himself or his grandfather. He wanted Happy to become a doctor, an engineer, or an inventor.

Ben encouraged Happy to study hard in school, to play sports, and to get involved in extra-curriculum activities after school. Ben tried to keep Happy away from farm chores and left them for himself and the three tenant farmers he had working for him.

When Happy was twelve years old and in the sixth grade, Ben was told that Happy had an extremely high IQ. His IQ was over 140, that of a genius, and Ben was told they should encourage his son to read a lot and study hard in school.

Happy became valedictorian of his 1973 graduating class from Rhinelander High School. He was president of both his junior and senior class. He was a tremendous athlete. He made all state both in basketball and football. He was the state champion in wrestling in the heavyweight class. He was also a standout swimmer, breaking multiple state swimming records. He was like a fish in the water.

Happy was offered multiple scholarships from many colleges. He selected the University of Wisconsin, where he was given both scholastic and athletic scholarships. Happy was very interested in the human eye. He wanted to become an eye surgeon and loved to invent things.

In 1974 Happy started his freshman year at University of Washington in Madison. He maintained a 4.0 average and was well on his way to his doctorate in medicine. In 1978 it all came to an abrupt halt. His father, Ben, died in a horrible accident on the farm in September of 1978. Ben had jumped off his large John Deere tractor and was making an adjustment to the massive thresher that was being pulled behind the tractor. Somehow the tractor reengaged into gear as Ben was lying on the ground in front of the thresher. The thresher ran over Ben and killed him instantly.

Happy left school immediately and went back home to attend the funeral and take care of the farm situation. His sister, Brandi—who had graduated from the University of Kentucky with her doctorate and was now a pharmacist and living in Louisville, Kentucky—was also there.

They had to have a closed casket at the funeral as Ben's body was so mutilated from the thrasher that it could not be viewed. Happy inherited the farm. He planned to take care of farm matters and his mother for a couple years, sell the farm, and return to school to become an eye surgeon.

Happy was a strong big young man, very good-looking, and very intelligent. He was a spitting image of his grandfather, Daniel, and had a very bright future in front of him. After running the farm for a year, he married his first love, his high school sweetheart, Phyllis Clark. They were married in 1979 and had a son in 1980 and named him Daniel, after his grandfather.

Dandy Dan Farms had grown into a massive four-thousand-acre farm with over twenty full-time employees and was making money hands over fists. Happy hired one of his cousins, who was the same age as Happy and the son of one of Happy's uncles. His name was Gus Peterson. Gus grew up on his dad's farm and was well versed in farming. Gus's dad had recently sold his farm to Ben before Ben died, and Gus had gone to work at Dandy Dan Farms, working for Ben.

After Gus had proven to Happy in 1982 that he could run and protect the farm, Happy made Gus part owner and partner in Dandy Dan Farms. He would give Gus 25 percent of the farm, and he would receive 25 percent of the net profit annually until such time as Gus could afford to buy Happy out. Gus could cut out twenty acres of land out of the farm and build a nice home for his family.

Happy was going back to school to get his doctor's degree and become an eye surgeon and inventor of medical apparatus. When Happy was finished with school and had all his degrees, he was going to return to the farm and build a laboratory and further his studies on the human eye and invent medical products.

While Happy was back in school, he would have his office and laboratory built on the same forty acres that his current home was located, but he would not be involved in any of the farm operations. He would meet with Gus once a month just to look over the books and get a monthly report on how the farm was doing.

Happy had his wife's blessings to finish his doctorate. Happy would come home on the weekends and holidays until he was finished in about three years. In 1983 Happy went back to the University of Wisconsin. He finished school and got all his degrees in 1985. He maintained his 4.0 average and was a genius. He was now Dr. Happy Benjamin Peterson.

When Happy returned to Rhinelander, the farm was doing great. Gus had done a great job and had landed two huge contracts with the two largest potato chip manufacturers in the states. Dandy Dan Farms had its most profitable year ever in 1984 and looked like 1985 would be even better.

Happy's son, Daniel, was now five years old and looked just like his dad. Phyllis was delighted to have her husband back on a full-time basis. Happy's office and laboratory were finished. Phyllis had decorated Happy's office, and it was beautiful. Happy had ordered some very expensive, elaborate equipment. He was expecting delivery on some of it in thirty days. Another piece of laser equipment that he had designed especially for studying the many facets of the eye would not be delivered for another six months. It was being made in Germany to Happy's specifications. No piece of equipment like this had ever been produced before, and no one knew exactly its capabilities except for Happy.

Happy was paying $700,000 for this piece of equipment, and it was taking over a year to manufacture. Happy spent over two years while in school inventing this laser eye equipment. That was a lot of potatoes.

Happy started out in his lab, inventing medical apparatus that was far superior to what was on the current market. Happy invented an optical shield that was bulletproof, improved clarity and vision distance by 30 percent, and would not fog up in any conditions. He had it patented and sold it to the military for millions of dollars. It could be used for eyeglasses, goggles, visors, and windshields for vehicles and planes.

Happy was making so much money on his medical inventions that he never started his practice as an eye surgeon. By 1992 Happy had become a multimillionaire from his medical inventions.

Happy and Phyllis built a beautiful mansion on an eighty-acre tract of land on the Wisconsin River with over two thousand feet of river frontage. He built a new laboratory and office within walking distance of their new mansion. He had a second lab built that would hold all types of animals and birds so that he could study the various eyes and what caused different reactions and vision capabilities in different mammals. He had parrots, eagles, hawks, owls, and many exotic birds of prey. He housed dolphins, seals, otters, beavers, wolverines, badgers, monkeys, and other exotic mammals. The second lab cost him over eight million dollars to build. It had the ability to have all the birds and mammals living in their natural element.

Happy was the foremost expert on vision and its relationship to the brain. Happy was contracted by the US military to research optical products. He was given huge grants and paid millions not to work with any foreign governments.

Happy would accept birds and animals from around the world. They all had serious eye injuries, and he would perform surgery on them, trying to save their eyesight and, at the same time, experimenting with the different facets of the various eyes. Happy did this at no cost to the owner or zoo. There was a long list of exotic patients awaiting to be admitted to Happy's new animal optic hospital.

Happy was very selective as to which animals or birds he would admit. Not only was Happy helping out the animals, but he was furthering his study of different eyes. One of Happy's goals was to invent the perfect artificial eye.

Over the course of years, while operating on various animals and fowl and studying their sclera, cornea, chambers, iris/pupils, lens, vitreous, retina, optic nerves, refractions, avascular, nerve fibers, specific viscosities, eye pressures, fovea, conjunctiva, fluids, and many other fascinating parts of the eye, Happy gained invaluable data to help him invent the perfect artificial eye.

Happy often worked with Dr. Harold Bennett, a well-known brain surgeon and one of Happy's best friends. They met at the

30

University of Wisconsin while they were getting their doctorate degrees. They often discussed the relationship between the brain and the eye. Happy's work was instrumental in the modern-day success of LASIK eye surgery.

After many years of surgery and experimentation on hundreds of various animals, Happy came up with the perfect mechanical eye. It was a mechanical eye that looked exactly like the human eye. Properly attached to the brain, it would have magical powers. It could allow blind people to see again, and with modifications, it could allow the eye to see through six inches of solid steel and produce a laser beam and a number of unheard of abilities.

Happy had used a seal with one normal eye and one completely blind eye for his last experiment. After four unsuccessful, very delicate, and life-threating surgeries, Happy called in his friend Dr. Harold Bennett to help him perform the fifth surgery. It was a success. The mechanical eye could see through most anything, including six inches of solid steel. It could emit extreme heat, had laser abilities, was nocturnal, and had many other abilities. Happy was elated. He had fulfilled his lifelong dream. This may be the most incredible invention of all time, including the invention of electricity.

No one knew about this incredible invention other than Dr. Bennett, not even his wife, Phyllis. Happy had been busy inventing other medical apparatus for the government as well as for the general public. Happy had buried himself in his labs from early in the morning until late at night for the last several years. Happy was so excited about his success that on May 6, he walked from his lab to his house to share this exciting news with his wife, Phyllis.

As he entered the house, he did not see Phyllis in either the kitchen or the den. He heard some moaning sounds coming from upstairs. As he climbed the stairs, the moaning became louder, and as he approached their master bedroom, the door was slightly ajar. As he peeked in, he saw his beautiful wife, Phyllis, with his farming partner, Gus, both half undressed and in a passionate embrace.

Happy almost passed out in disbelief. Happy remained silent and continued to watch through the partially opened door. Gus removed her bra and was kissing her breasts. Phyllis was very aroused and was moaning very loud, saying, "I love you. More, more!" Gus laid her on the bed and removed her panties and began performing oral sex on her. Phyllis was going crazy, shaking, withering, and screaming for more. Gus had a huge erection and jumped on the bed with her.

Phyllis started having oral sex with Gus. Now Gus was going crazy and screaming and moaning, as Phyllis's lips were going up and down around Gus's shaft. Happy was about to puke. Phyllis then shouted out, "Gus, I need you now. Please fuck me." As Phyllis spread her legs and her wet vagina was accepting Gus's shaft, she started shaking uncontrollably and came all over the bed. Gus now turned her over and mounted her doggy style while slapping her ass with the palm of his hand. Phyllis was now hollering, "More, more! Deeper, deeper! I love you."

Happy's head was spinning. He was pissed off, betrayed, and heartbroken. He went back downstairs to the den, opened a drawer, and pulled out a .357 magnum pistol. Happy went back upstairs and opened the door all the way. Now Gus was again performing oral sex on Phyllis. Happy walked up to the edge of the bed. Both Phyllis and Gus were so passionately involved that neither of them saw or heard him.

Happy hollered at Gus, "You motherfucker!"

Gus immediately raised his head out of her muffin. With his eyes as big as saucers, tried to say something to Happy, but nothing came out. Happy said "Adios, mother fucker" and shot him right in the balls then shot him right between the eyes. Blood was flowing all over the bed, and Gus's brains were lying on Phyllis's stomach. His testicles are nowhere to be found.

Happy said to Phyllis, "I should shoot you right now, you fucking whore." While holding the pistol to her head and listening to her cry and say how sorry she was, he reached in the second drawer of the nightstand and took out a black Magic Marker. He writes on her forehead "Whore" and, on her belly "I have been fucking Gus." He rolled her over and wrote on her back, "I am a worthless whore." Then on both cheeks of her ass, he wrote, "Free." He then grabbed her by her hair, dragged her down the steps, opened the front door, and pushed her outside bare-ass naked. Then he kicked her ass with his foot and locked the door.

Phyllis knocked at the door, screaming, "Please let me in." Happy simply walked away, went to the phone, and called the police. He gave them his name and address and told them he just killed a man and that there was a naked lady outside his front door, trying to break into his home.

The police arrived, arrested Happy, and took him to jail. They put up yellow "no trespassing" ribbons all around the house, wrapped Phyllis in a blanket, took her to a neighbor's house, and informed her she or no one else may enter the house until the police were through with their investigation, which would take a minimum of three days. The officer in charge did retrieve some clothing for Phyllis and told her no more request until after the investigation.

The year of the murder was 1998. Happy was forty-four years old and very wealthy. His son, Daniel, was eighteen and was about to graduate from high school. Daniel never had anything to do with the farm and knew nothing about farming.

The day after the shooting, Daniel went to visit Happy in jail and got all the details. Danny looked just like his dad and had inherited a lot of his dad's qualities, including a very high IQ. Danny and Happy were very close. Any spare time Happy had, he would devote it to Danny. This might be one of the reasons Phyllis was having an affair with Gus; she didn't get much of Happy's free time. It was later discovered that Phyllis had been having an affair with Gus ever since Happy went back to school in 1983. The affair had been going on for fifteen years.

Happy had taught Danny the importance of education and how to swim, hunt, fish, and play basketball, baseball and football. He taught him the importance of listening instead of talking and not to prejudge people until you got to know them.

During Danny's visit to the jail, he was told the whole story about his mother and Gus in detail. After all, Danny was eighteen and was becoming a man, and Happy was going to need his help. Happy told Danny he realized Phyllis was his mother and he could have any relationship with her that he wanted and he would understand. Happy told Danny that he had a trust fund set up for him and that he should never have to worry about money for the rest of his life. The trust fund wouldn't kick in until he was twenty-one years old. And it was irrevocable, so he couldn't change it. Happy would, however, set up an additional three-year trust so he would have immediate access to funds.

He told Danny that he was not sure of what might happen to him because of the murder. However, whatever happened, he wanted his son to live a full life and to live out his dreams. He told Danny his wishes were for him to go to college and get as many degrees as he could. He also told Danny that he would never put any pressure on him and would support any decisions Danny made.

He told Danny about projects he was working on, including the magical eye, but no one was to know anything about any of his projects because some of them were highly classified, as he was working with the US government, including the FBI, CIA, and US Army. He then gave Daniel a list of things he needed to do right away for him. Included on the list was having Happy's attorney, Gerry Kline, visit him in jail within the next twenty-four hours; to have Jonus Peppington, who was Gus's right-hand man on the farm, visit him immediately; to call General Dwight Smith with the US Army, who was in charge of all Army procurements and Happy's contact with his dealings with the Army. Danny was to introduce himself as Happy's son and give the general the details of what happened and that all their confidential projects would be on hold. Happy gave him a special phone number for the general and to never use it again unless Happy told him to.

He told Danny all the combinations to all the heavy security locks that were in the laboratories and that he would have to use a special key along with the combinations to enter the labs and all the secured areas. He gave Danny a list of all donors who gave him mammals and birds for his experiments. He was told to call all these people to come and retrieve their animals or donate them to different zoos. He was to get rid of all of them except for the seal.

Danny's only job was to daily check on the lab and make sure the room temperatures were always the same as the instructions printed on each thermostat until all the animals and birds were gone—except for the seal, who was kept in a special room. Then all thermostats could be set at seventy-two degrees except for the seal, who not only had his own environment but had a large pool and other apparatus. The seal must be fed a special diet of fresh fish every day between 4:00 and 5:00 p.m. A monthly supply of fresh fish was delivered the first of each month and kept in a special tank. Danny was told that eventually someone would be put in charge of the lab, but until further notice, it was his responsibility. There were other items on the list, but these four requests must be done immediately.

Happy's attorney, Gerry Kline, came to visit immediately after Danny phoned him. Gerry spent the rest of the day with Happy, getting all the details he could about the murder so he could start preparing for trial, which would be at least six months away, but there would be a court hearing within the next week to seek bail and other such court matters.

Gerry was also instructed to start divorce proceedings with Phyllis. Happy wanted Phyllis out of the house and off the farm immediately. He instructed Gerry to meet with her attorney and draw up a temporary-separation agreement. "Buy her a new home anywhere she wants. Give her some money and anything else she may want within reason. Just get rid of her."

Happy wanted to sell the entire farm and all the assets. The only thing he wanted to keep was his eighty acres on the river, his mansion, and all his labs. After Phyllis moved out, he wanted Gerry to work with his son on hiring someone to fence in electrically his entire eighty-acre estate with a guard shack at the entrance to the long winding driveway, manned by an armed guard and security dogs.

Happy told Gerry he knew he would be busy preparing for his hearing and trial so he could get someone capable from his office to get rid of Phyllis and sell the farm. Dandy Dan Farms was now the biggest potato farm in Wisconsin with huge contracts with most food processors that used potatoes in their products. "Contact all the large potato chip manufacturers to see if they have any interest in buying the farm. List it nationally. Put it on the internet. Just sell it, and get a fair price for it."

Happy's next meeting was with Jonus Peppington, a huge man with an infectious smile and a great sense of humor. He was Gus Peterson's right-hand man on the farm. He was hardworking, very knowledgeable of the farm operations, and a terrific mechanic, but he was not a good businessman or at least had no experience in finances or sales and couldn't be trusted to run the business end of such a large operation.

By now, the whole town of Rhinelander knew all the details about Phyllis and Gus and Happy shooting Gus right between the eyes right after he shot him in the balls.

Upon entering Happy's cell, Jonus jokingly said, "I hope you don't have a gun."

Happy, knowing Jonus's sense of humor, shot back, "Why? Were you fucking my wife too?"

Jonus didn't know how to take that, and he became very defensive, saying, "Absolutely not. I am sorry if I offended you, Mr. Peterson. I was just trying to lighten the air."

Happy said to Jonus, "I was just doing the same. Relax." They both smiled and laughed and called each other a son of a bitch.

Happy told Jonus his life was turned upside down right now and he didn't want to deal with the farm. "My intensions are to sell the farm, which I know you don't want to hear because it is your livelihood. I figure it will take me a year to sell the farm if I have to divide it up, as not too many people can afford to buy such a big operation. At any rate, I have an offer for you. If you can keep running the farm in good order until I sell it, I will double your current salary of $48,000 to $96,000—let's just make it a $100,000. Upon the sale of the farm, assuming you have done a good job, I will give you a $100,000 bonus and will ask the buyer to consider keeping you on as a manager of the farm. If the buyer does not decide to keep you, I will give you an additional $50,000. That will allow you to take a well-deserved vacation and look for another job with no financial pressures on you."

Jonus Peppington began to cry. He stood up and gave Happy a huge bear hug. "Happy, you can count on me." Then with a big smile on his face, he said, "I will even stay away from the house."

They both smiled and laughed, and Jonus began to cry again. He told Happy that he just made his life easier, that he and his large family had been struggling to make ends meet, and that this would allow him to send his oldest son to college. With that, Happy started to cry and told him that within two days, an additional $25,000 check would be delivered to his front door with no strings attached.

Happy then hugged Jonus and told him, "You are a good family man. Now get the hell out of here before I go broke, and if you cry again, I am not giving you the twenty-five grand."

Jonus cried anyway. They both laughed, and Jonus was on his way back to the farm. Jonus now knew what kind of a good man Happy Peterson was, and he didn't blame him for killing Gus.

Daniel had called the general and had a fifteen-minute conversation with him. The general asked many questions and told Danny to tell his dad that he was calling several meetings with very powerful people and that he could expect a visit from him in the near future. It might even be several weeks, but he would be there.

Danny also took care of the lab requests, had called all the donors to retrieve their birds and animals, and was already making arrangements with zoos around the country to donate some of the exotics that people did not want back.

Danny was also taking care of the seal and was becoming attached to him. Danny would feed and swim and play with the seal every day. The seal also became attached to Danny and would squeal and clap his flippers every day when Danny would arrive. Happy never named the seal. He was only referred to as project 99. So Danny named him Hoddie, a nickname often given to the Rhinelander hodag. Hoddie and Danny became inseparable, and Hoddie became Danny's special pet. Danny taught Hoddie many tricks. Sometimes Danny would put up a volleyball net across the pool, and they would play volleyball. After Hoddie got the gist of the game, he would beat Danny every time.

Now that Happy got the urgent matters underway, he felt better. His court hearing was in two days, on May 13, and he was hoping they would set bond for him. He didn't care about the amount; he just wanted out of jail and get back to his work at the lab.

At the hearing, Gerry Kline asked the court to allow bail because of the circumstances of the murder and that Happy was an outstanding citizen who had donated lots of money to different charities, helping many of the less fortunate and being instrumental in helping blind people.

The state's prosecutor asked the court to deny bail. He said that Mr. Peterson, regardless of what he had done in the past, was a murderer. Mr. Peterson was a flight risk as he was so wealthy; he could flee to anywhere in the world and start a new life.

The judge took a five-minute recess to go back to his chambers and think about each request. He returned and announced that no bail would be granted; however, he scheduled another hearing for ten days from today on May 23 to let both sides have further arguments on the bail issue. Happy was very disappointed, as was his attorney, Gerald Kline. But Gerald assured Happy that at the next hearing, they would most likely get bail set.

Two days later, on May 15, Happy got a visit from General Smith. The general flew in to Rhinelander from Washington, DC, on a military plane. Arrangements had already been made for Happy's release from jail for forty-eight hours under the supervision of General Dwight Smith, a three-star general on active duty in the US Army. No one knew of this arrangement but the sheriff, the district attorney, and the judge—not even Happy's son or his attorney. A gag order had been put out, and it was on a need-to-know-only basis.

When the general arrived in a car supplied by the sheriff's office and driven by a sheriff's deputy, he waited in the back seat in front of the jail. Five minutes later, Happy got in the back seat with the general and off they went to Happy's home. Greetings were extended to each other. They had met more than a half dozen times over the years, but never at Happy's home or lab. They had a very good relationship, and Happy was one of less than a dozen people who had the general's private phone number. The general and Happy were on first-name basis, and Happy simply called him Dwight.

On the ride from the jail to the lab, Dwight let Happy know he knew all the details regarding the shooting and many other things he knew about Happy, which surprised Happy. The general said, "I am not here to discuss these events." The general stated that he would have shot the son of a bitch himself. Dwight was there to discuss his upcoming hearing and the murder trial and to discuss the ongoing projects Happy was doing for the Army as well as future projects. Happy had produced some incredible inventions that were now being used very successfully in the Army as well as the Air Force and the Navy, and the General wanted to see that continued.

As they pulled up to Happy's home and labs, the general assumed no one would be there. Happy explained to the general that only his son, Danny, had access and that he came every day to oversee the lab and take care of some animals. "However, he will not be in our way because my office was not near the main labs." The general said that was fine and they would greet Danny upon his arrival, spend a few minutes with him, and explain some things.

Happy gave the general a tour of his labs. He showed Dwight some of the projects he was working on for him and the different development stages they were in. The general was very impressed with the layout, the security, and the very sophisticated equipment that was located everywhere in the labs. The general told Happy he had never seen any equipment quite like this. Happy told him the reason why was that there was no other equipment like this. He had it all designed to his exact specs; most were made in Germany at a very high cost, and no one knew what the equipment was for or what its capabilities were. After receiving most of the equipment, he would make some alterations, tweaking a few things, and finish the job here in the lab. No one could reproduce this equipment but him.

The general said, "This stuff has to be so expensive. Who pays for all this?"

Happy said, "You do." And he laughed.

The general laughed with him, and they retired to Happy's office.

While the general was sitting down, he said to Happy, "I noticed the seal you had in that special room. What's the deal with that?"

Happy said, "That's my son's pet seal, Hoddie."

The general said, "Let's get right to it. You only have forty-eight hours. I need the rest of the day with you, dinner tonight, two hours in the morning, and you will have from 10:00 a.m. to 4:00 p.m. to spend with your son or do whatever you want, but you must turn yourself back in by 4:00 p.m. I will not be taking you back. You are turning yourself back in, and we have reasons for that. Okay, Happy, everything I am saying and doing here today is for a reason. I had very high-up meetings before coming here, one which included the president. We pulled a lot of strings with the FBI, CIA, and the Justice Department. So hold all your questions until the end and listen intently. First, we fired your attorney, Gerry Kline, and he is off this specific case but involved in all your other personal agreements. He will not ask you any questions regarding this case. You are now being represented by Captain Patrick O'Conner, retired US Army. He will meet you two days before the next hearing. You are not to discuss what is said here today with anyone, including your son. At the hearing, bail will be set at $1 million dollars. A bond will be posted by the US Army, and you will be free to leave the courtroom. You may return to your home. Your wife will be gone and not able to return unless you give her permission. At least until your divorce is settled, we have nothing to do with that. Your attorney, your wife's attorney, and the courts will decide the outcome of that."

Just then Danny walked in and was shocked to see his dad. He ran up to Happy and gave him a big hug and said, "What the hell is going on?"

Happy introduced Danny to the general. Danny shook the general's hand, and they both held a very strong grip on each other's hand while looking into each other's eyes.

The general said to Happy, "Your son and I had a great conversation on the phone, and I must say I was quite impressed with the delivery of the very disturbing information you had him deliver to me."

Danny was a big tall well-built athlete. He was very handsome and looked just like his dad. Happy, being a very proud father, informed the general that Danny was an all-state football player and basketball player. He was undefeated and state champ in the heavyweight division in high school wrestling. He was also an all-star swimmer who broke some of his dad's longtime records in swimming. He was graduating in two weeks and was the valedictorian of his class. He had been offered many scholarships to many colleges.

The general raised his hand to stop Happy and said, "Like father, like son."

Happy said, "How did you know that?"

And the general said, "I have unlimited resources." He grinned. The general congratulated Danny on all his achievements and said, "I can see why your dad is so proud of you. If you ever decide to join the service, which I am sure your dad doesn't want you to, call me first. You have my number. Now, Danny, I am not in a position to discuss certain matters about your dad's situation, but I can assure you that everything is going to work out for your dad. I give you my word. But you can never repeat what I just said. If you do, I will know you can't be trusted and would deny it anyway."

The general stood up and said, "With that, your dad and I have a lot to talk about, and I have a feeling that you and I may meet in the future." They shook hands again, still with a viselike grip, again looking each other in the eye.

Danny said, "Thank you very much." And he gave the general a hug.

After Danny left to feed Hoddie, the general and Happy resumed their conversation. The general went back over the bail hearing, returning home, wife being gone, and then continued, "You will not be able to leave the county until after the trial. You will be free to do as you wish but must check in once a week with a court-appointed clerk. This can be done over the phone. After the hearing and before the trial, you are to resume working on our army projects. As time goes on, you will be given additional projects. You will continue to be paid handsomely and be given grants as you need them. I will remain your liaison should you have any problems. A court date will be set 120 days after the hearing. You again will be represented by Captain O'Conner, and you won't see him until two days before the trial. He will call you if he needs to, and you may call him if you need him. Use this direct number." Dwight slipped Happy Patrick's card.

The general told Happy the trial would be held without a jury, with the judge making the decision of guilty or not guilty and delivering the sentence. "You will be found not guilty by reason of temporary insanity. The judge will dismiss the court, and you will walk out a free man. In return, you will work for the US Army in the same capacity as you now do—only for the next five years, you work exclusively on our projects. After that, you can do whatever you want. Any questions?

Happy asked only one question. "How did you get my wife to move out of the house?"

The general said, "We made her an offer she couldn't refuse." Happy and the general went to dinner, drank some wine, and did not discuss any business.

The next morning, they had breakfast at the hotel the general had made arrangements with. They both had a slight hangover after three bottles of wine, some great storytelling, and a lot of laughs. Dwight and Happy were becoming pretty good friends.

They went back to Happy's office and discussed some ongoing projects, some deadlines, and the general left him with some briefs on future projects. He wanted Happy to get back with him on whether or not Happy thought they were doable and the approximate cost and time frames. The general left at 10:00 a.m. sharp, and Happy spent the rest of the day with Danny and Hoddie.

On May 23, the hearing was over, Happy was free in time to attend his son's graduation and see him be honored as the class valedictorian. On September 25, 1998, the trial was over, and Happy was a free man.

Happy was back home and working in his lab. His son, Danny, was working with him, not sure what he wanted to do. Two months later, his divorce was final. Phyllis got all her personal belongings and a $12 million dollar check. Happy had an offer from a food conglomerate for the farm in excess of twenty million, which he accepted. They agreed to keep Jonus on to oversee the farm at a $100,000 salary for a minimum of one year and then would reevaluate the situation.

Happy used that money to pay off the divorce settlement and gave Jonus Peppington a $250,000 bonus after the closing for doing a great job. It is now late August of 1998, and Danny had been working in the lab, helping his dad with some of the army projects since his graduation. Each day after 4:00 p.m., Danny would spend a couple hours playing with Hoddie after he fed him. Danny and Hoddie had a special bond. Danny had been told about his secret project with the magical eye and what a big part Hoddie had played in it. No one knew about this amazing eye project with the exception of Dr. Bennett, not even the general.

The eye needed some fine-tuning, and Happy had three working eyes—one was in Hoddie and the other two were used to improve the existing abilities and add new abilities to the eye. Every Tuesday, Happy and Danny would work strictly on the magical eye. Once a month, they would sedate Hoddie, remove the old eye, and replace it with the new and improved eye.

At this point, the magical eye could make a normal blind eye be able to see with 20/20 vision or see through six inches of solid steel; it could produce a laser beam and, if applied properly, could burn a hole through solid steel. All these functions had to be controlled by the brain. The eye could be set to do any one of these functions or all of them. In order to perform all functions with one eye, it would take the human brain to control them.

Hoddie, being a mammal and not having the ability of the human brain, could only process one function at a time. Happy continued experimenting with the eye and was making amazing progress.

On August 29, Danny told his father that he wanted to join the Navy and become a member of the elite division Navy SEALs. Happy told Danny he would prefer him to get his doctor's degree in a field of his choice but he would honor any decision that he made. Happy also told Danny that he might physically be able to perform the demanding training a Navy SEAL goes through; it was still very hard to be selected into that elite group. There were only a few openings and thousands of applicants, and he should talk to the local Navy recruiter and get more information.

Danny told Happy he would think about his options but that he needed to move on with his life.

CHAPTER FIVE

Daniel Peterson

Daniel Andrew Peterson was born in 1980 to Happy and Phyllis Peterson.

Daniel's father, Happy, was born into farming and inherited his farm from his father, Ben Peterson. Ben inherited the farm from his father, Daniel Peterson, who immigrated to America in 1917 from Sweden.

The immigrant Daniel, purchased the original land as timberland. He logged the land, sold off the timber to pay for the land, and made a farm out of the cleared land. The farm was located in the Rhinelander, Wisconsin, area and was named after his nickname, Dandy Dan, thereby becoming Dandy Dan Farms. He raised potatoes on the farm. Each generation expanded the acreage, and it eventually became the largest potato farm in Wisconsin.

As a small boy, Danny did very few farm chores, as his dad, Happy, did not want him to be a farmer. He wanted Danny to become a doctor. Danny was the only child, and his father, Happy, who also didn't want to be a farmer, became an eye surgeon and an inventor of medical apparatus later in life.

Danny did help his father around the farm until the age of twelve, at which time Happy removed Danny's responsibilities of farm chores and made him study and play sports. By the time Danny started his freshman year at Rhinelander High School, he had played Little League baseball, PONY league football, basketball, and junior swimming at the YMCA.

Danny stood 6 feet, 2 inches tall and weighed 220 pounds and was solid as a rock. He was extremely athletic and very handsome. He was very bright and, like his father, had an IQ that was in the genius range.

As a freshman, he played football for the junior varsity team. After the first game, he was moved to the Rhinelander varsity squad. Danny became a starting linebacker and was the second-string quarterback behind a very talented senior named Otis Taylor. He also played basketball and was on the swim team and wrestling team. He only wrestled in three team events after the 260-pound star senior wrestler Scott Davis was injured late in the season.

Danny won all three of his heavyweight matches. When the season ended and the state championships were starting, the coach had to make a decision. Scott had returned healthy. He was 12–1 for the season and had earned his way into the state championships. However, Danny was a better wrestler and had beaten Scott twice after his return to practice. The coach decided to bench Danny and send Scott to the state championships. Scott was a senior and could possibly get some scholarships if he did well at state.

Scott won four matches at state and made it to the finals of the heavyweight division. He would be wrestling last year's state champ from Milwaukee Central, who weighed over 300 pounds. He was undefeated since his junior year and had a 36–0 record. His name was Sylvester Samanski, and his nickname was the Pin Man. He had pinned thirty-four of his last thirty-six opponents.

Scott lost to Sylvester in the last seconds of the match on a two-point reversal. It was the most exciting match of the tournament and the score was 12 to 11. Scott was given a full scholarship to the University of Iowa, where he became an all-American.

The beginning of 1995 in Danny's sophomore year, he was named the starting quarterback and captain of the Rhinelander Hodag football team. The Hodags went 9–1, and Danny made second team all-state. After football, Danny had to make a decision—to play basketball, which he excelled at, or join the swim team, which he loved. He could only make one choice as their seasons were at the same time.

Both the basketball coach and the swimming coach wanted Danny. They both knew he was a star athlete, and not only would he help their team, but he would make them look good as coaches. They both started recruiting Danny even before football was over. Danny loved both sports but was won over by the swimming coach, who had a great personality and was a friend of his father, Happy. His name was Barry Wise.

Coach Wise told Danny that his father, Happy, still held four conference records in freestyle, the 100-, 200-, 400-, and 1,500-meter events as well as the 200 butterfly, 100 and 200 backstroke, and the 200 breaststroke. Happy still held the state record in the 400 and 1,500 freestyle, 200 butterfly, and the 200 backstroke.

Coach Wise reminded Danny that his father was still a legendary athlete at the high school and was often referred to as the Happy Hodag, a nickname given to Happy in his junior year. Coach Wise told Danny if he would work with him, they would try to break some of his dad's records. Danny, being very competitive, would love to take over some of his dad's records and keep them in the family. To the dismay of the basketball coach, Danny chose swimming.

In his sophomore year, Danny became the star of his swim team. He won many of his competitive swims and came within two seconds of two of his dad's records and within one second of another. The Rhinelander Hodags were conference champs.

When swimming was over, wrestling began. Danny wrestled in the heavyweight division and had to beat out two other heavyweight wrestlers to become the starter. It wasn't even close. Danny went 15–0 and wrestled some very good athletes in their North Woods conference. He also became state champ and finished 19–0.

It was a very good year for Danny athletically as well as scholastically. He retained a 4.0 average. He had classes in English, Spanish, algebra, science, US history, and biology. He was the most popular boy in school, and all the girls were crazy about him. All the girls wanted to go out with him, and Danny tried his best to accommodate all of them.

On Danny's sixteenth birthday, Happy bought him a customized van. It was baby blue, had a great stereo system, sunroof, all-leather interior, and it was loaded with every option you could imagine.

Happy had bought this vehicle for Danny because he was always hauling his athletic gear and friends around. He didn't want to buy him a sports car, in fear of him killing himself at such a young age. Happy knew that youth had no fear.

Danny was getting laid on a regular basis. His van turned into a love machine. His rear bench seat would be converted to a bed, and the girls loved it. He took many young girl's virginity in the back seat of that van. Danny had a mural of his pet seal, Hoddie, painted on each side of his van, with the inscription of "Sealed with a Kiss" below the seal's picture. Danny was getting more ass than a toilet seat.

In 1996 Danny began his junior year of high school. He was elected president of his junior class. He retained his 4.0 average throughout the year and was taking English 2, Spanish 2, Arabic, calculus, zoology, and world history. He was named all-state in football, and the Hodags went undefeated at 10–0. The swim team again won the conference championship, and Danny broke four of his dad's longtime swimming records that had stood for twenty-four years. Two of them were state records, the 400- and 1,500-meter freestyle events.

Danny went undefeated in the heavyweight division again at 15–0, went on to the state championships in Madison, and again won the state title by pinning all his opponents in the four matches. He again finished 19–0. He now has two state championships, and his unblemished career record was 41–0. His classmates nicknamed Danny the Happy Hodag, just like his father before him.

The girls were still flocking around Danny, and the back seat of the van had to be replaced. Danny had either screwed or got into the pants of every senior girl that he was interested in and now was working on the junior class. He had no long-term relationships with any of the girls. The only girl that he was interested in was a junior by the name of Shirley Adams. She was the homecoming queen and an absolute knockout, a real beauty.

She would not go out with Danny because of his reputation of "love them and leave them." Danny had asked Shirley out on three different occasions. She turned him down all three times and then turned him down again when he asked her to the junior prom.

The year 1997 had been another great year for Danny, with the exception of Shirley Adams. Danny spent the summer working with his dad, Happy, and spending time with his pet seal, Hoddie. Happy told Danny that he was so proud of him and he hoped Danny would break the rest of his swimming records next year.

Danny began his senior year in 1997 and again was elected president of his senior class. This year, he was studying French, Russian, trigonometry, health and the human body, physics, and psychology.

Danny continued his quest to try to lay every pretty girl in school and had already done a pretty good job. He continued trying to get Shirley to go out with him but kept getting turned down.

After another undefeated football season 10–0 and state honors and now holding the state record for most touchdowns scored in a high school career, Danny would be sought after by all the big universities looking for a star quarterback.

Danny was elected the homecoming king and Shirley Adams was again elected as the homecoming queen. This meant that Danny and Shirley would represent the royal couple at the homecoming dance. Finally, Danny was getting a date with Shirley.

At the homecoming dance, Shirley was dressed to kill in a stunning low-cut gown. She had the homecoming crown pinned to her beautiful blond hair. Danny was decked out in a tux with a red cummerbund and red bowtie. They were a beautiful couple and led the festivities off with an opening waltz.

Shirley would not allow Danny to pick her up before the dance; instead she met him at the homecoming dance. She had told Danny that both he and his van had a reputation that preceded themselves and she had no intentions of getting in his van.

They did spend the evening talking and dancing, and both were having a good time. In the beginning, Shirley held Danny at bay, not letting him get too close to her while they were slow dancing. By the end of the night and after a few glasses of champagne smuggled in by the senior class, they were dancing very close, and Shirley even kissed Danny on the cheek. Danny tried to talk her into letting him drive her home, but she refused and thanked him for a great evening. She gave him a kiss as the evening ended. Danny was infatuated with Shirley and was determined to win her over. He didn't know it, but he was falling in love.

Danny went on to break all of his dad's swimming records that year. The Hodags won their third straight conference swimming title. During the swimming season, Danny got Shirley to actually go out on a date with him. He picked her up in his father's car, and they went to an early movie and a late dinner. They had a great time and found out they had a lot in common. Danny drove her home and walked her to the door, trying to be a complete gentleman.

Shirley thanked him for a fun evening. She put her hands on his cheeks, gave him a big kiss, and stuck her tongue in his mouth.

Danny said, "Jesus Christ, you taste just like candy."

At that, she opened the door and said, "Good night. Thanks again."

Danny's heart was pounding, and he knew he wanted more candy.

Shirley started attending the season-ending swimming meets. After each meet, they would go to the local hangout and get a burger and fries. Shirley asked Danny if he would show her his pet seal. They made a date for the following Saturday, as swimming would be finished for the season. He told Shirley he would pick her up at noon and to bring a bathing suit and they would swim with Hoddie. He also informed her he would be picking her up in his van but that she would have nothing to worry about.

At noon on Saturday, Danny picked up Shirley. She asked him to come into her house and meet her parents. They knew who Danny was. He was in the sports section of the *Rhinelander Daily News* almost on a daily basis, but they had never met him. They spent about half an hour talking to her parents. They were very nice, and Danny felt comfortable around them.

They arrived at Danny's mansion about 1:00 p.m. He gave Shirley a tour of the house, and then they went to the lab. They stopped at the first lab, where Happy did all his research and had his office. Danny introduced Shirley to Happy, and they had a nice visit.

As they were departing to go into the other lab building, where Hoddie was, Happy said to Shirley, "You are a beautiful woman. I now can see why Danny is always talking about you."

Shirley blushed and said, "And I can see where Danny got his good looks."

They both smiled at each other, and Danny and Shirley headed for the other lab.

As they entered the large pool area, Hoddie spotted Danny and started his loud barking and was clapping his fins together. Hoddie swam up to Danny and gave him a big kiss. Danny then clapped his hands twice and pointed to Shirley's cheek and told Shirley to bend over. Hoddie gave Shirley a big kiss and started clapping his fins together.

Shirley immediately fell in love with Hoddie and started asking Danny a million questions about him. After about thirty minutes of sitting on the edge of the pool and answering all of Shirley's questions and going into some detail about the patch and Hoddie's blind eye, Danny asked Shirley if she would like to feed him. They went to the fish tank and threw Hoddie some fresh fish. Each time Shirley would throw him a fish, he would come out of the water, nod his head, and clap his flippers to thank her. Danny then made Hoddie show Shirley a variety of tricks that he had taught him. After the show, Danny told Shirley to feed him some more fish.

Hoddie was housed in a caged area just off the pool. There was a steel gate at one end of the pool that led to his housing quarters. When the gate was opened, Hoddie would swim into his berthing quarters, where he would spend the night. At 8:00 a.m., the gate would automatically open, and Hoddie would enter the pool, where he spent most of his day. The gate would remain open all day so he could come and go as he pleased. The gate would only close manually but could be opened anytime by remote control.

Danny told Shirley to go into the bathroom and change into her bathing suit and they would take a swim with Hoddie. While Shirley was changing, Danny slipped into his swim trunks and dove into the pool and started playing with Hoddie. As Shirley came out of the bathroom, she had on a very skimpy bikini, which showed off most of her beautiful body. She had let down her long blond hair, and she was stunning.

Danny was glad he was in the pool because he got an immediate erection. Shirley dove into the pool, and they began playing with Hoddie. After his erection was not so obvious, he put up the volleyball net, and the three of them played volleyball. Shirley couldn't believe how talented Hoddie was. After volleyball, Hoddie wouldn't leave them alone, so Danny opened the cage gate, and Hoddie swam into his quarters. Danny shut the gate, and they now had the pool to themselves.

They swam and played in the pool. Danny would get Shirley to stand on his shoulders, and he would send her flying through the air. Shirley swam into Danny's arms and gave him a kiss. Danny put his arms around her and kissed her back. He then said, "Can I have some candy?" She gave him another big kiss, only this time she stuck her tongue in his mouth. He was going crazy and got his huge erection back. Danny told her she was the most beautiful woman he had ever seen and he was falling in love with her.

They kissed again, and this time, she put her hand on his erection. Then she fell backward and said, "Wow, that thing is big." She pulled herself out of the pool, stood on the edge, and smiled at Danny. The tiny bikini showed off most of her large breasts and barely covered her bush. She slowly took off her top and then her bottom. She stood there, bare-ass naked. She slowly turned around and began modeling her body. Danny starting barking like a seal and clapping his hands together like Hoddie.

While laughing, Shirley dove into the pool as Danny was removing his trunks. She yelled at him "Catch me if you can!" and started swimming to the other side of the pool. Like a shark in the water, he caught up to her immediately. They embraced and starting kissing passionately. Danny started fondling and kissing her breast as she was massaging his shaft. Danny put his finger in her love canal, and she starting moaning. She whispered in his ear, "Be gentle. It is my first time."

Danny pulled her to the shallow end of the pool, and they began kissing passionately again. They were fondling each other and kissing each other all over. Danny told her to put her arms on the side of the pool and to lie back and relax. He then spread her legs and started kissing and licking her thighs. She started moaning, and then Danny started performing oral sex on her. She was going nuts. She was withering and humping and going spastic, and then she came all over Danny's face.

Her body went limp, and Danny said, "That's the best candy I have ever had. I love you."

They then reversed positions, and she spread Danny's legs and starting licking his thighs; now he was going nuts. She put her mouth over the tip of his cock and started sucking very slowly. Her lips were moving up and down his shaft. She could only get half his cock in her mouth, as it was so large. She started to pick up the pace, and wham, he shot his load all over her face. They both went limp and held each other in their arms.

They both began talking. Shirley said, "That was a first for me."

Danny said, "It wasn't my first, but it was my best." They both began laughing and kissing. Shirley reached down and grabbed Danny's cock. He already had another erection.

She said, "I am not sure I can handle that monster." They both laughed.

Danny said, "I don't want to hurt you. I am in love. Let's dry off and go back to my house." They both got dressed and went back to the mansion.

Danny took her upstairs to his bedroom, turned on the stereo very low, and played some sixties love songs. He laid her on his king-size bed and starting kissing her, and she passionately kissed him back. He started to remove her clothes, admiring and kissing each part of her body. When he got her completely naked, he started kissing her breasts and sucking her nipples. She began moaning, and he moved down to her clit and started kissing and licking her love nest. She was now going nuts again, and he removed all his clothes. Danny went to the bathroom and got some Vaseline. He told Shirley this would serve as a lubricant and help her accept him with more ease. He spread her legs and lubed her up with Vaseline and also put some on his cock.

He told Shirley, "If it hurts, tell me to stop. I will go slow and be gentle."

Danny now lay down beside her and began kissing her. He moved his hand to her vagina and inserted one finger. She began to moan; she was enjoying it. He now inserted two fingers and was massaging her clit. She was now going crazy and asking for more. He spread her legs wide open and lay on top of her. He inserted just the head of his cock and then slowly inserted a few more inches, and she was moaning and asking for more. The lubricant was working, and neither of them were dry. After he had about six inches inside her and moving in a faster rhythm, she went crazy. Shirley asked him to fuck her with his whole cock. He obliged her and now was grinding as hard and fast as he could. She was screaming and moaning, and wham, he shot his whole load inside her. He went limp, and so did she. They lay together, snuggled, and fell asleep.

When they awoke, it was getting dark, and she had to go home. One of her two older brothers was coming home for the weekend. He worked in Milwaukee, about four hours away. She had two brothers and one sister. Her sister was two years older than her and was in college at the University of Wisconsin in Madison. Her name was Candace, and she was majoring in criminology. She wanted a career in law enforcement.

Danny drove her home, and neither could stop talking or keep their hands off each other.

They had both fallen in love with each other. They would get together almost every day after wrestling practice. Every Sunday, they would swim with Hoddie and make love in the pool and then in his bedroom. They would use her bedroom when her parents were away, and sometimes during lunch hour at school, they would use the van.

The remainder of their senior year, they were together every day. Shirley would attend each one of his home wrestling matches. They talked about going to school together at the University of Wisconsin. They talked about what they might major in and about getting married after college and raising a big family.

Danny told her every time they kissed or made love that she tasted like candy to him because she was so sweet. He told her he was going to start calling her Candy. She said that he couldn't do that because her older sister's name was Candace and her nickname was Candy. Danny said he didn't care. Her sister wasn't here, and he would only call her Candy when they were alone. She agreed to that. She wanted to know if she could call him Big Dick, and he said only when they were alone. They both laughed and needled each other.

Danny again went undefeated in wrestling 15–0 and again was going to Madison for state finals. The finals were held on Saturday and Sunday. Danny was 56–0 for his career and had three more matches to win to get to the championship match.

No one had ever been 56–0 in their high school career in the state of Wisconsin. There were two other wrestlers from Rhinelander going to the state finals: Sam Donelson in the 165-pound division and Michael Bloom in the 120-pound division.

Candy had planned to drive to Madison Saturday morning to watch Danny wrestle and spend the night in hopes of watching him wrestle on Sunday for his third consecutive heavyweight state title.

Happy was also going to the state finals for the weekend to watch Danny wrestle. They all decided that Candy would drive with Happy and he would get separate hotel rooms for him and Candy. They would be staying in the Renaissance Hotel, the same hotel the wrestlers were staying in. They could all have dinner on Saturday night, and Danny could retire early to be rested for hopefully the championship match.

Danny and the other two wrestlers drove up in the coaches' van on Friday night so they could get a good night's sleep and get ready for their matches on Saturday.

Danny had three matches on Saturday—one at 10:00 a.m., one at 1:00 p.m., and one at 4:00 p.m. The championship match, if he made it that far, was scheduled for 11:00 a.m. on Sunday.

It was a three-hour ride to Madison, so Candy and Happy had to leave at 6:00 a.m. to be there for the first match. Danny won his first match. Sam Donelson and Michael Bloom also won their first matches. Danny spent about a half hour with Happy and Candy then had to meet with his coach and the other two wrestlers for a late lunch and discuss strategy for their next matches.

Danny won his second match by pinning his opponent in under a minute. Both Sam and Michael lost their second-round matches and were out of the tournament. Then at 4:00 p.m. in the semifinal match, he wrestled a three-hundred-pound farm boy who smelled like an old hog and was stronger than a bull. The smell was awful and distracted Danny quite a bit. He fell behind 6–3 with two minutes remaining. He scored 5 points in the last two minutes and won his match 8 to 6 and was now 59–0 and going to the state championship match at 11:00 a.m. the next morning.

Danny, Candy, Happy, and the coach had dinner together at the hotel at 6:30 p.m. They all had a nice meal and talked until about 8:30. Danny made fun of the three-hundred-pounder he beat in his third match and said he almost forfeited the match because he thought he was going to pass out from the smell. The coach said he could smell him from the bench and said he saw the referee making disgusting faces.

They all laughed, and the coach said to Danny, "Get to bed early and get plenty of rest. You have the toughest match of your career tomorrow. This guy you are wrestling tomorrow is also undefeated this year and has a great coach."

Danny had slipped Candy a note under the table, telling her to unlock her door at 9:25 p.m. and that he would be there at 9:30 p.m. She was on the second-floor, three rooms from his dad's room. Danny's room was on the fifth floor.

Before leaving the restaurant, the coach told Danny to meet him for breakfast at 8:00 a.m. sharp. They would have a light breakfast, go to the gym, have a workout, and talk about his opponent and their strategies.

At 9:30 p.m. Danny was in Candy's room. She was in a satin see-through negligee and smelled just like candy. Danny took off all his clothes and had a huge erection. They made mad, passionate love all night long. They had sex in positions they never had before. They loved, laughed, and giggled all night long.

They had left a wakeup call for 7:00 a.m. so Danny could get to his room, take a shower, and meet the coach at 8:00 a.m. When the phone rang at 7:00 a.m., they were still going at it like two horny monkeys. Danny got up, put his clothes on, kissed Candy, told her he loved her, and said that was the best night of his life.

When Danny got out of the elevator, the coach was getting into the elevator. The coach said, "I just knocked on your door." Danny said, "I got up early and took a walk, thinking about my match. I had a lot on my mind. I will meet you for breakfast at 8:00."

Danny picked up the phone and called Candy's room. When she picked up, he said, "I just called to tell you I love you and I have another erection."

She laughed and said, "Take a cold shower and start thinking about your match. I am going to take a two-hour nap and dream about you." They hung up, and Danny took a shower, got dressed, and met his coach for breakfast.

The guy Danny was wrestling today was from Eau Claire Wisconsin. He was big, fast, and undefeated. His name was Red Savage. He had red hair and a small red beard and was very muscular. The two best heavyweight wrestlers in the state would be facing off against each other this morning. One would no longer be undefeated.

As the coach and Danny were discussing the strengths and weaknesses of Red Savage, the coach looked at Danny and said, "You're pale and look weak. Did you get a good night's sleep?" The coach didn't ask him why, but he knew. Coach said, "There is no way you can last six minutes with this guy. He will kick your butt." They strategized that if Danny was going to beat Red Savage today, he would have to do it in the first two-minute round. That meant Danny would have to pin him. Coach told Danny that Red was very aggressive and liked to try to throw his opponents to the mat at the opening bell and fall on them for a two-point takedown. They decided that Danny would let Red throw him to the mat and as Red dove on top of him, Danny would do his lightning reversal escape and try to get his right leg under Red's armpits and the back of his neck and apply his 220 pounds to Red's upper-body area and try to pin him immediately. It was called the claw hold, a move Danny had not used since his sophomore year.

The University of Wisconsin gym was packed and Happy and Candy had front-row seats. Both wrestlers were introduced. The announcer made note that they were both undefeated this year and that Danny was undefeated the past three years, had a record of 59–0, and was the reigning state champ the last two years. They both received standing ovations and went to their bench for last-minute instructions from their coaches.

The coaches were friends and had both wrestled for the Wisconsin Badgers back in the midseventies. In fact, last summer, they went on a fishing trip together in the backwaters of Minnesota, a trip they took every other year together for the past ten years. They fished the boundary waters for bass and walleye in a canoe and made camp in a tent. Their lives revolved around wrestling, fishing, and hunting, and both were very competitive.

This match meant as much to the two coaches as it did to Danny and Red. Coaches were paid in accordance to their team's performances, their conference records, and how they did at the state championships. It wasn't just about their competitive nature. It was about money.

The wrestlers were called to the center of the ring. The referee made them shake hands, pushed them apart, blew his whistle, and the match began.

The two wrestlers circled each other for about fifteen seconds. Then Red made his aggressive takedown move, and Danny let him easily throw him to the mat. Red quickly dove on top of Danny and got a two-point takedown, but no sooner was Red on top of Danny than Danny did his lightning reversal move while successfully applying the unescapable claw move to his head and shoulders. Within less than one minute, Red was pinned, and the match was over. Danny was now 60–0 and a three-time heavyweight wrestling champ. The Happy Hodag was exhausted. Danny and Red shook hands. Danny and the coach hugged each other, the two coaches shook hands, and Happy and Candy ran out on the floor. Happy shook Danny's hand and gave him a big hug.

Danny picked Candy up off the floor and gave her a big hug, and as they kissed, she ran her tongue down this throat. He stepped back and said, "Don't do that. I will get an erection out here." They both laughed and started mingling with other people from Rhinelander who came to see this historic wrestling legend.

Sam, Michael, and Danny all had to ride back with the coach. It was school policy. School was on Monday and less than two months to graduation on June 1. Candy and Danny decided to swim with Hoddie after school on Monday.

It is now the first of April, and Danny and Candy are head over heels in love. They were inseparable. They would be graduating on June 1, and they both planned on attending the University of Wisconsin together in Madison. Danny had already accepted a full athletic scholarship and would be wrestling for the Badgers.

Candy had already applied and was awaiting acceptance. What Candy didn't know was that Danny had told the head wrestling coach that his acceptance of his wrestling scholarship would depend on Candy being accepted at UW.

Every coach in the country wanted Danny. He had plenty of leverage. The coach assured Danny that she would be accepted, but no one could know of this arrangement. Nothing would be in writing, and she would have to go through all the standard procedures, including a visit in July to tour the campus and meet with the dean of admissions.

Candy and Danny spent a lot of time at the lab, helping Happy and playing with Hoddie. While still in school, they would go out to his van at lunch hour and have some afternoon delight. The end of April, Danny proposed to Candy and gave her a beautiful diamond engagement ring. They had been planning their lives together for some time. They would not set a wedding date for several years but were making a commitment to each other. They planned a huge engagement party for June 5, four days after graduation. Candy's parents loved Danny, and Happy loved Candy. Neither family had any problems with their engagement.

A trip to the University of Wisconsin in Madison was planned for Candy's acceptance, registration, and indoctrination for July 13,

14, and 15. It was a trip she must take with her parents without Danny, as he was told to lay low until after she was accepted. Life was beautiful. Love was in the air, and everything was perfect.

Then on May 6, Danny's father, Happy, shot and killed Gus Peterson, his farming partner. Happy walked in on his wife, Phyllis, and Gus as they were having sex in his bed. He shot Gus right between the eyes after he first shot him in the balls.

Happy went to jail. There were two hearings and a trial. Everyone's life was turned upside down, and of course, being from such a small town, the rumors were flying. Very high-ranked military and political figures got involved. Happy was working on top secret programs for the Army. After Happy's second hearing on May 23 and one week before Danny's graduation, Happy was out on bail. Bail was set at $1,000,000. He was free to do whatever he needed but could not leave the county. A trial date was set for September 25.

Now that Happy was out of jail, things began to calm down. His wife, Phyllis, had moved out of town, and they were going through divorce proceedings.

Happy attended the graduation on June 1 where his son was honored as the class valedictorian. He finished his entire four years of high school with a 4.0 grade average. He also attended the engagement party that had over four hundred people: the entire senior class, all their friends, neighbors, and relatives. Happy did not stay very long, as he was getting bombarded with questions about his situation. The party was a huge success—live music, delicious food, and plenty to drink. It went on until 3:00 a.m.

After graduation, Danny and Candy spent every day at the labs. Happy had both of them on his payroll; they were making nice salaries. They would leave Rhinelander every weekend and travel to different places around the state.

On the Fourth of July, they had a big party at Happy's house. They hired a professional in pyrotechnics to set off major fireworks. It was a wonderful gathering. Flags were flying, fireworks were going off, a band was playing, and everyone was dancing and drinking.

Danny and Candy spent the night together at his house. They didn't wake up until 10:00 a.m. Candy rolled over and cuddled next to him and said she had some news. She told Danny she was pregnant. You could have heard a pin drop. Then Danny grabbed Candy, kissed her, and said, "I guess we will be starting our family sooner than expected." Candy was so happy that Danny was not mad. In fact, Danny was just the opposite and was ecstatic about the news.

They talked about what they should do. Danny's first suggestion out of his mouth was, "Let's not tell anybody until you and I can figure out what we should do and weigh all our options. One option we do not have is abortion. We will not abort this baby." He then kissed her belly and put his ear on her navel and said, "Talk to me, kid." They both laughed.

Danny told Candy that they both needed to think about their situation and not tell anybody about her pregnancy until after she returned from her enrollment process in Madison on the July 15. They both decided that was the right thing to do rather than making any quick decisions they may later regret.

On July 13, Candy and her parents drove to Madison and began her enrollment process. While they were there, they would visit her sister, Candace, who was in her third year at the University of Wisconsin. Candace was majoring in criminology. Candace and Shirley were very close. Not only were they sisters; they were best friends.

Shirley was dying to talk to someone about her pregnancy even though she and Danny agreed not to tell anyone until Candy returned from Madison. When Candace and Shirley were alone on Saturday, Candy told Candace. Her sister was very concerned about her sister's situation. She also knew that she loved Danny and they were engaged to be married and was sure they would work things out. Candace agreed not to say anything about this to her parents, as they would find out soon enough and should be informed by Shirley, not her.

On Sunday afternoon, Shirley and her parents said goodbye to Candace and headed back to Rhinelander. That afternoon of July 15, they were involved in a head-on collision with a tractor trailer. The driver either fell asleep behind the wheel or had a heart attack. All four of them died at the scene.

Danny did not find out about it until the next morning. The sheriff pulled into Happy's driveway and informed Happy of the horrible accident and that they all died at the scene of the accident on Highway 51, just outside of Wausau, only about sixty miles from home. Happy went limp and almost fell. The sheriff caught him, and they sat down. The sheriff told Happy that his office would start notifying the next of kin that morning. The sheriff thought he should notify Happy and Danny first because he was aware of Danny and Shirley's relationship and their engagement.

Happy thanked the sheriff and tried to gather himself before he told Danny. Danny was in the pool, playing with his pet seal, Hoddie. Happy went to the pool, stripped down to his underwear, dove into the pool, and swam over to Danny and Hoddie. Happy was crying, and Danny grabbed his dad and said, "What's wrong, Dad."

They swam to the shallow end of the pool, where they could stand. Hoddie followed them. Happy put his arm around his son and gave him the bad news. Danny's body went completely limp, and his dad had to hold him up. Danny started immediately crying and started yelling. He hollered, "This can't be true! Tell me it not true!" Happy assured him it was true and that the sheriff was notifying their relatives this morning. Happy told him that Shirley and her parents were all killed yesterday in a head-on collision just outside of Wausau.

Danny was crying and screaming. He scared Hoddie, who swam up to him and put his flipper around his shoulder. Danny just melted, and his dad lifted him out of the pool. Danny lay motionless on the floor for fifteen minutes, his dad by his side and Hoddie staring at him from the pool.

Danny and Happy went back to the house. Danny went to his room and grieved. He did nothing for two days—never left his room and spoke to no one. The third day, he ate breakfast and looked at all the calls on his phone. Happy explained to Danny that the funerals would be in two days and that Shirley's sister has been trying to get hold of him since Monday. Today was Wednesday, and the funerals were Friday.

Danny picked up the phone and called Candace. She was at her parents' home with her two brothers. They were planning the funerals. Candace told Danny that she knew he was devastated, but they all were, as he might imagine. Danny agreed to meet them at their house and try to help with arrangements. Danny had met the entire family on several occasions, so he knew Candace and the two brothers fairly well.

As Danny entered the front door, Candace met him with a big hug. She could have been Shirley's twin sister, only about three years older. The brothers shook his hand and gave him a hug. All four of them began crying. Danny spent the next two days with the three of them preparing for the funeral and burial. They would all three be laid to rest together in the cemetery that also housed her grandparents. Earlier, Candy's parents had bought six burial plots next to the parents of Candy's dad, with the intention that one day his whole family would be buried there. That day came too soon.

Before the funerals, Danny and Candace went for a walk. They talked about Shirley and the special relationship they both had with her. Candace explained to Danny that she knew much more about him than he might think. Shirley and her were not just sisters but best friends, and Shirley confided with her on most everything. Candace didn't want to go into everything Shirley had told her, but she let him know that her sister told her about the pregnancy.

Danny told Candace it was all he could think about the past few days. He was glad that Shirley had told her because now he had someone to talk to about the issue. First, he wanted to know if she had told anyone, including her brothers. She assured him that she had not.

They walked for over two hours and discussed many topics. Danny told her that his pet name for her sister was Candy. To Danny's surprise, she said she knew and that it was because he thought she tasted like candy. Danny blushed, and Candace said, "Don't worry. I told you I knew more about you than you can imagine. I know you took her virginity, that you were very gentle with her, that you were a great lover, and that you have a pet seal. Most of all, I know you are a real man with real feelings and that you loved my sister. As you know, my nickname is Candy—not because I taste like candy, but because Candy is a common nickname for Candace. Everyone calls me Candy, so feel free to do the same unless it would bother you." Then Candace continued. "Let's talk about the unborn baby. Tell me what you have been thinking."

Danny said he thought about telling his dad and also telling her and her two brothers and to ask for advice. Obviously, the baby was dead, and no one would know she had been pregnant. "I assume you were the only one she told."

Candace assured Danny she was the first and last person to know, unless Shirley had told their mom and dad on the way home before the accident, but she doubted that very much, as Shirley was anxious to get home and discuss this with Danny so that the two of them could make plans.

Danny said to Candace, "After much thought, I have decided not to tell anyone." A part of him died the day Shirley died, and he thought it would be nice for Shirley to be buried with her unborn baby inside her, thereby having the child with her for eternity and also having a part of him with her.

At that, they stopped walking. Candace hugged him and gave him a kiss and said, "That's the most wonderful sincere thing I have ever heard from a man. I agree with you 100 percent. Let's drop that subject and talk about you. I know you are devastated by her death, but life will go on. I hope you will continue with your original plans of going to college and getting your doctor's degree. You have got the whole world by the balls. You can go to any school you want on full scholarship. Do not let that go to waste. Please continue your education, even if you decide to wait a year and let all this pass."

Danny gave Candace a big hug and thanked her for the advice and agreeing with him about Shirley and the baby. He said, "I feel like I now have someone to talk to that reminds me of my Candy, and if you don't mind, I would like to call you Candy."

Candace said, "That makes me feel good. Please keep in touch with me. You have my phone number."

The viewing was on Friday, and the funeral was on Saturday, the twenty-first. Danny spent all day and all night Friday at the funeral home, never leaving Shirley's casket. He decided to name the unborn baby Sam—Samuel if it was a boy and Samantha if it was a girl. Sam covered both. Danny shared that with Candace, and she loved it. After the burial, Candy had to go back to school, but before leaving, she gave Danny her phone number, her address at school, and her e-mail address and told him to stay in touch with her.

Danny went back to work with his dad, working on the classified Army projects, playing and training Hoodie, and working on the magical eye with his dad. Happy's trial was just over sixty days away. Danny delayed his commitment to school for at least a semester, as he was going nowhere until his dad's trial was over and he was certain his dad was a free man.

For over thirty days after the funeral, Danny couldn't get Candy and the baby out of his mind. He had thought about many options he had, but he knew he had to leave town once his dad's trial was over and he was set free. Danny had been visiting the local Navy recruiter, getting information on the Navy SEALs. The recruiter knew all about Danny, his athletic accomplishments, all his state titles, etc. Danny was showing real interest in joining the Navy if he could get into the Navy SEAL program.

The recruiter told Danny that his chances of getting into the SEAL program was more than a hundred to one. If he were lucky enough to get into the program, he was sure Danny could survive the rigorous training, which would last six months. He told Danny that if he didn't know a congressman, senator, admiral, or general, his chances were very slim even with his outstanding résumé.

Late in August, Danny told Happy he wanted to join the Navy SEALs, get out of town after the trial, and put the death of Shirley behind him. He wanted to spread his wings and see what would happen. It was time for him to leave the nest, but he was not interested in college at this time. He also told his dad he had no shot of getting into the elite SEAL program unless he knew someone in high places. He related to his dad what he found out from his recruiter.

Happy would prefer Danny go to school now rather than later, but basically, he had done the same thing when he had to return to the farm and finish his education later. Danny asked his dad if he would mind if he called the general. After all, he remembered the vicelike grip and the eye-to-eye contact he had with General Smith and the general saying to him, "If you ever decide to join the military and need my help, call me. You have my number."

Happy said, "Go ahead. Call him. I just talked to him last Thursday, and he was asking about you."

Danny called General Dwight Smith on September 1, 1998, twenty-five days before his father's trial. After a few pleasantries on the phone, Danny reminded the general of his comment about calling him if he ever decided to join the military.

The general acknowledged saying that and told Danny he just spoke to his dad last week. The general also congratulated Danny on winning his third straight state championship in wrestling and gave Danny his condolences in the loss of his fiancée. He also said, "Happy had told me that you were going to the University of Wisconsin on a full athletic scholarship. So what's this about the military?"

Danny explained to the general that he needed to make some changes in his life and put off his education until a later date and that he would like to join the Navy and become a SEAL. He explained to the general that the local Navy recruiter told him it was all but impossible to get into the SEAL program unless he knew someone in high places.

The general said to Danny, "If you want to go into the military, how about going to West Point and becoming an army officer? I know I could get you in there, and they would love to have you." Danny told him he had been offered a scholarship to West Point, but right now he wanted to become a Navy SEAL and he wanted to experience some combat and serve his country.

The general knew he had been offered athletic and scholastic scholarships to almost every college in the country. The general asked Danny if he was 100 percent sure he wanted to do this, and Danny simply answered 100 percent yes. The general told him he would see what he could do. He had some admiral friends in the Navy. He said he couldn't make him any guarantees, but he thought he might be able to help him. The general would call him back within two weeks and let him know.

Danny thanked him and told him he was nervous about his dad's trial on the twenty-fifth. General Smith told Danny he had nothing to worry about and that it was all he could say. They bid each other goodbye, and Danny said, "I will look forward to your call."

The general called Happy the next day and asked him what he thought about Danny wanting to join the Navy and become a SEAL and if he wanted the general to get him in? Happy told the general, "I would rather Danny pursue other options, but I know my son is special. I am not worried about Danny's future. I want Danny to be happy and to do what he thinks he must do, so yes, I would like you to help him become a SEAL."

The general said, "I need to talk to you about another project anyway. Let's set up a meeting on September 18, a week before your trial. I will be there for two days. We will discuss this new project, existing and ongoing projects, and some possible improvements to the old C7 visual shield. We will also discuss your trial and meet with Danny with my findings."

The meeting was set, and the general told Happy to tell Danny to be available for those dates. Happy told Dwight to plan on staying at his house during his two-day stay, and the general agreed.

On the eighteenth, Happy picked up the general at the airport. The general flew in on his private jet. On the way to Happy's lab, the general informed him he was able to get Danny admitted to the elite SEAL training program and would go over the details with both of them at dinner. Happy said that they would be having some huge grilled porterhouse steaks, fresh corn on the cob, and twice-baked potatoes with a surprise desert and that Danny was going to be the chef. The general said, "Christ, Happy, is there anything that kid of yours can't do?" Happy simply said no, and they both laughed.

Happy and the general spent the next three hours in Happy's office, discussing business matters. At 5:00 p.m. when they were finished, the general asked where Danny was and Happy told him he was either in the other lab with his pet seal or at home, getting ready to prepare their dinner. The general asked to go into the other lab that hosted the seal to see if Danny was still there.

As they entered the lab, Danny was taking down the volleyball net, and Hoddie was barking and clapping his fins at the sight of Happy. Danny jumped out of the pool, and Hoddie came right behind him.

Danny shook the general's hand, looked him square in the eye, and said, "It is great to see you, General." The handshake was just like the last one. It was a vicelike grip, and each was trying to squeeze harder than the other.

Hoddie, standing next to Danny, extended his fin to the general, and the general shook his fin and said, "Nice to meet you, Hoddie." Hoddie barked twice and nodded his head. The general laughed and said, "Here I stand beside someone who wants to become a SEAL and another one who already is." They all three laughed, and Hoddie barked with them.

Danny said, "Let me put Hoddie away and feed him, and I will meet you two at the house and start preparing dinner."

Happy said, "No, we will put Hoddie away and feed him. You go home now and start preparing dinner. We are starving." Happy let the general feed Hoddie, commanded a few tricks from Hoddie, and the general was amazed.

He said, "That's one smart seal. I assume he lost an eye, therefore the permanent-looking patch."

Happy explained to the general that Hoddie was one of numerous mammals and birds that Happy had acquired to use in his many experiments. Those experiments helped Happy invent some of the products that he was now supplying to the US military. Danny had gotten so attached to Hoddie that he let Danny keep him as a pet and that, yes, Hoddie was blind in one eye.

Happy did not reveal to the general that Hoddie was an invaluable tool being used in the development of the magical eye that only four people knew about—Happy, Danny, Dr. Harold Bennett, and Candy, though Candy was now dead.

Dr. Bennett was the brain surgeon who helped Happy successfully attach the magical eye to Hoddie's brain. Harold Bennett graduated from the University of Wisconsin with Happy. They had been friends all through college and got their doctor's degrees at the same time. Dr. Bennett was now a well-known brain surgeon working with the Mayo Clinic in Minneapolis, Minnesota. Although they generally only saw each other twice a year, they stayed in contact via phone on a weekly basis. They hunted and fished together. Harold was Happy's best friend and the godfather of Danny. Harold was one of the first people to visit Happy when he was locked up for killing Gus Peterson.

As Happy and the general were about to put Hoddie away for the night, Hoddie jumped out of the pool and shook the general's hand again and gave Happy a kiss. The general just shook his head, and they went to the house.

Danny had the big porterhouse steaks marinating. The twice-baked potatoes and the fresh corn on the cob could all be ready in twenty minutes. He would just wait for the word. He knew they would have cocktail first.

Happy and the general freshened up and came down to the kitchen, where the general saw these huge porterhouses and said, "Danny, it looks like you're about to feed the whole Army."

Danny said, "I am."

They laughed and made cocktails and walked into the big porch, where Danny had set the table. On the porch was a big built-in grill, a bar, and a huge fireplace, which was now burning some seasoned oak. There were four lounge chairs and a sofa with coffee tables facing the fireplace.

As the three of them sat and took their first sip of their twenty-year-old Kentucky bourbon on the rocks, the general took over. The general first told Danny that he admired all his scholastic and athletic achievements and acknowledged that at such a young age, he felt Danny was already a man and would be able to accomplish any task that he decided to tackle. The general went on to tell Danny that he would make the perfect military officer and that West Point would always be open to him if he decided to alter his direction.

"That being said, I was able to get you into the elite SEAL team training program. However, there are a few stipulations. You must attend regular Navy boot camp for twelve weeks in San Diego, California. You will then attend sixteen weeks of communications training in Bainbridge, Maryland, as a radioman. You will then be sent to Coronado, California, to the elite SEAL team training program. You will spend six months in Coronado, and if you survive that, you will be sent to an undisclosed destination for further training to become combat ready. If you become a combat-ready SEAL, you will be assigned to a six-man team and become a member of SEAL Team Six. At that time, you will be serving your country by being deployed into highly classified, dangerous locations around the world.

"You are to never mention my name, never mention the fact that it was predetermined that you would be going to radioman school and then on to SEAL training. You will act like all other sailors in boot camp, wondering where your next active-duty station will be. You must enlist locally with your local Navy recruiter for four years. Do not discuss with your recruiter any of this discussion. Immediately after boot camp in San Diego, you will be given two weeks' leave before reporting to radio school in Bainbridge, Maryland. After radio school, you will be given two more weeks' leave before reporting to Coronado for your first six months of SEAL training. You will officially enlist on October 1, 1997, one week after your dad's trial date. Any questions?"

Danny said, "What if my dad's trial is not over by October 1?"

The general said, "It will be."

At that, Happy said to Danny, "Let's eat."

And Danny started preparing dinner, while Happy made him and the general another bourbon on the rocks. As the general finished his delicious steak prepared to perfection as well as his twice-baked potato and corn on the cob, he said to Danny, "The best steak I have ever eaten. Are you sure you don't want to join the Army and become my personal chef?"

They all laughed, and Danny served them a slice of his famous rhubarb pie topped with vanilla ice cream and a special caramel sauce.

After dinner, while they were enjoying a small glass of cognac and a cigar, both Happy and Danny thanked the general for all he had done. They asked the general if there was anything they could do for him.

The general said, "Yes, there are two things. First, become the best goddamn SEAL the Navy has ever produced. And second, when Captain Patrick O'Conner comes here two days before Happy's trial to defend him, put him up in your magnificent home and cook him this exact meal you cooked for me."

They both said, "Done."

The general raised his glass and made a toast to Danny's next step in life, and then they all retired to bed.

On September 23, Captain Patrick O'Conner arrived at the Rhinelander airport on General Smith's private jet at 10:00 a.m. Both Danny and Happy picked him up and took him home with them.

They spent the day going over proceedings that would occur in court on the twenty-fifth. Happy was instructed what to say when asked specific questions while on the stand. He was also instructed to say "I do not recall" if he was asked any questions regarding the shooting—before, during, or after the shooting—and also the fact that he didn't remember calling the police. Danny was told he would be called to the stand by the captain and asked three specific questions. First was, how often he saw his father during the day. The answer would be never, that he was buried in his work at the lab and normally would come to the house between 7:00 p.m. and 8:00 p.m. for dinner. Second was, how often did he see his uncle Gus and where he would normally see him. The answer would be quite often, maybe three or four times a week, and always in or around the house. Third was, if he was aware of any guns in the house. The answer would be that he knew they had many guns in the house, as his dad and him were avid hunters. There were three loaded pistols in three separate areas of the house, which his mom, dad, and him were all aware of. They were there for their protection in case of a break-in.

Patrick told them both not to offer any information that wasn't asked and not to expand on any questions asked by the prosecuting attorney other than a simple yes or no. Patrick told them the trial would be over the next day on the twenty-sixth at the latest. There would be no jury, and the judge would make the ruling and the sentence.

Danny made the captain and Happy the same meal the general had. Patrick commented that it was as fine a meal as he had ever had and that he had been looking forward to it ever since his last meeting with the general, who had told him he was in for a special treat.

After dinner, the captain asked Danny if he would show him his pet seal that the general had told him about. They went to Hoddie's lab, turned on the lights, and opened up Hoddie's gate. He swam out into the pool, barking at them. Danny took the captain to the fish holder and told him to throw Hoddie a few fish. After Hoddie devoured about a half dozen large fish, he jumped out of the pool and slid up to the captain and extended his flipper. The captain shook his flipper and laughed. Danny had Hoddie perform a few tricks, and they put him back in his house and shut the gate. The captain was quite impressed and stated he never knew seals were so intelligent. Danny assured the captain that that seals were intelligent, but not to the degree that Hoddie was; he was special.

On September 25, at 9:00 a.m., the judge entered the courtroom, and the bailiff asked all to rise. The judge acknowledged the prosecution, the defense, and the packed courthouse and asked them all to be seated. The bailiff announced the case number, docket number, and charges brought against Happy Peterson by the state of Wisconsin. The judge asked the defendant to rise and asked him how he pleaded.

Captain O'Conner told the judge that the defendant pleads not guilty by reason of temporary insanity.

The judge looked at Happy and said, "Is this your plea?"

Happy simply said, "Yes, Your Honor."

At that, the judge called the court to order, and the trial began.

The prosecutor called some witnesses to testify, and after they all had testified, he then called Happy to the stand and grilled him about the murder for over an hour. All responses from Happy were yes and no or that he couldn't remember or didn't recall. The judge then asked Happy's attorney if he would like to cross-examine any of the witnesses that had testified.

The captain said that the only witness he wanted to cross-examine was the defendant, Happy Peterson but first he would like to call his only witness, Daniel Peterson, Happy's son. The judge said, "Please proceed."

The captain asked Danny how often he would see his father during the day, how often he saw his uncle Gus and where, if there were any guns in the house, and if so, where they were kept and who knew about them. Danny answered all the questions just like they had rehearsed.

Then Patrick called Happy to the stand, told the court of Happy's reputation, generosity, and involvement in the community. He then asked Happy the last thing he could remember the day of the shooting.

Happy answered, "Standing in the doorway of my bedroom, watching my cousin Gus Peterson making love to my wife while she was moaning and screaming how much she loved him and for him to give her more."

The captain asked Happy if he remembered retrieving the .357 magnum, and Happy said no. Patrick asked him if he remembered shooting Gus in the balls and then in the head, and Happy said no.

Patrick then said, "Do you remember dragging your wife downstairs and pushing her outside?"

Happy said no.

The captain asked Happy if he remembered calling the police, and Happy said no. The captain asked Happy the first thing he could remember after witnessing his wife making love to his cousin and business partner. Happy said, "Waking up in jail."

Captain O'Conner then recapped Happy's testimony by saying, "Mr. Peterson, what you are telling this court is that you cannot remember or recall anything from the first time you witnessed the scene in your bedroom until you woke up in jail. Is that your testimony?"

Happy responded by saying, "Not only is that my testimony, it is the God's truth."

Captain O'Conner said, "I have no more questions."

The judge asked the prosecution if they would like to cross-examine Happy. The state's prosecutor simply said, "No, we rest our case."

By this time, it was late in the day, and the judge said, "This court is adjourned until 9:00 a.m. tomorrow morning, when I will deliver a verdict and pronounce sentence."

Harry, Danny, and the captain were starving. They didn't want to go to a restaurant as they would be hounded by many of the local residents, so they ordered a couple of pizzas and had them delivered to the house.

While they were eating pizza and drinking a few ice-cold beers, Danny asked the captain why the prosecutor didn't cross-examine either him or his father. Patrick looked them both in the eye, winked at them, and said, "That's a question for the general." They all smiled and knew the answer. They then went to Hoddie's lab fed him some fish, watched him perform some more tricks, and then retired to bed in anticipation of tomorrow morning's verdict.

They all rose early in the morning of the twenty-sixth, had some breakfast, and prepared for the day. They arrived at the courthouse an hour early, got some coffee, and sat in the courtroom, awaiting the arrival of the judge. The captain had made both Happy and Danny confident that the decision would go the right way for them. Both Happy and Danny knew that life was full of uncertainties and that sometimes unfortunate things happened in your life. It was never over until it was over. It was now 9:00 a.m., and the judge entered from his chambers into the packed courtroom. There were reporters from all across the state. Relatives and friends were crammed into the courthouse, and another hundred or so were standing outside on the courthouse steps.

The bailiff bellowed out, "All rise!"

The judge took his seat and asked everyone, "Please be seated." The judge pounded his gavel on the desk and said, "This court is in order." The judge picked up a single sheet of paper and read from it. "This court finds Happy Peterson, the defendant, innocent by the reason of temporary insanity. He is a free man. This court is adjourned."

And just like that, it was over. Happy and Danny took the captain to the airport. They exited through the back of the courthouse to avoid all the reporters. They shook hands on the tarmac, gave each other hugs, and the captain was off on the general's private jet. Happy and Danny went back home to celebrate this burden that had been lifted off their chests.

Shortly after entering their home, Happy popped open two cold beers, and as they clicked bottles, Happy's private phone rang. It was the general. Happy informed him he was putting him on speaker so that they could both talk to him. The general congratulated Happy on the verdict and told them both that he could feel their relief. The general went on to tell them how close he had grown to them and considered them family. Nothing else had to be mentioned about this matter, and they were not to ask him any questions. The only thanks he wanted was a promise from Danny that he would become the best Navy SEAL that he could be and a promise that one day he would cook him another meal as good as the one he had just experienced with them.

Danny shouted out, "You got it, General! And thank you from the bottom of our hearts."

At that, the general said, "I am sorry, guys. I have to go. I look forward to seeing you both in the future." And then he hung up.

Happy and Danny had grown very close to the general, but even now Happy's magical eye was still a secret and not shared with the general. A lot of the functions from the magical eye were used to invent optical-type equipment that Happy invented and sold to the military. Happy was not going to share any information about the magical eye with anyone besides Dr. Bennett and Danny. Besides, Happy was not supposed to work on any private ventures for five years per an agreement he earlier made with the general.

Happy figured he would be completely finished with the magical eye in about two more years. The eye could already cure some blindness and could create such heat it could melt or bore a hole through eight inches of solid steel. It could allow someone to see through clothes, walls, rock, and steel. Happy wanted to improve on these features and add additional ones. With Dr. Harold Bennett's help, he'd be able to attach this magical eye to the human brain and have the human brain control the eye to do single or multifunctions.

Happy was currently working on a laser function for the eye that would allow the eye to produce a very strong laser beam, which would give the eye many more abilities. Danny's pet seal, Hoddie, was a key element in Happy's scientific experiment, but he knew one day it would have to be tried out on humans. Once completely perfected, this eye and the variations of the eye would be worth billions of dollars.

On October 1, 1998, Danny was on his way to basic training in San Diego, California.

CHAPTER SIX

The Navy

Danny arrived at the San Diego airport at 11:00 a.m. with his limited luggage he was told to bring. He and about thirty other recruits were loaded on a naval bus and driven to the naval station, where they were unloaded and processed.

At boot camp, there are eighty sailors in a company. Each company was assigned a barracks that all eighty sailors would call home for the next twelve weeks.

Danny's company was number 109. Each company had four platoons with twenty men in each platoon. Each company had a chief petty officer, who was in charge, and he was called the company commander.

The chief would assign one recruit to each platoon to be the platoon leader. The chief would read all eighty résumés to determine whom he would pick as his platoon leaders. All companies would compete against one another for different awards at the graduation ceremonies. The company commanders were graded upon how well their companies did at graduation.

They marched everywhere they went, and they exercised three times a day. Reveille was at 5:00 a.m. each morning, and lights out was at 8:00 p.m. At 5:00 a.m. each morning, a loudspeaker would blast out, "Reveille! Reveille! All hands on deck. The smoking lamp is now lit in all berthing areas."

At 6:00 a.m. their bed was made, and the barracks were clean, and they marched to the mess hall for breakfast. After marching back from breakfast, the day began with an hour's worth of exercising.

A typical day consisted of marching, exercising, classes in everything you could imagine—firefighting, swimming, survival, hygiene, tying knots, gas masks, hand-to-hand combat, and a variety of other courses, including evaluating their skills to determine what rate they would become in the service. This in most cases determined where their next duty station would be, at sea or on land.

Danny was named one of the four platoon leaders. He was in charge of twenty men and responsible for their performances, good and bad. The four platoon leaders would meet every day with the company commander and evaluate their men. Company 109's commander was Chief Manny Rodriguez from Puerto Rica. He was very loud and boisterous and very tough and demanding, but Danny thought he was fair. His job was to get the most out of his recruits and make them into good sailors. He had been commanding recruits the past three years.

The first few days at boot camp consisted of getting properly fitted for clothing, eye examinations, physicals, dental examinations, and haircuts. Every recruit got a burr haircut. After the first week, there was a regular routine; it was quite grueling both mentally and physically, but Danny knew this was nothing compared to what he would experience in SEAL training.

Each recruit was issued an M-1 rifle, which from that point forward would always be called their piece. They had to assemble and disassemble their piece every day as well as clean and oil it. They would go to the firing range twice a week and learn how to shoot. They had to march with their piece, eat with their piece, and sleep with their piece. Their piece would become their best friend. If they were going to have any sex over the twelve weeks of training, it was going to be with their piece.

They were issued a seven-digit service number, which would remain with them the rest of their lives. It was their military social security equivalent. They had to memorize it. Danny's number was

774-05-42. This number was tattooed on all their clothes and military possessions.

Chief Manny had studied Danny's résumé very closely and took an interest in Danny. He spent more time with Danny than any of the other platoon leaders, and when the chief would be away for any period of time, he would leave Danny in charge.

Chief Manny had lucked out with this group of sailors in company 109. He usually had a couple of dead beats that wouldn't graduate, but this group was eager to learn and followed orders well. By the end of the twelve weeks, all his men would graduate, and he knew that they would perform well at the graduating ceremonies.

Company 109 was given four individual first-place honors for marching, marksmanship, firefighting, and survival training. They came in second in the other three categories. There were twenty-two companies competing with one another. Company 109 was given the overall award, and this was a first for Chief Manny, another feather in his hat. All the sailors had been given a rate and their new duty stations. Some would be gunner mates, boatswain mates, corpsmen, firemen, etc. Danny was made a radioman. The last day at boot camp, everyone in company 109 was given their second stripe and became E2s, seaman apprentice. It would take another six months before they could take their E3 seaman exam and make more money.

Danny had become good friends with one of the other platoon leaders, Rudy Simpson. Rudy had also been a standout athlete at his high school in Louisville, Kentucky, and they had a lot in common. Rudy was also selected to become a radioman, and they would be in the same class in Bainbridge, Maryland.

Company 109 was dismissed, and all headed home for two weeks' leave before reporting to their next duty stations. All of them had grown most of their hair back, and they all were physically fit. They all lost between fifteen and forty pounds.

On January 25, 1999, Danny was picked up at the Rhinelander airport by his father, Happy Peterson. Danny was all decked out in his dress Navy blues and looked very handsome and fit. He had his naval duffel bag with him and looked like a sailor.

Happy had planned a welcome home party the next day on Saturday for Danny. On the ride home, Danny asked Happy how Hoddie was doing. Happy said the Hoddie would probably go crazy when he saw Danny. Happy had hired a friend of the family, Sally Shields, to watch after Hoddie in his absence. Sally also cleaned the house and the labs.

Sally was a forty-five-year-old widower without any children. Happy hired her full-time and moved her into the mansion to clean, cook, and do a few secretarial duties for Happy. Danny knew Sally and liked her. She was very attractive and had a great personality. Danny asked his dad if he was violating Sally, and they both laughed as Happy said, "No, not yet."

When they arrived back at the mansion, Sally met them at the front door, gave Danny a big hug, and told him, "I have been telling Hoddie all week that you were coming home. He kept looking around like he knew what I was talking about. Every time I mention your name, Hoddie barks!"

After Danny put his duffel bag in his bedroom, he slipped on a pair of trunks and headed to the lab. When Hoddie saw Danny, he went nuts. He started barking and clapping his flippers. He slid out of the pool, wrapped his flippers around him, and started kissing him. Happy and Sally witnessed this, and all started laughing, including Hoddie. Danny fed Hoddie and played with him the rest of the day before putting him away for the evening.

Back at the house, Sally had prepared a big meal of fried chicken, mashed potatoes, homemade gravy, and green beans. The three of them sat at the table had a glass of wine, and Danny told them about his twelve weeks of boot camp and that he was on his way to radio-man's school in Bainbridge, Maryland.

Sally got up from the table, served the meal, and it was delicious. After dinner, Happy and Danny went to the porch and brought each other up to speed on what had happened since Danny had left for boot camp. Then Danny retired to bed as he was worn out from the long flight and the day's events.

Danny woke up the next morning at 8:00 a.m. It felt great to be home and get a good night's sleep in his wonderful bed. He knew the party was starting at 2:00 p.m. He ate some breakfast and went to spend a couple hours with Hoodie. The crowd started arriving around 2:00 p.m. It was very cold, and there was snow on the ground, a lot different than San Diego at this time of year.

The mansion was big enough to hold a hundred people, which was about the number of people who showed up. All their neighbors and friends were there as well as some of Danny's classmates and all of his cousins and aunts and uncles. The only relatives that didn't show up was Gus Peterson's family. Even Candice Adams, Candy's sister, was there. She had driven from Madison for the weekend to see Danny.

Happy had the event catered, and the food was delicious. The booze was flowing, and they had a disc jockey playing music. They had two hours of karaoke, and fun was had by all.

Danny had to spend time with everyone, and the night flew by. When Danny saw Candy, she gave him a big hug and a kiss. They talked briefly, and Danny asked her if she could join them for breakfast Sunday morning around 10:00 a.m. before driving back to Madison. She agreed.

The party was over at 1:00 a.m., and Danny went to bed, feeling no pain, leaving the cleanup to Sally and the caterers.

The next morning, Candy arrived early at 9:45 a.m., and Sally made them all a big breakfast of bacon, sausage, scrambled eggs, pancakes, and homemade biscuits with honey. Danny asked Candy when she had to leave for Madison, and she said by 2:00 p.m. She then asked if they could go visit Hoddie, and the two of them walked to the lab.

Hoddie was excited to see them. He barked and clapped his flippers. Danny let Candy feed him. She loved that seal. They then sat on a couch by the pool, and Candy asked Danny about the Navy, and Danny asked her about school. Danny asked Candy why she chose criminology as her major, and she said she was always interested in the law but was not interested in becoming an attorney. She chose law enforcement, and she loved it. It was her desire to be hired by the FBI or the CIA and become a field agent.

They discussed many topics, as they had a lot in common. They were both having feelings for each other. Two hours flew by, and it was time for Candy to go. Danny grabbed her hand and told her how beautiful she was and how much she reminded him of her sister. Then tears came to his eyes.

Candy wiped the tears away with her fingers and said, "It has been six months since she passed away. It is time for your mourning to end and move on with your life. She will always be in your heart and a part of your life. She would want you to move on."

With that, she grabbed Danny for a big hug and gave him a long passionate kiss while sticking her tongue down this throat. They held that embrace and kiss for what seemed like five minutes. While they were tightly embraced, Danny got a huge erection. Candy said, "Whoa, boy." She reached down and grabbed his cock and said, "That will have to wait for another time." Danny was embarrassed, and she grabbed his hand as they walked back to the mansion.

After saying goodbye to Happy and Sally, Candy then gave Danny another kiss and said, "Call me."

The rest of his time was spent with Happy, Hoddie, and a few friends from high school. Danny asked Happy how the eye was coming and was told by Happy that he planned on spending more time with it as soon as he finished up a special project for the general. Danny waited a few days before calling Candy, as he didn't want her to think he was forcing himself on her. On the third day after her departure, he called her around 7:00 p.m., knowing she would be done with her classes. She already had her bachelor's degree, was halfway through her master's, and would need an additional two years to get her doctorate. She should be finished with school by the end of 2002. She was working part-time in the Madison sheriff's department, doing some fingerprint work, shipping out DNA samples to the lab, and anything else they would allow her to do.

When she answered the phone, she said, "I was just thinking about you."

And Danny said, "Isn't that a coincidence? I have been thinking about you for the last three days and was trying to get the courage to call you."

They both laughed and talked for two hours. Candy asked Danny if he could come to Madison for a few days before leaving for Maryland. He could stay at her apartment. Danny said he could come Friday evening and leave Sunday to pack for Maryland and his tour at radioman school.

She said, "Perfect. I don't have to work that weekend, and we can spend the whole weekend together." A big smile came on both their faces, and Danny got an immediate erection.

Danny arrived on Friday evening, January 16, found her apartment, and knocked on the door. Candy opened the door. She was dressed to kill. She was beautiful. She told Danny she was taking him out to her favorite restaurant and for him to go get his things out of the car, freshen up; they were leaving in half an hour.

They had a wonderful dinner and split a bottle of wine. After a dessert of banana foster, Danny asked for the check, and the waiter said it was already taken care of. Danny looked at her, and she just smiled. She told him they were going to meet a few friends of hers at the Diamond Nightclub. Once there, she introduced him to two of her girlfriends and their dates. They talked and laughed and had a few cocktails and danced. The third dance was a slow dance, and as Candace held her body close to his, Danny again got an erection.

Candy said, "Well, I guess it is time to go home." And she patted his cock. Once they got back to her apartment, they kissed in the foyer, and Candy said, "Let's take a hot shower together." Her apartment was fairly large for a one-bedroom apartment. It had a very large bath off the bedroom with a huge shower.

As they walked into her bedroom, they started kissing and undressing each other. Candy was beautiful with long blond hair and a magnificent body. Candy grabbed Danny by his cock and led him into the shower, telling him he was her new pull toy.

The shower had two large showerheads across from each other. As they stood under the showerheads, they started lathering each other up. As their hot, wet, lathered bodies touched each other, they began to kiss. Danny lifted Candy off the shower floor and held her up with his hands gripping her buttocks. Candy wrapped her leg around his waist and guided his hard lathered-up shaft into her soapy love canal. The ease of entry was smooth and swift. Danny's whole shaft was in her immediately. Candy began to moan uncontrollably as she clawed his back and thrust forward with all the power she had. Danny immediately exploded inside her. Candy screamed out, "Wow!"

As Danny's member slipped out of her hot oyster lips, Candy turned around and spread her legs and put her hands on the shower wall while the hot water from the showerheads ran all over her body. Danny mounted her from the rear and thrust deep inside her with fast, powerful strokes. They were both moaning and shouting uncontrollably. Candy shouted out, "I AM COMING!" And as she did. So did Danny. They both slid to the shower floor, holding each other in their arms as the hot water from the showerheads covered their bodies. They both lay there for several minutes and then started laughing.

Candy then said, "I have never experienced anything like that."

Danny said, "Nor have I."

They left the shower, got two large fluffy towels, and dried each other off. Candy then grabbed Danny by his cock and pulled him into her bedroom and folded back the comforter and silk sheets on her queen-size bed. She told Danny to lie down. She then started slowly massaging Danny's cock with her warm, soft hands, and within seconds, Danny's large cock was again standing at attention, harder than a rock.

Candy giggled. "I can't believe I just took his beautiful, massive cock inside me." She then said to Danny, "Just relax." Candy then started kissing his balls and taking them into her mouth. As she was gently sucking them, she was humming, and Danny was going crazy. She then put her lips around the tip of his shaft and slowly began rotating her tongue and lips around the tip of his shaft. Danny was now going completely nuts. Candy then began slowly taking his entire shaft into her warm mouth and again began humming. Now she started moving her lips up and down his shaft at an alarming rate of speed. *Pow!* Danny exploded in her mouth, and he went completely limp. She lay next to him and said, "Thanks for the candy." They again both laughed and started some small talk.

Then Danny rolled her over on her back. He spread her legs and moved down to her feet. He started sucking her toes then started kissing her calves and then moved to her inner thighs and, with his hot breath, began kissing and sucking her thighs. Candy now began moaning again in a soft, comforting style. She was in bliss.

Danny now moved to her sweet-tasting vagina and went to work. He was darting his tongue in and out of her then gently sucking her clit. At this point, Candy had gone crazy. She was hollering and twisting and yelling, "Don't stop!" She was uncontrollable and then exploded in Danny's face. Danny exclaimed, "More Candy!" They lay together, holding each other in their arms, and fell asleep.

When Danny woke up, Candy was not in bed. He got up went to the bathroom and washed his face and hands. He then went to the kitchen, where he smelled bacon frying. Candy was standing there, cooking bacon and eggs, in only an apron with nothing on underneath the apron. Danny was standing there, wrapped in a towel. Candy shut the stove off and ripped off Danny's towel then gave him a big passionate kiss and grabbed his cock. Danny removed her apron, and they went at it on the kitchen floor like a couple of drunk monkeys.

When they were finished, Candy got up, put on her apron, and finished cooking. Danny got up, put his towel back on, sat at the kitchen table, and said, "What's for breakfast?" They both started laughing, kissed each other, and ate breakfast.

They never left her apartment the rest of the weekend; neither even answered their phones. All they did was make love, laugh, and talk. They talked about their feelings toward each other, about what others might say or think about them because of Danny's engagement to her sister, who had only been gone six months.

They decided to hell with everyone else, that they were the only two that mattered, and that they both felt like this would make Shirley happy as both Danny and Candace were the two people she loved the most. And if she couldn't have Danny, she would want her sister to have him, and if Danny couldn't have Shirley, he should have her sister. They decided they would spend as much time together as they could with her being in Wisconsin and him being in Maryland; they would work things out.

On Sunday afternoon, Danny left for Rhinelander to gather his Navy gear and head to Maryland. They embraced and told each other how much they loved each other and that they would cherish this weekend forever.

Danny arrived in Maryland on January 20, checked into processing, and was assigned a barracks. When he got to his barracks, his good friend from boot camp, Rudy Simpson, was already there. They were assigned to the same barracks and the same class.

The first two days, there were classes explaining the layout of the base, the rules and regulations, the class schedules, and what was expected out of the newly arriving sailors. School hours were eight to five Monday through Friday. The radioman school was divided up into two semesters, three months each. After the first semester, there would be a four-day break before the start of the second and final semester.

After school was dismissed at 5:00 p.m., they could leave the base if they were not assigned some kind of duty but had to be back on base by midnight. After the first month of school, if they were in the top 20 percent of their class, they could apply for weekend passes.

Normally, they were assigned some kind of duty every other day. It could be shore patrol, KP (working in the galley), front gate watch, or barracks watch. Shore patrol was the best duty, as they traveled around the base in a golf cart. The Waves (women sailors) had their boot camp in Bainbridge, and while on shore patrol, the sailors could ride over there and witness the same thing they went through at their boot camp, except it was women with women company commanders.

It was said the first thing the Waves company commanders told the new women recruits was "There is thirty miles of dick on this base, and you aren't going to see six inches for three months."

The communications classes at radioman school consisted of Morse code, typewriting, transmitters, receivers, portable radios, antennas, teletypes, and preventive maintenance. They had to be able to send and receive Morse code at twenty words per minute, type at thirty words per minute, and operate and maintain transmitters, receivers, portable radios, antennas, and teletypes.

It was nice having Rudy around. After classes, they would go to the enlisted men's club and play pool, drink a few beers, or take in a movie. Occasionally, they would leave the base and go to Baltimore, which was only about forty minutes away. Sometimes they would take in one of Baltimore's well-known restaurants or go to the Block, which was a block-long stretch of gentlemen's clubs with nude dancing. Even Blaze Starr, the famous burlesque queen, had a club there.

There were forty sailors in their class, and both he and Rudy were at the top of their class.

Danny and Candy talked most every night, some nights for an hour and some nights just long enough to tell each other they were in love. Danny was getting a weekend pass on February 20. He was flying into Madison late Friday night and had to fly out at 11:00 a.m. Sunday, the twenty-second. He wasn't telling Happy as he didn't have time to see everybody, so it was a secret between him and Candy. Danny also informed Candy that he was getting a four-day break between semesters. That would be March 22 through 25. He would have to be back by the evening of the twenty-fifth. He would fly out of Maryland after school on the twenty-first to Rhinelander, arriving around midnight. The plan was for Candy to make arrangements to drive to Rhinelander the morning of the twenty-second and depart around noon on the twenty-fifth. That would give them three and a half days together and also be able to visit Happy and Hoddie.

Danny made his two visits to spend time with his new love and just fell more deeply in love with Candy. Everyone was glad to see Danny, including Happy and Hoddie.

Danny finished first in his class. He could send and receive Morse code at forty words per minute. He could operate a speed key, could type eighty words per minute, and could set up and tear down any piece of radio equipment the Navy had. He knew more about antennas than his instructor. He also was the only one in his class that was given top secret clearance.

Graduation was on May 15, 1999. Everyone was given their next duty stations. Rudy was going to the USS *Enterprise*, the largest aircraft carrier in the Navy. It was the home to over five thousand sailors and airmen. Danny was being sent to Coronado, California, for six months of SEAL training.

Danny had two weeks' leave from May 15 through June 1. Candy would be finishing her semester on May 10, and her summer semester would not begin until June 15, so she would be with Danny his whole two-week leave.

Danny had told Happy about his relationship with Candy and had gotten Happy's blessings. In fact, Candy stayed at Happy's home during Danny's last visit to Rhinelander. Danny arrived at the Rhinelander airport on May 15. Both Happy and Candy met him at the airport. Candy had been staying in Danny's bedroom since her semester ended on May 10. Candy and her brothers had sold their parents' home, so she really had no other place to stay—or at least that was a great excuse. Candy had been taking care of Hoddie for the past three days.

Danny was met with a big hug from his dad and an even bigger hug and kiss from Candy. When they arrived back at the mansion, Sally had prepared them supper. She was an excellent cook, and she was now Happy's girlfriend. She had moved from the guest bedroom to Happy's bedroom. He had not seen his dad this happy in years. After dinner, they all had several glasses of wine, had some laughs, and then retired to bed.

Danny told Candy, "Now there are two couples living in sin under the same roof." They both laughed, and Danny jumped in the shower. While he was cleaning up, Candy slipped into a new crotchless, see-through silk negligee. She was waiting in bed for him; she was beautiful. They made mad passionate love until 3:00 a.m. Then they both passed out. It was a great two weeks. They spent a lot of time with Hoddie, Happy, and Sally. They learned a lot about Sally, and Sally learned a lot about them.

Danny informed Candy that once he got to SEAL training, he would not be able to leave until graduation six months later on December 1, 1999. He then would have two weeks off till December 15 before reporting to Camp Lejeune, North Carolina, for combat ready training. After Camp Lejeune, he would have thirty days' leave from May 1 to June 1 before being deployed to the Middle East.

Danny didn't like the fact that he would be away from Candy for that long period of time, but he had to finish this four-year commitment he had made to himself, his dad, the general, and the US Navy.

Candy started to cry and said, "If anything happens to you, I will be devastated, heartbroken, and will just want to die. You are the love of my life and all that I have dreamed of."

Danny assured her that nothing was going to happen to him, that he was gifted and could take care of himself better than most. Danny then pulled this big beautiful diamond ring out of his pocket, kneeled down, grabbed Candy's hand, and said, "Will you marry me?" Tears formed in her eyes, and a huge smile came on her face as she yelled, "YES!"

Danny told Candy he wanted to get married on May 15, 2000, that she had one year to plan the wedding with no cost restrictions. He would not have any time to get involved with the planning. She was in complete control.

They were going out to dinner that night with Happy and Sally at a very nice restaurant in Eagle River, Wisconsin, about thirty miles away. As they sat down for dinner, Happy asked why they were both smiling and acting so nervous. Candy held up her hand and showed off her ring and announced they were getting married. Happy and Sally both got up and gave them a big hug and said, "Congratulations!" The owner of the restaurant overheard the announcement and sent them over a nice bottle of champagne.

Danny announced the date of the wedding, which was May 15, 2000, about one year from now. Danny told Happy she had carte blanche and could make any arrangements she wanted with cost not being a factor. Happy was elated, and so was Sally. Sally told Candy she would be more than happy to help her with the wedding arrangements. Happy announced that the cost of the wedding just went up. They all laughed and proposed a toast.

Danny said his goodbyes to everyone at the airport, shook his dad's hand, hugged Sally, and planted a two-minute kiss on his fiancée. Danny was in the air and on his way to Coronado to become a Navy SEAL.

When Danny arrived at Coronado, he went through two days of orientation, was issued all his gear including two rifles and a pistol. All his gear had 7740542 engraved on them. That was his military service number. If you were ever captured by the enemy, the only thing you could give them was your name, rank, and serial number.

Danny's drill sergeant was a marine sergeant. His name was Sergeant Rock. He was 6 feet, 4 inches and weighed about 240 pounds. He had muscles all over his body, including muscles bulging out of his neck. He looked like a large chunk of granite. His head was shaved clean, and when he talked, it sounded like his voice was coming out of a loudspeaker.

There were eighteen recruits in Danny's platoon. They were from all over the country. There wasn't an ounce of fat on any of them. On their first day of training, they were lined up in three rows, six to a row. They were all standing at attention when Sergeant Rock arrived on the scene. He had a belt holster around his waist that carried a .44 Magnum pistol, twelve rounds of ammunition protruding from the belt, and a sheathed twelve-inch bowie knife also attached to his belt.

Sergeant Rock stood in front of his recruits and announced, "I am Sergeant Rock. I am the meanest son of a bitch in the valley. Welcome to SEAL training at Coronado, you fucking maggots. You will not speak unless spoken to. You will address me as Sergeant Rock, sir. You will finish each sentence with sir. If you need to piss, you will ask permission to piss by saying, 'Sergeant Rock, sir, requesting permission to use the head, sir.' If you are given permission to take a piss, you will say, 'Thank you, Sergeant Rock, sir.' If you are not granted permission to use the head, you will hold it or piss in your pants—whatever hits your hot button. Do you understand?"

All eighteen recruits answered in unison, "Sir, yes, sir!"

Sergeant Rock said, "You are going to go through pure hell while you are here. Half of you won't make it, and the other half will be saying to yourself, 'What the fuck have I done?' I will work you so hard you will puke. While you are here, you will be running twenty miles a day, crawling through snake-infested swamps, and swimming miles in freezing conditions. You will learn all about various weapons. You will participate in hand-to-hand combat and many other unpleasant things. Now some of you are wondering if this .44 Magnum I have strapped on my waist is loaded with live ammo." Sergeant Rock pulled out his .44, aimed it at a beer can forty paces away, and fired. The beer can went flying. "Any questions?"

"Sir, no, sir!" was their response.

"You will march everywhere you go. Reveille is 5:00 a.m. every morning, unless you piss me off or disappoint me the day before. Then it will be 3:00 a.m. Lights out are at 9:00 p.m. unless you pass out before then. If you think you are in good shape now, you are fucking crazy. You fucking maggots are the lowest dog shit on this planet. I plan on making men out of you faggots. If you think you hate me now, just wait until tomorrow and each day after. If you are a smoker, your last cigarette is the one you smoked before falling into line here this morning. If you get caught smoking or even smell like a cigarette, you are out of here. No second chances. Any questions?"

"Sir, no, sir!"

"Just so you know, I can kick the shit out of any of you right now. If you were to try to attack me with a weapon, any weapon, I could kill you with my bare hands. If there are any doubters out there, please step forward."

Nobody moved.

"Each morning, after reveille, you will fall into line, and we will march to chow. After chow, you will fall back in line, and we will march to one of our many training sites and begin our daily training. After our first day of training, you will be so sore you will wish you were dead. I expect at least four of you will quit before the second day. Do you fucking maggots understand me?"

"Sir, yes, sir!"

"What is my name?"

"Sir, Sergeant Rock, sir!"

"Who is the meanest son of a bitch in the valley?"

"Sir, you are, sir!"

"Very good, gentlemen, I will now turn you over to Captain Crimshaw, who will spend the rest of today with you in the classroom for your final indoctrination. Enjoy your day. It will be the last day you enjoy for the next six months. See you at 5:00 a.m. tomorrow morning. Fall out!"

For the next six months, life was pure hell, almost unbearable. Only eight of eighteen made it through training. By the end of the first week, we were down to twelve. We lost four more before the end. Sergeant Rock was a son of a bitch in the beginning. Then after two months, he was just a prick, and after four months of training, he became their friend—but was still tougher than a pit bull. At this point, they now trusted their life with Sergeant Rock and the remaining recruits.

On different days of training, they would run twenty miles, swim ten miles, paddle small rafts for thirty miles, and crawl five miles through swamps. They were sent in the swamp, naked, with nothing but a bowie knife, and had to survive for three days. It was relentless, but at the end of the six months, they were men among men and soon would be headed to Camp Lejeune for combat-ready training. The last day at camp was graduation, the easiest day in six months.

There were only 24 recruits out of the 120 that started training in June that survived to graduation. That was only 1 out of 5, or 20 percent that made it. Out of Sergeant Rock's platoon, an outstanding rate of 44 percent made it, and his platoon won the majority of the merit awards at graduation. Even though Sergeant Rock was the toughest drill sergeant there and only one of two marine drill sergeants, he was the most successful instructor at camp, even if he was the meanest son of a bitch in the valley.

Danny took first-place merit awards in marksmanship, speed swimming, and endurance swimming. He was also awarded the iron man award for compiling the most points during the entire six months of training.

At the closing of the graduation ceremony, Captain Roy Matthews pinned the Navy SEAL ribbon on each recruit's chest and shook their hands and welcomed them into the elite family of

SEALs. After graduation, Sergeant Rock met with just his recruits for a private meeting.

He congratulated all of them for their achievements and entry into the elite SEAL program. He asked them all if they thought he was still the meanest son of a bitch in the valley, and Terry Harper shouted out, "Sarge, you are just a big pussy!" They all laughed, including Sergeant Rock. He shook their hands, gave them a bear hug, and told them safe travels. Sergeant Rock's parting words were "If you only remember one thing that I taught you, remember to always watch your back. You can always see what is in front of you but never behind you—unless you look. This advice may one day save your life. Remember it, especially when you are on a mission."

Danny was headed home for two weeks' leave before reporting to Camp Lejeune on December 15 for advanced combat readiness training. While he was in SEAL training for the past six months, he received over a hundred letters from Candy and sent her about thirty.

Danny knew that Candy had been working on the wedding, which was now only six months away, and that they would have plenty to talk about when he came home. Candy would be graduating in January of 2001, six months after the wedding, with her doctorate in criminology. Her semester break from May 1 to June 10 was perfect timing for the wedding.

When Danny arrived in Rhinelander on December 1, 1999. He was decked out in his dress Navy blues, proudly displaying his SEAL ribbon. Candy, Happy, and Sally all met him at the airport with big smiles on their faces. It was 2:00 p.m.

On the ride back to the mansion, Happy announced, "Dinner will be served at 7:00 p.m., so you two lovebirds have four hours together before dinner."

Big smiles and laughter broke out among all four of them. After four hours of trying to make up for being apart for six months, they both were starving.

Sally had prepared a delicious meal, and after dinner, they all sat around the fireplace and listened to Danny brief them on his last six months, including stories about Sergeant Rock, the meanest son of a bitch in the valley. Actually, Danny had grown quite close to

Sergeant Rock. At the end of training, Sergeant Rock told Danny he was the best recruit he'd ever trained, and he had trained hundreds of them. After Danny was through talking about SEAL boot camp, Happy said, "We have some news of our own."

Happy told Danny that he and Sally have decided to get married, and Sally held up her hand with a big diamond on it and a huge smile on her face. Happy told Danny, "Candy suggested we have a double wedding. We didn't want to make a decision without talking to you in person. The last thing we want to do is take anything away from your special day. I know Candy has been going nuts the past thirty days, keeping this a secret from you."

Danny jumped up and gave Sally a huge hug and kiss, shook his dad's hand, and said, "Congratulations!" Danny thought it was wonderful and it would only make their special day even more special.

He then looked at Candy and said, "I will punish you tonight for keeping this secret from me."

Candy said, "I can't wait." And they all laughed.

During Danny's two weeks' leave, a lot was discussed. Danny spent time with his dad discussing improvements to the magical eye. It was Happy's most proud invention, and he told Danny he was about two years away from perfection. Happy and Dr. Bennett had successfully attached the eye to the brain of a great horned owl and another seal.

They couldn't perform any more surgeries on Hoddie. They did, however, implant the magical eye into Hoddie with only one function, a 20/20 vision. Hoddie was no longer blind in one eye. He had perfect vision in both eyes, and he now had a new playmate by the name of Heidi. She was a female seal, and they got along great. Hoddie had actually already taught Heidi some of his tricks. They even played volleyball together. Heidi would now be Happy's new patient for the magical eye and its various functions. Heidi had lost her sight in her left eye several years ago in the San Diego Zoo.

One of Sally's duties was to feed, entertain, and care for the two seals. There were now five people who knew about the magical eye. Happy, Danny, Dr. Bennett, Candy, and Sally. This amazing invention would be worth billions after its release to the public. Surgeons from all over the world would be trained to perform this surgery by Happy and Dr. Bennett. There would be eyes available with only one function, to correct vision. Other eyes could do multifunctions, and there would be a special eye only for the military that could be used in combat conditions. June of 2003 was the projected date of completion of the magical eye.

They talked about the wedding and their honeymoons. It was decided that the double wedding was to be on May 15 at the mansion. Breakfast would be served at 10:00 a.m. A buffet lunch would be at 2:00 p.m. The wedding vows were at 5:00 p.m., with the reception beginning after the wedding and dinner to be served at 7:30 p.m. Happy would use ten of his eighty acres to hold the affair. There would be ten circus-type tents, which could seat up to forty people each for dinner with plenty of room to spare. There would be smaller tents spread around in case of foul weather. There would be multiple bars set up all around the grounds. There would be four different bands playing live music.

The wedding tent would take up a whole acre and could seat as many as five hundred people. There would be special seating assigned to special guests. There would be forty portable toilets with running water set all over the grounds.

They would hire a world-class company to organize and manage the event. This company would meet with Sally and Candy to coordinate all functions related to the wedding, including caterers, bands, tents, seating, bathrooms, floral arrangements, parking, invitations, food, beverage, transportations, hotel accommodations, etc. They would handle any special requests from Candy or Sally.

The process was to begin immediately, and Happy would get involved with any potential problems that the girls were not sure of or couldn't handle. Danny's involvement was zero; all he had to do was finish training and give them a list of special invitees he would like to see attend his wedding, or at least be invited to it. The invitations would be sent out within thirty days with an RSVP by February 1, 2000, in order to get an approximate head count so they could properly plan the wedding.

Danny's list was fairly short but consisted of about twenty of his classmates and spouses, all seven of the seals he graduated with, Sergeant Rock, General Dwight Smith, Captain Patrick O'Conner, Barry Wise, Rudy Simpson, his wrestling coach and football coach from high school. And that was Danny's list. Danny knew that Happy, Sally, and Candy would have all their friends and relatives on the list.

Danny asked Candy if she thought it would be okay if he invited all the girls he had sex with in high school. Candy promptly replied, "According to my sister, Shirley, we don't have a big enough tent." They all laughed.

On the invitee list would be all the prominent politicians, business owners, judges, police and fire chiefs, and the sheriff of Oneida County.

They talked about their honeymoons. Should they be separate, or should they go to some exotic island together? After all, they would have their own private quarters and probably wouldn't see much of each other anyway. Happy came up with an idea. They'd charter a one-hundred-foot yacht with a crew and just set sail for a week. They'd be visiting some small islands and doing some fishing, snorkeling, and scuba diving. This idea sounded very interesting to all of them. It would be very expensive, but Happy was given the task of looking into it.

This whole affair was going to be very expensive. Happy didn't care about the cost. He was a multimillionaire about to become a billionaire in a couple of years, and this was a once-in-a-lifetime event.

On December 15, after a blissful two weeks with his love, he was off to more SEAL training and would return on May 1, 2000. He was leaving all the wedding arrangements to the three of them.

After arriving at Camp Lejeune and two days of indoctrination, the best of the best began their combat readiness training. They were broken up in groups of six. It was no longer a matter of being physically fit; it was a matter of reaction to life-threating situations.

They were issued new gear that would be theirs for life. Again everything of a personal nature, such as their weapons, were engraved with their service numbers. In Danny's case, it was 7440542.

They were issued four different assault-type rifles, three different handguns, four separate types of knives, silencers, sheaths, holsters, special ammo belts, night goggles, scuba gear, and many other items. These items were theirs and theirs alone. They obviously would not use all these on the same mission, but some would be used on every mission. Other items would be given to them right before a specific mission, such as grenades, landmines, kill pills, radios, secret codes, etc.

This training was rough and very thorough. They were taught to kill with their bare hands or with a knife, bringing their enemy to immediate death without making a sound. They were taught how to attend to knife, shrapnel, and gunshot wounds. They trained mostly at night, under the cover of darkness. They learned how to sleep, eat, shit, and kill in the dark without making a sound.

They were taught that if they ever came face-to-face with another human that could either be an enemy or a friendly villager, they should always treated them as their enemy. The Navy could live with a dead villager but not a dead SEAL. They not only would be protecting their own life but also the lives of their fellow SEAL. They were taught that they never left another SEAL behind, dead or alive. They were taught the cruelty of battle, the smell and taste of blood.

They were taught how to eat ants, rats, grunts, snakes, and anything that crawled; how to squeeze water out of certain types of vegetation; how to wipe their ass with a cactus and like it; and how to live in pain and sew up their own wounds.

In short, they were taught survival in the absolute worst conditions, that their mind and their ability to act lighting fast was their best weapon. After four months of the most intense training possible, the course was over. It seemed like only two weeks, not four months.

All six of the new SEALs that Danny trained with were like brothers, and all members of the elite SEAL Team Six. All seal units consisted of six SEALs, and all units were given a code name. All of Danny's new brothers would be sent to different SEAL units, either replacing a SEAL who had retired or severely injured or killed.

Before they left Camp Lejeune on their thirty days' leave, Danny invited all five of them to his wedding. Four of them were single, and one was married. Danny told them to call him within three days and he would send them airline tickets and put them up in a hotel in Rhinelander with their spouses or girlfriends. There would be no cost to them, and if they couldn't make it, he would understand. Danny would fly them in on the fourteenth and out on the sixteenth. He would have rental cars at the airport for them with directions on how to get to the hotel and mansion.

Should they decide to come, he promised them two hours of his busy schedule to meet his pet seal, Hoddie, and his mate, Heidi. He promised them a volleyball match with his seals. It would be the five of them against Danny; his fiancée, Candy; and the two seals. And he promised them Hoddie's team would kick their ass.

All four of the single guys committed right on the spot. They were now SEALs, and they wanted to meet Hoddie. Danny got their addresses and phone numbers and would send them tickets in the next couple of days.

Dave, the only married guy, said, "I want to come, but I have to clear it with my wife." They all called him a pussy. Dave said, "Fuck it! I am coming. I will call you and tell you if my wife is coming or not, no later than tomorrow night, but I am coming."

They all shook hands, and Danny declared the volleyball match was on—the SEALs against the seals. Danny informed them he would have the local newspaper there to report on the event so they couldn't back out. Danny reminded them, "You never leave a SEAL behind."

They were all off for their homes and would see one another in two weeks.

Danny was met at the airport by Candy as Happy had to fly to DC to meet with the general. The general had sent his private jet for Happy, and he would be back tomorrow. Sally was having a meeting with the wedding manager.

As Candy and Danny kissed in the airport, he told Candy he could take her right there on the floor. When they got in the car, he said, "I could take you right here in the back seat."

Candy laughed and said, "We are only twenty minutes from home." The airport hotel was right there.

DANIEL GARBER

Danny said, "I have waited for four months. I can't wait another twenty minutes."

They pulled up at the hotel and parked in the registration parking space right in front of the door. Benny Thompson, a classmate of Danny's, was behind the counter.

Danny said to Benny, "Give me the closest room to this desk and give me the keys. Here is my credit card. I will fill out all the bullshit in an hour or so." He winked at Benny, got the keys, and grabbed Candy's hand, and they were in the room within thirty seconds.

They ripped each other's clothes off, and without any foreplay, they were screwing like two drunk monkeys. After about a half hour of nonstop lovemaking, there was come all over them and the sheets. They both rolled over and started laughing uncontrollably. They got up and took a hot shower together. They lathered all up and made love in the shower.

After cleaning up and drying off, they went to the bed, ripped off the top sheet, and threw it on the floor with the wet towels. Candy gave Danny oral sex, and he exploded. He then crawled between her legs, and he gave her oral sex until she exploded. They lay in each other's arms for a while, and Danny said, "You still taste like candy."

They got up and took another shower and dried off on what was left of the towels and wash clothes. Everything was thrown on the floor, including the sheets and comforter and pillows. It looked like a tornado had gone through the room. They put on their torn clothes and headed back to the car. Danny stopped at the desk, signed the credit card receipt, winked at Benny, gave him a fifty-dollar bill, and told him to call the maid.

They got home, changed their clothes, put on their bathing suits, and went to visit Hoddie.

Before leaving the house, Danny called his dad on his private number. His dad answered the phone and said, "Welcome home. I am in a meeting with the general."

The general grabbed the phone from Happy and said, "Congratulations on becoming a SEAL."

Danny asked the general if he was coming to the wedding. The general said he wouldn't miss it. Danny then told the general about the SEALs-versus-seals volleyball match scheduled for the day before the wedding. The general said he would have to shuffle a few things around but he had to witness the SEALs-versus-seals. He asked if he could bring an army photographer with him.

Danny said, "Sure. I know that you and Dad are busy, so I wanted Dad to tell you about the seals match. But now you can tell Dad. He doesn't know anything about it. I look forward to seeing you in a couple of weeks." Then he hung up the phone.

Candy said, "What's this SEALs-versus-seals volleyball match?" Danny explained everything to her. She told Danny, "That is the day before our wedding. It is going to be chaotic around here. I will be getting my hair done, nails, and all that beauty stuff so I can be the most beautiful bride for my SEAL."

Danny promised he wouldn't get her involved in anything the day before the wedding. "We are paying a manager a lot of money to handle this kind of stuff."

Candy kissed him, and they were off to see Hoddie and Heidi.

Danny knew that after he called the newspaper about the SEALs-versus-seals match, there would be others wanting to witness this event. He told the wedding manager he wanted one hundred seats set up at the poolside in lab 2 for May 14. He invited Barry Wise, his swimming coach, to attend and be the referee.

Sergeant Rock had accepted the wedding invitation and was coming in a day early to see the SEALs-versus-seals event. The word traveled fast, and Danny was getting overwhelmed with phone calls of people wanting to attend. He even got a call from Captain Roy Matthews, the commander of SEAL training in Coronado, California, and he asked Danny if he could attend. He thought it would be great advertising for the Navy SEAL division. Danny extended an invitation to him and his wife to not only attend the SEALs-versus-seals match but also to attend their wedding. He accepted. Danny told Captain Matthews that General Dwight Smith from the US Army would be there. The captain said, "Hell, I know Dwight very well. This gets more interesting all the time."

Danny had newspaper people coming from Milwaukee and Madison as well as Minneapolis. The governor wanted to come, as did the senators and two Wisconsin congressmen. It was getting out of hand. There were now about 150 people who would attend the SEALs-versus-seals event.

Danny had to have a meeting with the wedding manager. He would now have to make arrangements for 150 people to watch the match. A special section was to be set up for the press and photographers. Another special section was set up for the general, the captain, Sergeant Rock, the governor, the senators and congressmen, the mayor, and the police chief. There would have to be at least ten extra seats in all sections just in case of overflow.

The manager was to call the offices of the governor, senators, and congressmen and also extend them an invitation to the wedding. The manager would have to have someone sitting at the entrance door to lab 2 with a list of invited guests, and if you were not on that list, you couldn't get in. It was by invitation only.

There would be programs handed out at the door with the pictures and names of all the Navy SEALs, plus pictures of Hoddie and Heidi with their names printed under their pictures. There would be mention of all the special attendees, from the general down to the mayor. Danny would give him that list of names so they would be included in the programs. The program would explain the matches. There would be three nine-point matches, with the six Navy SEALs, including Danny, rotating teams so that all six Navy SEALs got to play on the real seals' team. It was four on four. Four Navy SEALs versus two Navy SEALs and the two real seals.

The fourth and final match would be Hoddie and three Navy SEALs versus Heidi and the other three Navy SEALs. There would be no losers. It was a win-win situation. After the matches were over, there would be a reception with cocktails and appetizers served under one of the massive tents set up outside the lab.

Barry Wise, Danny's swimming coach, was to be the master of ceremonies and the volleyball referee.

It seemed like every day there were meetings with the wedding manager, who had a staff of four who controlled all the arrangements from seating, food and beverage, entertainment, floral, photography, last-minute cancelations, and last-minute invitees. Two people were in charge of hotel and flight reservations. It was quite a production. At last count, there would be five hundred people in attendance. A valet service was hired to park all the cars in a designated area away from the festivities. Everything was being handled professionally by the management company hired by Happy. This was going to cost Happy a bundle, but as Happy said, it was all worth it.

Time flew by, and it was now three days before the wedding. The four of them had dinner each night at the mansion, prepared by a chef who had been hired to do all the cooking starting ten days before the wedding. There was also a maid service cleaning up the messes left by the different contractors every day. All the tents were already set up with bars, tables, and chairs set in place.

The wedding tent was all set up with chairs already in place. There would be ushers taking guests to their assigned seats. The four of them designed the seating arrangements for the wedding with the immediate family, military, and high-ranking politicians sitting in the front rows. Danny's best man was Rudy Simpson from boot camp and radio school. Happy's best man was Dr. Bennett. Candy's maid of honor was Heather Baldwin, her best friend from college, and Sally's maid of honor was her sister, Betsy, from Dallas, Texas.

On the evening of May 12, three days before the wedding, they all sat down to discuss last-minute details. Most everything was now in the hands of the wedding manager, Dominik Perkowski, who had done an outstanding job.

Candy and Sally let Danny and Happy know that beginning Thursday afternoon, the thirteenth, they would not see much of them until the day of the wedding. They had personal woman things they needed to take care of. Danny was in charge of the SEALs-versus-seal event, and all the classified equipment had been sealed off from the pool area. Happy informed everyone about the honeymoon arrangements. He had leased a 110-foot yacht off the coast of Costa Rica. They would fly to Costa Rica on a private jet Monday, the seventeenth. They would board the yacht called *You Must Be Dreaming* on the morning of the eighteenth and would sail to nowhere or anywhere. They had to be back in port by the evening of the twenty-fourth. A private jet would take them back home on the twenty-fifth. The yacht had a crew of ten, including a world-renowned chef. The captain was very experienced and had captained *Dreaming* for the past five years.

There were two private master suites with all the amenities. There was a large pool and many sunning decks, three hot tubs, and a sauna. There was a small basketball court, skeet shooting, an arcade, and a small disco, along with other things. There'd be breakfast in bed, if so desired; international meals; a kitchen open for twenty-four hours; and plenty of fabulous wine and top-shelf booze. There was a workout room and a plush movie theatre. There was a ski boat and four personal watercraft. The honeymoon was all set.

The weather forecast for the wedding was perfect, mideighties, and sunny. Everything was running smoothly.

Danny's SEAL brothers were all arriving on the thirteenth, a day before the original SEALs-versus-seals match. They would be having dinner at the mansion on the evening of their arrival with Danny, Candy, Happy, and Sally. The SEALs-versus-seals match had grown into a huge event. Candy was no longer involved in the volleyball matches, and it was now all SEALs. The event was to start at 1:00 p.m., and the actual matches would begin at 2:00 pm.

Danny had made six all black wet suits with the names of each Navy SEAL and the SEAL emblem embroidered on their wet suits. He also had the same company make two red capes with Hoddie and Heidi embroidered on them along with an emblem that read Real Seals.

The five SEALs arrived together on time. They flew into Minneapolis from different destinations, and Danny had a private jet fly them from Minneapolis to Rhinelander. Danny picked them up in a large van he had rented for their use. They drove to their hotel, unloaded their gear, and drove to the mansion.

Danny took them to the lab to visit the seals. Danny introduced them to Hoddie and Heidi, who were barking and clapping with excitement. Danny had the seals preform some tricks and had each Navy SEAL feed them some fish. Danny then said, "Watch this." He threw Hoddie a volleyball, clapped his hands three times, and

Hoddie flipped the volleyball high into the air, sprang out of the water, and spiked the ball, using his tail with much force.

The Navy SEALs were in awe. They put on their trunks, put up the net, and started practicing. They had a ball. They couldn't believe how athletic the real seals were. They divided up into equal teams as the program would state. All of them got to play with the seals both together and apart. They were all close matches. However, Hoddie could score at will when he spiked the ball with his tail.

After about three hours in the pool, they put the seals away, took a shower, and got dressed. Before they left the lab, Danny gave them their game suits. They were impressed. Then he showed them the real seals' capes, and they all laughed. They all wanted pictures. Danny informed them he had hired a professional photographer and a video guy to shoot the whole event. They could get whatever poses they wanted.

They all went back to the mansion for cocktails before dinner. Danny showed them around the mansion. He took them into the trophy room, which Happy had built for all of Danny's trophies he had amassed in high school. The seals were amazed as they saw all the state football, swimming, and wrestling titles Danny had won. A plaque showing Danny's 60–0 three-time heavyweight state champion record was in the center of the wall. Along with all of Danny's accomplishments, there were mounts of trophy deer and bear scattered around the room that he and Happy had shot. It was a real man cave.

They then retired to the porch, where a waiter took their orders for cocktails. A short time later, Candy came down and looked astonishing; she was breathtaking. One of the SEALs, Dave, jumped up and said, "I hope you are not taken." Candy gave him a smile and said, "Yes, I am." And she gave Danny a big hug. They all laughed. Danny then introduced Candy to all his SEAL brothers. "Dave here is our class clown. Dave Matthews, Tom Akins, Billy Kennedy, Bones O'Hara, and Hank Armstrong."

They all kissed her hand and said, "This is not fair. Danny always comes in first." And they all laughed again.

Happy and Sally entered the room and were also introduced to all the SEALs. They were having their second cocktail and enjoying one another's company, asking one another many questions. The chef came out onto the porch and asked Happy what time they would like to be served dinner. Happy said, "In half an hour." And the chef went to work.

They had a lovely dinner of beef tenderloin, lobster, and a medley of veggies, then apple crisp for dessert. After dinner, they had a night cap and left for their motel, and everyone else went to bed. Danny told the SEALs to be there no later than 10:30 a.m.

Danny arose at 6:00 a.m., had some breakfast, and went to the lab for some last-minute preparations.

Barry Wise, the receptionist, and all others working for Danny in the SEALs-versus-seals event were told to be there no later than 11:00 a.m. The 150 guests would start arriving around 1:00 p.m. Two ushers would be there to escort the dignitaries and press to their assigned seats. Everyone showed up on time. The programs arrived yesterday, and they looked great. They were in full color and had explanations of the events and pictures of all the SEALs, including the real seals, with their names under their pictures. Special invitees were named on the program, including the general, the captain, the senators and congressmen, the governor, and Barry Wise, who was the master of ceremonies and the referee of the volleyball matches.

Once all were seated, Danny would welcome everyone there, acknowledge the dignitaries and introduce Barry Wise, who would take over the podium. Danny had given Barry a written script to go by, which he had basically memorized. After Barry was finished with his presentation, Barry then would turn over the podium to Captain Matthews, who would say a few things and then introduce his SEALs by name and their hometowns. When he was finished, he would say, "Let the games begin!"

It was now 1:00 p.m., and the guests were arriving. By 1:30 p.m., all were seated, and Danny welcomed everybody. More than 150 people showed up, and some who were not on the list were turned away. Danny turned the podium over to Barry, who did a fine job with his presentation. Programs had been handed out at the door. Now Captain Matthews took over and introduced his Navy SEALs one by one. He announced that these young men were the finest the Navy had to offer and that he was proud to be their commanding officer. At that, Danny clapped his hands, and Hoddie and Heidi slipped out of the pool and stood next to the Navy SEALs. Danny put their capes on, and they began barking and clapping their flippers. The audience went crazy with applause.

Photographs and videos were taken for about five minutes, and the captain declared, "Let the games begin!"

The matches were all very close and exciting. The real seals were the hit of the games. Every time Hoddie would make one of his powerful spikes, the whole crowd would go crazy and applaud. It was a smash hit. Everyone was astonished at how well trained the real seals were.

At the end of the final match, Danny addressed the crowd and told them to stay seated for about fifteen minutes and he would have his two seals perform some astonishing tricks. The seals were given standing ovations after each trick. The seals would bark at them and clap their flippers. Then Danny thanked them all for coming and told them there were refreshments and cocktails under the big tent outside the entrance door.

The crowd mingled under the big tent for two hours. The governor and congressmen congratulated all the members of SEAL Team Six and thanked them for their service and for a very entertaining afternoon. The press was interviewing everyone. Photos and videos continued. It was a super affair, and fun was had by all.

After the reception was over, General Smith, Captain Patrick O'Conner, Navy Captain Matthews, and Sergeant Rock, along with the six SEALs, returned to the mansion for a little surprise. They sat on the porch, opened up some special wine, and were all handed a solid gold plaque, which had their names on it and read, "I attended the SEALs-versus-seals special event in Rhinelander, Wisconsin, in May of 2000."

They all shook hands and thanked Danny for such an unusual experience. They all went on their way. The wedding was tomorrow, and they knew Danny had things to do.

All nine of them decided to meet for dinner that night, and the general said the evening would be on him.

Sergeant Rock said, "No, sir, I would like to pick up this evening's tab."

Captain Matthews said, "Sergeant, that is very thoughtful of you, but you are outranked. And, Dwight, you don't have a chance. You are outnumbered by the Navy. This one is on me."

They all had a great evening. They had many laughs and way too many drinks. It was not often that enlisted men got to go out with high-ranking military officers and be treated as equals.

The event made headlines in all the local and state newspapers; it was broadcast on all local and national news channels. ESPN ran a special on the event.

The wedding festivities began at 10:00 a.m. Breakfast was being served, and music was already playing. All the bars were open. There were already two hundred invitees there. By noon, most of the over five hundred guests had arrived.

The double wedding was a huge success. The brides were beautiful and decked out in unbelievable gowns. Four different bands were playing. Candy must have danced with fifty different people, including all the military personal and the politicians. There was a twist, jitterbug, and limbo contest. Bones, the Navy SEAL, won the limbo contest, Captain Patrick O'Conner won the jitterbug, and the chief of police won the twist contest. The food was fabulous, and the booze ran until the reception ended at 2:00 p.m. The chief of police was so drunk they took his keys away from him and put him into one of the spare bedrooms in the mansion. There was a staff of drivers at the valet stand that would take those too drunk to drive back to their homes.

The whole weekend was a success. The weather had been perfect, and there were two newlywed couples who slept until 10:00 a.m. on Sunday morning. All four of them met for a late breakfast at 11:00 a.m. Crews were almost finished taking down the tents, removing all the chairs, and cleaning up the mess.

They all ate a big breakfast and talked about the wedding. They laughed and told different stories about the night. Candy said she thought she had danced with the whole town of Rhinelander and her feet were killing her. The local Sunday paper was given to them at the table. On the front page was a picture of all four of them at the altar. Below that picture was a picture of all eight of the SEALs in their wet suits and capes.

Articles were written on both the wedding and the SEALs-versus-seals event. It was declared the biggest private event ever held in Oneida County. They all laughed again. Then Happy said, "Who the hell is paying for all this stuff?" Everyone laughed again. They had less than twenty-four hours before their departure to Costa Rica.

Monday morning, they all got up at 6:00 a.m. Their bags were already packed for their honeymoon. They had a nice breakfast and headed to the airport. A twelve-passenger jet was waiting for them.

They landed in Costa Rica in the afternoon. A limo picked them up at the airport to take them to their luxury hotel. The limo driver informed them that he was supposed to drive them to the marina where *You Must Be Dreaming* was docked. The captain wanted to meet them and give them a tour of the yacht before they sailed in the morning.

When they arrived at the marina and saw the 110-foot yacht, they were in awe. It was massive and beautiful. The captain met them at the gangplank and welcomed them aboard. His name was Rusty Miller, and he had fire-engine red hair. He gave them the complete tour but didn't spend much time at each station. He showed them their staterooms. They couldn't believe how big and decorated their stateroom were. They looked like they were staying in the honeymoon suite at the Waldorf Astoria. There was even a hot tub and sauna in each stateroom. The yacht seemed like a small city and had a crew of ten.

The captain invited them to spend the night on the yacht. His crew was all aboard, and the chef was there and could cook their dinner. He would make arrangements to cancel their hotel reservations. The boys looked at the girls and said, "What do you think?" Sally was still in awe of the yacht. She said, "Our hotel room can't be this nice, and we won't have to fool with our luggage." They all laughed and agreed. The captain laughed with them and sent four mates to retrieve their luggage and take them to their staterooms. The captain said he would meet them for dinner in the main dining room at 6:30 p.m. He would talk to them about the yacht and what their options were as far as where they might want to sail. There were brochures in their rooms, explaining things about fishing, snorkeling, scuba diving, island hopping, etc. There were also maps showing them how to get to different areas of the yacht. The captain tipped his hat and said, "See you at six thirty for cocktails. Don't worry about your hotel. I will take care of that."

As they entered their suites to unpack, they were surprised at the large his and hers closets, big bathroom with a huge shower, sauna, and his and hers facilities. Happy said to Sally, "Now I know why this goddamn thing cost so much." They both laughed.

They all met at six thirty for cocktails with the captain. The captain explained to them all about the yacht and answered all their many questions. Happy told the captain they wanted to do some snorkeling and some scuba diving and would like to stop at one secluded island with a nice beach; other than that, it was in his hands.

The chef prepared their dinner of fresh lobster, scallops, shrimp, and local fish. It was outstanding. The chef's name was C. J. Junior, and he was simply called cookie. After dinner, the four of them walked around the yacht, exploring. They found the movie theatre, and the women spotted the spa, where they met the woman who was in charge of pedicures, manicures, hair, makeup, and massages. Her name was Ingrid, and she was beautiful with a great personality and was from Sweden.

When they returned to their rooms, their beds were turned down. Flowers and chocolate were placed on their pillows, and all the linens were silk. They were to meet on the main deck at 8:00 a.m. They would be introduced to the entire crew and told what their duties were. All crew members wore white uniforms with their names printed on their shirts. They would go over life raft drills and other safety precautions. The lines would be cast off, and they would be on their way.

The honeymoon was fantastic. They were waited on like royalty. The whole crew was over the top. The chef was outstanding, and the captain became their friend. They snorkeled in coral reefs that held thousands of beautiful fish. It was like swimming in an aquarium. The boys did some scuba diving and a little fishing. The girls had spa day every day. They dove for some lobster, which they had for dinner one night. They stopped at a secluded island for a day, where they rode the personal water craft, skinny-dipped, sunned on the pure white beach, and played some volleyball. Candy and Sally bonded on this trip and became very good friends.

Both Happy and Danny enjoyed a much-needed vacation. They talked no business except for a two-hour conversation about the magical eye and some of its improvements. The last day of the cruise, the captain stopped the yacht and anchored in about one hundred feet of aqua-blue water. The whole crew, including the captain, took a swim in the ocean with them. After the swim, they all gathered in the main dining room and had a buffet lunch that the chef had made in advance.

They all talked and laughed. The guests all thanked the captain and the crew for an incredible cruise and the over-the-top service. Happy then handed each crew member an envelope and said, "This is a little thank-you for the best vacation any of us has ever experienced. Each crewman thanked and hugged all four of them. After lunch, the anchor was lifted, and they sailed back to Costa Rica.

The next day, they were on their private jet and headed back to their normal lives. Happy would be back on his military projects. Sally would be caring for the seals and lab 2. Candy had only three semesters left to get her doctorate, and Danny would be heading to his first deployment as a Navy SEAL in less than a week.

When they arrived back at the mansion, it looked like nothing had taken place the week before. Danny and Candy spent their last week together, making love and talking about their future plans after she graduated and he was discharged. They also spent time with the seals.

During the time the general was at the wedding festivities, he had a nice talk with Danny and Candy. He told Candy that he understood that she was getting her doctorate in criminology and wanted to become an FBI agent. He gave Candy his private number and told her to call him when she began her last semester. He might be of some help getting her interviews with the right people at the FBI. Candy smiled and gave him a big hug and a kiss and couldn't thank him enough. Danny shook his hand and said, "You are the man." The general just smiled and wished them both the best of luck.

The mansion was full of articles from papers around the country about the SEALs-versus-seals event. Some photos of the seal event and the wedding had just arrived. Danny sent pictures to all the seals, Captain Matthews, Sergeant Rock, and the general. On June 1, Danny was off to San Diego.

Once Danny arrived in San Diego, he was assigned to Bravo team. He was replacing a SEAL who just retired. Bravo team was being deployed to Afghanistan in five days. He was introduced to all five members of the Bravo team, a unit of SEAL Team Six. Chief Brad Bennington was the team leader, Jake Olson was a first-class petty officer, Randy Jackson was also a first-class petty officer, Hector Lopez was a second-class petty officer, while Ed Zulch and Danny were third-class petty officers. The chain of command was Brad, Jake, Randy, Hector, Ed, and Danny—in that order. These were all seasoned veterans except for Hector, who had only been a SEAL for nine months, but this was his second deployment.

They all got to know Danny during these five days and was told what was expected of him as the team rookie. News traveled fast in the military, and his new mates had heard and read about the SEALs-versus-seals event. They asked Danny a million questions and took an immediate liking to him.

While being deployed, Brad filled Danny in on what he could expect in Afghanistan. Brad had been on over thirty missions, and eight of them were in Afghanistan. Brad questioned Danny about his abilities, knowledge of his weapons, and overall training. He asked Danny if he had ever killed another human being. They talked about the SEAL code of never leaving another SEAL behind even if you were putting your own life in jeopardy. Danny liked Brad, and Brad felt comfortable with his new rookie.

Once they arrived in Kabul, Afghanistan, they were transferred to a forward operating base near the Afghan-Pakistan border. SEAL team Bravo was directed to a berthing tent that would serve as their temporary quarters. It was hot and humid. They were surrounded by desert and mountains.

After settling into their quarters, they got a visit from the base commander, Commander Wilson. He welcomed them to the base and shook Brad's hand as he had commanded Brad on prior missions. The commander said to Brad, "You just can't get enough of this shit, can you? You just keep coming back."

Brad laughed and said, "I see you're still here."

The commander laughed and said, "I guess neither of us can get enough." He told Brad he would like to see him in an hour at his headquarters, which was nothing more than a little larger tent. There was one concrete structure used as a latrine and shower.

After Brad's meeting with the commander, he came back to the Bravo team and told them they would be going on a mission in three days, more information to follow.

The next day after another briefing with the commander, Brad came back to Bravo team and laid out their mission. He had maps of the terrain. Intel showed about twenty Afghan rebels occupying some caves at the base of Tiger Mountain. The reports said that each morning the rebels would come out of the two caves and bathe in a small pond. Their mission under the cover of darkness was to dig foxholes on the other side of the pond, plant explosives at each cave entrance, and plant landmines immediately to the east and west of the cave entrances. In the morning, as the last rebels approached the pond, they were to blow up both entrances to the caves, pop out of their foxholes, and open fire on the rebels.

The SEALs would be dropped off about four miles from the caves, and with their night vision googles (which were invented by Happy) they would make their way to the pond, dig the foxholes, plant the explosives, lay out the landmines, and wait for the morning sun. If the mission was not successful, they were to withdraw and make it back to another checkpoint ten miles away, where they would be picked up.

The day of the mission, Danny was getting goose bumps. He was not frightened but excited. It would be his first action. They were dropped off two hours after nightfall and made their way to the ponds. Danny was in charge of the radio, and Brad's last words to him were "Make sure that goddamn thing is shut off until we need it." They had to be as silent as possible.

The foxholes were dug, the explosives planted, and the land-mines laid out east and west of the pond. Now they just waited. It seemed like an eternity to Danny. Everyone's faces were blackened with charcoal, and they lay motionless.

As the sun rose, all six were buried in their foxholes. Brad had a small periscope protruding out of his foxhole. That would show him the movement of the rebels. The rebels slowly emerged from their caves—two, four, eight of them. Within minutes, more came out. Brad counted twenty-one. After two minutes, Brad saw no more and shouted, "Now!" They rose out of their foxholes and opened fire. The rebels went for their rifles lying next to the pond. Jake set off the explosives, and the cave entrances were sealed shut. Rebels were falling everywhere while being fired at by the SEALs. Those who were not already dead tried escaping by running both east and west of the pond. They hit the landmines, and in a matter of five minutes, it was over.

Brad said, "Check all bodies. No prisoners." He turned to Danny. "Call in the Huey." Danny heard a few shots, indicating that a couple rebels were still breathing. The rebels were searched for maps or anything that could be informative. The Huey was there in ten minutes, and they were gone.

Back at base camp, the commander congratulated them on their successful mission. He asked Brad for a head count, and Brad said, "Twenty-one."

"Any survivors?" asked the commander.

Brad said, "None.

As the commander left their tent, he said, "Job well done. You guys relax, and I will send Messy over here with some cold beer." Messy was the mess sergeant in charge of rations and probably the most important person to be on the right side of.

Most military bases had daily mail call; however, because of the rapid movement of SEAL Team Six units, their mail was sent to a special PO box and then sent to whatever base that particular SEAL team was last sent. Sometimes the team may be transferred to another camp before the mail even arrived. Mail sometimes took two to three weeks to find them. If they were lucky, they would get their mail in ten days.

SEAL team Bravo's next mission was to free an American maritime captain and three of his crew that were captured off the coast of Somalia by some Somalian pirates. They seized their ship and took the four hostages and demanded $10 million in ransom.

Intel showed them being held in the town of Berbera off the Somalian coast near the straits of Aden. Bravo would deploy to Saudi Arabia and begin their mission there. Somalian pirates had been regularly capturing unarmed freighters in the straits of Aden, hijacking the captain and a few crew members and holding them for large amounts of ransom. Because of this, all maritime captains had a tiny beacon chip implanted in their body that would emit a signal for about a mile in distance. For security's sake, all the captains were sworn to secrecy, and no one, not even the crew members, knew about the chip.

This was the first American ship ever seized by the Somalian pirates. Drones were flown over Berbera, and the captain and the crew's exact location was discovered. Intel was able to get the layout of the building they were being held in.

Team Bravo had everything they needed. Under the cover of darkness, they were dropped off by a Huey ten miles from shore. They motored their raft to within two miles of shore then paddled in to shore.

Before they left, their commander told them to leave a message that would discourage them from seizing another American ship.

As the six men from Bravo eased their way into Berbera and located the building where the hostages were being held, it was 2:00 a.m. and pitch-black. They had on their night vision goggles and were well armed. There were two guards at the entrance of the building; one was sleeping in a chair, the other standing and smoking a cigarette. Within seconds, both their throats were slit, and they were placed back in their chairs. Danny was left to guard the door, which would be their exit choice. Brad turned on the beacon finder and saw that the captain was in a room two doors up on the left.

Brad and Jake entered the room while Randy, Hector, and Ed stood nearby with their weapons raised. All their weapons had silencers on them. All four hostages were tied up, and there were two guards watching them. They were immediately shot between the eyes. Hector was motioned into the room to untie the hostages and wait for exit instructions. Ed had a razor-sharp machete and was instructed by Brad to chop the right hand off of everyone they killed.

Brad, Jake, and Randy entered all the other rooms, killing an additional thirteen people. After Ed had chopped the right hands off the two guards in the hostage room, he followed behind the others, chopping everyone's hands off. After they had cleared all the rooms, they placed two explosives powerful enough to level the entire building. The explosives were set to detonate at noon, time enough for all bodies to be found and the message received. On the way out of the exit door, they saw two more pirates on the floor inside the building.

Danny killed them as they were approaching the two dead guards in the chairs. They probably had come to relieve them. Both of them had their throats slit and had bullet holes right between their eyes. Ed stopped and chopped of their hands and then operated on the two dead guards in the chairs.

Danny looked at Ed and said, "What the fuck are you doing?"

Ed whispered, "Orders."

As the SEALs and the hostages made their way back to the raft, Danny called the Huey for rendezvous arrangements. They paddled out about a mile, started the engine, and headed to the pickup point.

On the way to the Huey, Brad said to Ed, "Did you get them all?"

Ed said, "Yes, I feel like I chopped a whole cord of wood."

They all laughed. Ed had a diamond ring in his hand, held it up, and declared it a souvenir. He said, "One of the victims was a woman. The bitch must have been engaged to one of the pirates or was a pirate herself. One of the hostages said there was a woman with the pirates when they seized their ship." At this point, it didn't matter.

Bravo team was sent to a base in India to await future orders. The next several months, they did some surveillance missions in both Pakistan and Afghanistan and two in Iraq, gathering important intel.

The end of November 2000, Bravo team was to hook up with two other SEAL Team Six units, Charlie and Foxtrot. The three units trained together in Kuwait for a mission into Iran, where there was a large terrorist training camp and the headquarters for one of the Taliban's leaders.

Bones, one of Danny's original six SEALs, had been assigned to Foxtrot team, so they got to work together on this Iranian mission. They got to spend some time together during their training mission, had a few beers, and talked about the SEALs-versus-seals match. One evening, all eighteen SEALs got together for some cold beer. They had all heard about the SEALs-versus-seals match and Danny's grand wedding and that their commanding officer, now Admiral Matthews, was in attendance at these events. Danny never talked in detail about the events, but there were some articles printed in the *Seal Times*, which was a small Navy publication distributed to all special forces.

Bones started elaborating on the events and was talking about the two incredible real seals, Hoddie and Heidi. All the SEALs were listening with intent and laughing all through Bones's monologue. The members of team Bravo had grown fond of Danny as he had proven himself as a combat-ready SEAL and someone they could count on to have their back. This was something you had to earn as a seal, and you couldn't earn it unless you had proven yourself in combat. The Iranian mission was set for December 9.

The three SEAL teams would encircle the terrorist camp in a one-mile radius and slowly close the circle while eliminating any guards. When the circle got to within one hundred yards of the out-skirts of the camp, all visible guards should have already been killed. Foxtrot team would place landmines all around the perimeter of the camp, leaving only a thirty-yard exit route for the SEALs. The exit route would also be mined by Foxtrot when the last SEAL made it through the exit.

Team Charlie was to eliminate any guards that were standing duty in and around the barracks that housed the terrorist trainees.

Then team Charlie would place explosives in and around the same areas with detonators to go off at 5:20 a.m., right before sunrise. After that team Charlie was to also place explosives around the Taliban headquarters while Bravo team was inside, preforming their duties.

Bravo team was to enter the Taliban headquarters by eliminating the guards and cutting the throats of any Taliban sleeping in the complex. Their main objective was finding and killing Abudal Ronashan, the Taliban leader. While Brad, Randy, Hector, and Danny were killing Taliban, Jake and Ed would be looking for tapes, discs, maps, and other intel they could take with them.

The rendezvous point at the exit was 0200 exactly. If they were not finished with their assigned task, they were to leave immediately at 0155, regardless.

They arrived on the beach in Iran at 10:00 p.m. that night. They were about three miles from the terrorist camp. They had paddled in from four miles out in three separate rafts. When they arrived at their starting point, it was midnight. By the time they eliminated twelve guards that encircled the camp, they were ready. They had exactly one hour and fifteen minutes to complete their mission.

Foxtrot began planting the landmines. Charlie and Bravo were swiftly entering the barracks and headquarters building. Foxtrot killed three guards inside the barracks and silently slit the throats of those sleeping closest to the exits. They then began placing the explosives in the appropriate locations.

Bravo was already in the headquarters. They slit the throat of one sleeping guard. Jake and Ed went to the office area and started gathering critical intel. Hector stood watch at the entrance while Brad, Randy, and Danny went searching for Abudal Ronashan, killing all those they encountered during the search. Danny came out of one room with a bloody knife and a smile on his face, grabbed Brad while holding up a picture of Abudal, and pointed to the room he had just killed him in. Brad entered the room, pulled out a small camera, and took Abudal's picture. Brad told Danny to stand next to Abudal and smile. He took his picture with the dead Abudal.

Brad got Randy, and the three of them got into the offices where Jake and Ed were gathering data. Brad signaled five minutes to departure. Now all five were gathering intel, and Brad was taking pictures of everything with his small camera.

At 0200 all eighteen were at the exit—no casualties, not even a shot fired. As they left, mines were placed behind them. Brad told Danny to radio the Huey for rendezvous on the beach where they hid their rafts. They jogged the three miles to the beach. The big Huey was there in less than five minutes. They collected all the rafts, all eighteen SEALs jumped in the Huey, and they disappeared from Iranian soil.

At 5:10 a.m. the Navy sent four drones to encircle the camp and take videos of what was about to happen at 5:20 a.m.

Back in Kuwait, the base commander was briefed by the three team leaders. All intel and Brad's camera was turned over to intelligence. That afternoon, the base commander went to team Foxtrot, Charlie, and Bravo and thanked them for a job well done. He informed all of them that they would all receive the Naval Distinguished Medal Award. He also gave them all three-day passes to get off the base and go into Kuwait City, the capital of Kuwait. He told them all to enjoy themselves but not to get into any trouble. He gave them all $500 from a slush fund he controlled. He winked at them, shook all their hands, and said, "Now get the hell out of here and have some fun."

They all got nice hotel rooms supplied by the base commander, toured the city the first day, and had a fine dinner that night. The second day they were there, they spent the afternoon in a strip joint, drinking beer. All eighteen of them were together, laughing, telling stories on one another, and just having a good time. There was a table of about twelve marines sitting not too far from them.

Jake went to piss, and as he was standing at the urinal, a marine came to the next stall to relieve himself. As Jake was headed to the door, the jarhead said, "We marines usually wash our hands after we piss." Jake replied by saying that SEALs didn't usually piss in their hands. The jarhead said, "You SEALs think you are so fucking tough compared to us marines? You are a bunch of pussies! I ought to kick your ass."

Jake locked the door, turned around, and said, "Take your best shot, asshole." The marine lunged at Jake. Jake sidestepped him and kicked him in the ass while smashing his head into the door. Jake then grabbed him by the throat and said, "You are lucky you are on our side, or I would break your fucking neck." He then leveled a mighty blow to his nose and mouth. Jake broke the guy's nose and knocked out several of his teeth. The jarhead was out cold.

Jake removed the marine's shoes, unlocked the door, walked by the table full of marines, gave them the shoes, and said, "Your buddy has some problems in the head."

Jake returned to the SEALs table and told them what happened. Brad said, "Oh shit, boys, trouble is coming. Get ready."

Two minutes later, all the marines except the one in the head walked up to the SEALs table and said, "Which one of you pussies did this?"

All eighteen stood up and said, "I did." The biggest toughest-looking marine said, "Someone is going to answer for this."

Brad stood up and said, "You don't want to fuck with us. Not only will you get the living shit kicked out of you, but you will be embarrassed when you go back to your base with broken bones and your tail between your legs."

The tough marine sergeant said, "Then why don't just you and I go outside and settle this matter, you fucking maggot?"

Brad said, "Great idea."

They all walked outside and formed a circle. Brad and the sergeant faced each other. The marine threw the first punch. Brad grabbed his arm, brought it up behind his back, and raised it over his neck. You could hear it break. The sergeant screamed out in pain. Brad kicked him in the nuts, and as he fell to the ground, Brad looked at the other marines and said, "Next."

You could have heard a pin drop. Brad said, "I will let any two of you pick out any one of these SEALs and try to kick his ass."

One marine stepped forward and called out another marine by the name of Charlie and said, "We will take that skinny fucker." They pointed at Bones.

Bones immediately jumped out of the pack and said, "You dumb fucking marines will never learn." Like a cobra, Bones struck first with two fingers extended on each hand and buried them into the eye sockets of both marines. He then hit them both with a karate chop to their neck. They both were on their knees and couldn't breathe. Bones was about to deliver a lethal blow when he was grabbed by Brad and Danny and pulled away from his victims.

Brad then said to the remaining marines, who were standing there with their jaws open, "Gather up your tough buddies and get the hell out of here. Don't bother to pay for your drinks. They are on us. Just remember. Don't ever fuck with a Navy SEAL. Someday we might save your life."

As the marines gathered up their injured and their belongings and walked out the door, one marine whispered to Brad, "Thanks for the drinks."

The SEALs all laughed, ordered some more beers, and laughed some more. Danny said to Bones, "I think you were going to kill them."

Bones simply replied, "I was."

Brad raised his beer and said, "I would like to propose a toast. Here is to team Charlie and Foxtrot, our new friends. I hope we serve on many more missions together. You are the best."

After their three-day pass was over, they were all called to the commander's tent to review their recent raid on the terrorist camp in Iran. The commander had gotten back all the videos from the drones, had Brad's pictures developed, and gotten the reports back from Intel regarding their findings from what Bravo had gathered.

The commander said to all of them that he understood from his marine counterpart on the base that they had met some marines over the weekend. Brad stood up and said, "Yes, sir, they seemed like a nice group of guys." All the SEALs laughed, and the commander could not keep himself from smiling. The commander then showed a picture of Abudal Ronashan, the Taliban leader, with his throat slit then another picture of Abudal with Danny standing beside him with a bloody knife.

Jake yelled out, "Can I get a copy of that picture?"

The commander said no, and they all laughed again. Then the commander reported that the intel they gathered was extremely valuable. They got locations of other camps, addresses of other leaders, future terrorist plans of where and when, and cave and tunnel locations all through Afghanistan and Pakistan. They also got information about certain Pakistan officials that were collaborating with the terrorists. Then he began showing the videos of the drones.

The videos first showed the blowing up of the barracks then headquarters. They were both reduced to rubble, and what few survivors emerged from the remains were running in all directions. They were killed by all the landmines. There were no survivors. It was 100 percent successful with no American casualties. The SEALs were all cheering, and the commander gave them a loud applause and said, "Job well done."

Foxtrot and Charlie were sent back to their home base, and all six members of Bravo were going home for thirty days' leave. It was January 1, 2001. Before Danny left, he was called to the commander's office and given a color photo of him standing next to a dead Abudal Ronashan. The commander slapped Danny on the back and said, "Do not show this to any of your team members. I don't know where you got it."

Candy was home on semester break. She only had two more semesters before graduation in January of 2002. She picked Danny up at the airport in Rhinelander and drove him straight to the airport hotel. She took his hand and led him to the honeymoon suite. It was even better than last time. There was soft music playing. The king-size bed was turned down and a bottle of champagne iced down next to the bed with a fruit and cheese tray.

They made mad, passionate love for quite a while. They tasted each other and made love in numerous positions. They popped open the champagne and slid into the hot tub located in the huge bathroom and just relaxed and talked for over an hour. They got dressed and went back to the mansion. They were going to have dinner with Happy and Sally.

When they walked through the door, Danny was greeted by Happy and Sally. As Danny was hugging them both, there was a small puppy jumping on Danny's leg. He bent over and picked up this small beautiful black-and-grey toy poodle puppy.

Danny said, "Who is this little guy?"

Sally said, "It's a she, and her name is Lexi. She's mine, but she already seems more attached to you than me!"

The little poodle was kissing Danny's face over and over again. They all laughed, and Danny put the dog down. The dog followed Danny everywhere he went. Danny now had a new friend.

They had a wonderful dinner and afterward went out to the porch to continue all the conversations that were started at dinner. Candy talked about school. Sally talked about the SEALs and her new puppy, Lexi. Happy spoke briefly about some new projects he and the general were working on, and Danny told them about the missions he was on, holding the bloody details, which he would share with Happy until later. They all retired for the evening and would meet at 8:00 a.m. for breakfast.

At breakfast, they discussed Danny's time while on leave. He and Candy would fly to Florida for some warmer weather tomorrow on January 3. They would stay at Disney World for four days and then go to St. Augustine for two days and return on the tenth. Candy had to leave on the fourteenth for Madison and school. Danny would stay and spend time with Happy, Sally, the SEALs, and Lexi. Danny would leave on the twenty-third for Madison, where he and Candy would spend the remainder of his leave together. Danny had to be in San Diego on the thirty-first to meet up with team Bravo.

After returning from sunny Florida, Danny and Candy came home to a snow blizzard and minus-ten below zero. They spent the next four days with Hoddie, Heidi, and Danny's new friend, Lexi, the puppy. Candy left for Madison on the fourteenth for school. Danny would join her on the twenty-third.

For the next ten days, Danny spent working with his dad in the lab. Happy showed Danny the latest project he was working on for the general. It was a laser light attached to the helmet of a soldier. That would light up a path in front of him forty yards wide by one hundred yards long. It would make that area look like twelve noon when it was midnight and pitch-black. You could not see the laser's discharge, only the area receiving the laser. In other words, the enemy couldn't see you, but you could see the enemy. Happy had also invented a small handheld device that could detect landmines within fifty yards. This device would save many lives when approaching unknown areas that had been mined.

Happy informed Danny that he had made big inroads into the magical eye. He now had perfected a magical eye that could do five different functions: (1) make a blind eye normal with 20/20 vision; (2) power vision, able to see through eight inches of solid steel or three feet of granite; (3) heat vision, able to burn holes through solid steel or start fires; (4) nocturnal eye, able to make darkness into light; (5) laser eye, which had multifunctional capabilities, able to produce a laser beam up to one thousand yards that could direct a bullet fired from a firearm to hit a target dead center of where the beam was shining. This may be used as a floodlight with capabilities of lighting up a whole football field. The laser could be increased or decreased in intensity depending on the need.

Happy had made each of these eyes individually. He had tested each eye on either Hoddie or Heidi—but mainly Heidi because of all the prior operations on Hoddie. Happy could also produce the magical eye that could perform any combination of the five eyes or all five of them. Unfortunately, he had not been able to implant a combination eye, yet as it would take a human brain to make it change functions.

Happy also informed Danny that the general was told about the magical eye but only about the normal eye-correcting blindness and restoring 20/20 vision, not about the multifunctional eye.

The general gave Happy a $20 million grant to supply the army thirty of these eyes. Dr. Bennett and two army doctors had already done six operations, and they were 100 percent successful with no aftereffects. The first one was installed six months ago. Five more surgeries were taking place this month, also being performed by Dr. Bennett.

Dr. Bennett had been training six different surgeons on the eye-to-brain surgery, and one of the surgeons had already done a successful solo. The Army was paying Dr. Bennett a lot of money for his services for one year. The general was releasing Happy from his contract in two years, and he could go public with the eye, which would make Happy a billionaire. The general still didn't know about the multifunctional magic eye even though all the functions had somehow been used by the Army in many of Happy's inventions.

Happy had been assured by Dr. Bennett that the multifunctional eye could be implanted just like the normal one, with only one additional procedure. That procedure would be done at the same time as the normal operation. Happy and Dr. Bennett had implanted a multifunctional eye into Heidi three months ago. They could change the function in her eye mechanically by remote control, but she couldn't do it on her own. It would take a human brain to do that.

Once Happy's contract with the Army was finished, he was going to approach the general with the multifunctional eye, which would change the course of war. The USA would control the largest most efficient military in the world, and Happy would become a multibillionaire. By then, the magical eye would probably have a few more functions.

Both Hoddie and Heidi no longer wore patches over their eyes, as they both now had 20/20 vision in both eyes. Hoddie and Heidi would no longer be used in any on the eye experiments; they had served their purpose. They would remain at the lab as Danny's pets. Danny was amazed about all of this and very proud of his father.

Danny had long talks with his dad about his missions overseas. He was very graphic about the bloody details and how many men he had killed. He showed him the picture of him standing next to Abudal Ronashan with his throat slit and Danny holding the bloody knife.

Happy asked Danny if it bothered him to kill another human being. Danny replied, "Not if he is my enemy. Out there, it is kill or be killed." He told his dad he actually got a natural high when on missions and that the more people he killed, the higher he got. Danny also told Happy about the many medals, ribbons, and awards he had received in such a brief period of time and that he was proud of that.

Happy gave Danny a big hug and said, "I am proud of you, son. Go kick some more ass." They both laughed.

Danny said his goodbyes and left for Madison on the twenty-third. It was cold and snowy. He was anxious to see Candy but also anxious to get back to his SEAL unit.

Danny and Candy had a wonderful week together. They had plenty of sex and had many long conversations about their futures, the love they had for each other, the blessed life they were leading, and all the fun and excitement they had already experienced in their young lives. They were indeed blessed not only financially but with their health, their friends, their families, and their futures.

They reminisced about the SEALs-versus-seals match, their magnificent wedding, their beautiful honeymoon, and the wonderful sex they enjoyed with each other. Candy asked Danny, "How much do you think your dad spent on the wedding, the honeymoon, and all the festivities that surrounded these events?"

Without hesitation, Danny said, "Over $2 million, including the honeymoon."

Candy asked Danny if he knew what was in the envelopes he handed the crew when they departed the yacht. Danny told her, "Each crew member got $5,000. The chef got $7,500, and the captain got $10,000. That is around $60,000, all cash."

Candy told Danny that she and Sally gave Ingrid, the spa girl, another $1,000 each.

Danny left Candy on January 31, 2001, for a rendezvous with Bravo team in San Diego. Candy had about a year before her graduation in January 2002.

Bravo team spent ten days in San Diego and then deployed to a SEAL base in India. Once in India, they had a briefing with their new company commander, Captain Archie Proctor. Archie had come up through the ranks. He went to Annapolis for officer training and had been in the Navy for twenty-eight years, including eight years with SEAL Team Six.

Captain Proctor welcomed Bravo team to his base. He informed them that because of intel they had gathered when they killed Ronashan, the Navy had destroyed four terrorist training camps, killed over two hundred Taliban, and assassinated six Taliban leaders. They were informed of their next mission, which would begin in about fourteen days. They were all given top secret intel, territorial maps, a layout of a Syrian terrorist camp, and a picture of Rasha Bakka, a Syrian terrorist commander with a $1 million bounty on his head. Rasha Bakka had been responsible for at least twenty American deaths.

There were twelve handpicked terrorists led by Rasha Bakka that were going to poison New York City's water supply and poison tens of thousands of New Yorkers in May of this year. All twelve of the terrorists with their leader were all stationed in a planning-and-training barracks in Aleppo, Syria. The terrorists were scheduled to arrive in New York on April 15.

Bravo's mission would be to eliminate all thirteen participants under the cover of darkness without firing a shot, gather whatever intel they could from the barracks and office area, and depart to a rendezvous point. They would be joined on this mission by SEAL Team Foxtrot. Brad, the senior SEAL in this group of twelve SEALs, would be the team's leader.

On March 10, after several weeks of dry runs, team Bravo and Foxtrot were dropped off in the Cathi River, which ran through Aleppo. They were to drop off their rafts three miles from the barracks, which would be their rendezvous point. They jogged three miles to Aleppo. The barracks were located in a fenced-in area on about five acres, close to the downtown area of Aleppo. While wearing their night vision goggles and under the cover of darkness, they made their way to the fence.

They cut four big man-size holes in the fence to speed up their exit when they completed the mission. They got within two hundred yards of the barracks. There were two barracks, one very large barracks that housed about one hundred insurgents and a much smaller barracks that held the thirteen targets.

Three guards were spotted, one at each entrance to the large barracks and one walking around the small barracks. Team Foxtrot was to eliminate the guards and place two SEALs at each entrance to the large barracks and one SEAL at each entrance to the small barracks.

All twelve seals crawled to within sixty yards of the barracks. Brad sent Foxtrot in first. Once they eliminated all three guards and took their stations, Brad and Bravo would enter the small barracks from each entrance, three from each entrance, slitting the throats of all the terrorist working from the ends to the center. Once each terrorist was eliminated, they took a head count and only counted twelve. Brad saw a door leading into another room, which would be the office area. Brad and Danny entered the office area. There was a bigger bed with a man sleeping in the bed. It was Bakka. Brad signaled Danny, and he quickly slit his throat. Brad told Danny to take a picture of the now dead Rasha Bakka. Brad went back into the barracks and told Ed and Hector to take pictures of each dead terrorist and told Jake and Randy to come in the office and help him and Danny collect intel. Danny was still standing over Bakka and Brad said, "Get your ass over here and help us collect intel."

After gathering all portable intel, they took pictures of maps and data hanging on the walls, equipment, communications devices, and weapons lying around the complex. Brad gathered up all the SEALs and made their way to the fence. Brad told Danny to call the Hueys for pickup. They made it back to the rafts, and within two minutes of their arrival, a Huey and an attack helicopter were there. They loaded up their rafts, equipment, and intel they had gathered, and they were off to their base.

On their flight back, Brad congratulated them all for completing their mission without firing a shot. Jake said, "Shit, now we have to sharpen our knives again." They all laughed.

Danny was looking into a sack, and Brad said, "What do you have there?"

Danny pulled the bloody head of Rasha Bakka out of the sack and showed him off.

Brad said, "You sick bastard. I told you to just take his picture."

Danny responded by saying he wasn't sure his camera was working. They all laughed. Brad just shook his head.

They arrived back at base at 4:00 a.m. Captain Proctor was waiting for them. He counted twelve live SEALs and had a big smile on his face. He had a short conversation with Brad, and his smile even got bigger. He told them all to hit the sack and he would meet with them at noon in their barracks. The captain had four of his men unload the choppers and bring all the goodies to his office.

Bravo and Foxtrot slept till 10:00 a.m. They took a shower, had some breakfast, and were ready to meet Archie at noon. The captain stood in front of all twelve seals and congratulated them on a job well done. He told them that the intel they gathered was invaluable. That there would be a million New Yorkers who would never know about this mission that would be drinking fresh water for the next year, not knowing what possibly could have happened.

Archie said, "You SEALs did all this without firing a shot and we have positive identification on all thirteen of their elite terrorist." Then with a concerned look on his face, Archie pulled the head of Rasha Bakka out of the sack. "Was this necessary?"

Danny stood up and said, "Sorry, sir, I didn't think my camera was working."

Both Foxtrot and Bravo broke out in uncontrollable laugher.

The captain could not help himself and laughed with them. Archie said, "Sorry, guys, you are not going to get the $1 million reward that was offered for this head. But you are all getting three day passes and some cash to enjoy yourselves in town. I only ask that you don't meet up with any more friends like you did in Kuwait City."

They all laughed and said, "We promise."

The captain then shook their hands and let them know they would be receiving a special Navy medal.

For the next ninety days, Bravo was sent to Afghanistan, Pakistan, Lebanon, and Syria, doing recon missions. On July 14, 2001, team Bravo was sent to Tel Aviv, Israel, to work with some Israeli Special Forces. There was a big buildup of Lebanon forces in the town of Tyre, just south of Beirut, Lebanon. They were planning a big attack on Jerusalem sometime in September. The US and Israel got some reliable top secret intel on this buildup. The US and Israel were going to make a preemptive attack on the area and destroy all their tanks, artillery, and long-range missile sites.

They needed exact coordinates on these locations before the offensive so they could make an aerial attack on Tyre. Seal team

Bravo was given the task. A four-man team of Israel's elite would get them inside Tyre. It was then up to Bravo to pinpoint the different arsenals and report back to Tel Aviv with the intel. At that time, an immediate attack would be launched by the air forces of Israel and the US. The SEALs were to work under the cover of darkness. This would be a four-day mission. They would deploy at midnight, work until 4:00 a.m., meet up with their Israeli counterparts, give them their intel, and get ready for the next night's work.

After the fourth night and all intel was gathered, Bravo and the Israeli's team were delivered back to Tel Aviv. Two days later, a massive air attack was launched. All target areas were destroyed. The whole area was leveled. Thousands were killed, and all tanks, armored cars, artillery units, and missile sites, including launching pads and silos, were destroyed. It would be years before they could replace what they lost. Bravo was sent back to base camp in India.

On September 5, Bravo team was given two weeks' leave and were to report back to San Diego on September 20.

Candy was on semester break when Danny arrived home. She had to start her final semester on September 15. She had a job interview with the FBI on October 1. She was very excited about having Danny home, her last semester, and her upcoming job interview. When Danny arrived home, it was fall. The leaves were changing, and the North Woods of Wisconsin was full of life and color. Danny and Candy took a three-day vacation and drove to the upper peninsula of Michigan. It was beautiful. They stayed in a few bed and breakfast, made love, and talked about all that had gone on since he left.

When they returned to Rhinelander, they played with Hoddie and Heidi. The seals were now leading a more relaxed lifestyle, as there were no more experiments being done on them. The four of them swam together and played volleyball. The seals were very happy to have both Danny and Candy back home. Danny and Candy took a canoe ride on the Wisconsin River, enjoying the leave changes and watching the deer, wild turkeys, otters, and bald eagles. The beautiful black-and-white loons would soon be migrating to the south.

Danny spent time with Happy in his lab. Dr. Bennett and the Army surgeons had now preformed over one hundred eye operations with 100 percent success rate. There were three operations they couldn't attempt because the patients had brain damage, which prevented them from doing the operation. The general was ecstatic. They had given over one hundred military personnel the gift of sight. He kept getting Happy millions of dollars in grants.

September 14 came so quickly, and Danny and Candy left for Madison, as her last semester would begin the next day. She would graduate in January of 2002. Candy was so busy with school the first few days that she only saw Danny at night. One morning, Danny drove to Green Bay to watch the Green Bay Packers practice at Lambeau Field. Danny wore his full Navy dress blues with his SEAL hat and all his ribbons pinned on his chest, hoping this might give him the opportunity to meet some of the players.

The guard at the gate asked Danny if he had any credentials, and Danny said, "Just these." And he stuck his chest out, displaying all his metals.

The guard said, "That is good enough for me." He winked at him and let him in.

Danny strolled down the sidelines and saw Coach Mike Sherman, Brett Favre, Donald Driver, and many other Packer starters. Danny stood there, just watching, when Brett Favre walked up to him and introduced himself to Danny. He asked Danny what brought him here, and Danny said he was home on leave, was a big Green Bay fan, lived in Rhinelander, and was a Navy SEAL going back on deployment in a few days.

Brett put his arm around Danny and thanked him for his service and said, "Come with me." He introduced Danny to the head coach, Mike Sherman, and then to Donald Driver, Antonio Freeman, Dorsey Levens, and the others. They all asked Danny questions about the SEALs, his duty, etc. The coach walked up to Danny and said it would be their honor if he would join them after practice and attend their team meeting and then have dinner with them in the team's cafeteria. Danny said he would love to as long as he could be back to Madison by 9:00 p.m. Madison was two hours away. Coach said the meeting was at four, chow at five, and they would have him on his way home by six thirty. Danny was as happy as a pig in shit.

Danny had a blast. The team meeting was cut short and only lasted about fifteen minutes. The coach stood up and said to Danny, "You can ask any of us any questions you want, and then we are going to ask you a few questions."

Danny's first question was to the coach. "Are you going to the Super Bowl this year?" His answer was yes. Danny asked Brett Favre what his most memorable moment as a Green Bay Packer was. Brett answered, "Meeting you." They all laughed. Danny was having a ball and asked many questions.

Coach Sherman said, "Okay, now it is our turn. First, tell us a little bit about yourself, and then we will ask you some questions."

Danny told them, "I was a Hodag from Rhinelander, Wisconsin. I made all state twice as a football player and was heavyweight state champion three years in a row with a 60–0 record. I still hold most of the state swimming records and I am a huge Packer fan and I have a picture of Brett Favre hanging on my bedroom wall. I am a well-decorated Navy SEAL and proud to be an American. I am married to the most beautiful woman in the world, who soon will be graduating from the University of Wisconsin with a doctorate in criminology. After graduation, she hopefully will be working for the FBI. Her name is Candy, and she is probably wondering where I am right now. I am being deployed in two days for my third tour of duty to the Middle East, fighting terrorists. I have two pet seals and a toy poodle named Lexi. My father's name is Happy, and he is a genius. He is currently helping blind soldiers see again. And that is about it."

Brett Favre stood up and said, "Call Candy right now and put her on speaker phone. We want her to know where you are and why you will be late."

Danny called Candy and put her on speaker phone. She said, "Where are you?"

And he said, "Green Bay."

She said, "What are you doing in Green Bay?"

He said, "Having dinner with the Green Bay Packers."

Candy said, "You are full of shit."

All the Packers broke out in laughter, and Danny said, "You know who Brett Favre is?"

Candy said, "Everyone knows who Brett Favre is."

Danny said, "Here he is. Talk to him."

Brett said, "Hi, Candy. Nice to meet you. I hope you don't mind us taking your husband hostage for a few hours. We promise to have him home before nine."

All the Packers in unison said, "Hi, Candy!"

Danny took her off speaker and said, "I love you. Be home around nine, and tell you all about this incredible experience."

She said, "I love you too. Drive carefully."

Then Coach Sherman said, "Our turn, and I get the first question. Are you the guy who put the SEALs-versus-seals event together that we all read about and saw on the news?"

Danny said, "Yes." And he fielded many questions about Hoodie and Heidi. He then answered questions about his huge wedding; his father, Happy; SEAL Team Six; and what countries he had been deployed to. He was then asked if he had killed any terrorist, and he said yes. He was then asked how many, and he said all of them. They all laughed.

Donald Driver asked him seriously, "How many do you think you have killed?"

Danny said, "Not enough."

They all stood up and gave Danny a standing ovation. They then left for the Packer dining room. Danny sat between Coach Sherman and Brett Favre. Coach Sherman rarely ate with the team, but he did this on occasion. Coach Sherman gave Danny his private number and said, "Any time you or your family want Packer tickets, you call me." Brett Favre did the same.

After dinner, all the Packers shook Danny's hand and thanked him for his service and wished him the best. Coach Sherman told Danny there was a state trooper waiting outside the gate for him and he was going to escort Danny back to Madison in record time.

The trooper met Danny at the gate, shook his hand, and thanked him for his service. He said, "You follow me closely. My lights and flashers will be on, and when we get to the Madison City limits, I will leave you."

They drove in excess of a hundred miles an hour and arrived in Madison before 8:00 p.m. The trooper pulled over at the city line, and Danny pulled in behind him. Danny thanked him for the escort, and they shook hands. Danny was in Candy's arms by 8:05 p.m. She wanted to hear all about it. Candy was also a huge Packer fan as everyone from Wisconsin was. Brett Favre was her idol.

Danny gave Candy Brett's private number and said, "Call him some time."

She said, "He gave you this?"

Danny said, "So did Coach Sherman. We can have tickets whenever we want."

Candy screwed Danny all night long, and when she went to school in the morning, she said to him, "I will be home at one o'clock. I have no afternoon classes. Don't go on any more excursions. We only have one day left."

On the nineteenth, Danny gave Candy a big hug and wished her the best on her job interview in October. He told her he was going to do his best to be back for her graduation and that he was so proud of her. He was on his way to San Diego to meet his fellow SEALs.

Bravo team was deployed to a forward base near the Afghan-Pakistan border. After only being at the base for less than a month, Bravo team was sent to El Paso, Texas. They were to work with drug enforcement who were trying to break up a large cartel in Juarez, Mexico. The cartel's name was Moccasin, and they were manufacturing and distributing heroin into the States. Moccasin was led by Frederico Sanchez, a savage killer with no concern for human life. Moccasin was one of the biggest cartels in Mexico. Most of their operations were underground with many tunnels leading in and out of the complex. Some of the tunnels were so large you could drive vehicles through them. Many of the other tunnels were used for escape routes via foot.

Seal team Bravo settled into their barracks in El Paso and were having daily briefings with drug enforcement and boarder security.

Drug enforcement was able to get their hands on complete blue-prints of the entire operation, including all the tunnels. It looked like a massive spider web.

Moccasin was shipping tons of heroin and cocaine through California, Arizona, New Mexico, and Texas. They were also moving drugs into Tampa and Miami by freighters.

The mission was to completely destroy the cartel's labs and destroy the entire tunnel network. Many months of surveillance and undercover work by Mexican undercover agents allowed drug enforcement to gather all the intel they needed. Now it was time to come up with the right plan and execute it. Drug enforcement had come up with several plans; they wanted Bravo to read over their plans, improve them, or come up with a better plan.

Bravo had two weeks. They studied all the blueprints, drawings, sketches, and other intel that had been gathered. They interrogated the undercover Mexican agents for four days, picking their brains about minute details and asking them questions about those working in the labs, those guarding the tunnels, the type of weapons the cartel had, what type of vehicles were used in transporting the drugs, what times were the vehicles actually transporting drugs, if there were decoy vehicles sent out with no drugs, etc.

Bravo learned that Sanchez had a mansion located about three miles from the labs. There were two tunnels from the lab that led to Sanchez's office, and from his office, there was an exit that gave Sanchez direct access to his mansion. The drive from the mansion to the lab was only used by Sanchez and his lieutenants. The drive was lined on both sides with huge overlapping trees. That made it look like a tunnel. You could not see movement from the air. There were three black hummers either parked at the cave entrance or at the mansion. That would determine where Sanchez was. The three always traveled together and were heavily armed. Sanchez always rode in the one with a big star on each side.

Sanchez spent most of every day from nine to five, in his office, counting money, making drug deals, and working his money-laun-dering operations. About two hundred yards from the main entrance to the lab was a big parking lot area that housed from fifteen to twenty eighteen-wheelers. Forklifts would carry pallets of drugs from the lab to the parking area, where the drugs were loaded onto the big trucks.

Moccasin had the Juarez police department in their pocket and had free access from the labs to the major highways. They had Mexican manifests already approved by the Mexican government, stating that they were transporting coffee beans. Sacks of coffee beans were scattered over the pallets of drugs.

There were thirty tunnel exits, all funneling down to four main exits leaving the compound. One exit went to Sanchez's mansion to the south; one exit to the east was used strictly for the eighteen-wheelers. One exit to the west and one to the north were used by employees or visitors. There were parking lots by the west and north entrances and exits. Employees were shuttled in from the parking lots back to the labs and offices. It was actually an engineering marvel to build such a complex, not to mention the expense. Each entrance had two armed security guards. The lab ran twenty-four hours a day, seven days a week, with three eight-hour shifts: seven to three, three to eleven, and eleven to seven. There were sixty employees working each shift.

The mansion had four armed security guards that changed shifts every eight hours. Sanchez's four lieutenants also lived in the mansion. The mansion was set on ten acres of lush landscaping and had four gardeners maintaining the property from eight to five, five days a week. They lived on the property in a small house. The property was completely fenced in with barbwire on top of the eight-feet-high fence. There was a small airstrip capable of landing small private jets and a large helicopter pad where Sanchez's private helicopter was kept.

Bravo did not like the Feds' plans. They came up with their own plan and met with the director of drug enforcement and his second in command and with the director of border patrol and his second in command. Bravo laid out their plan. The Fed officials had never been involved in covert operations, and they knew team Bravo had been involved in many and were the best, so they listened intently.

Brad brought out a much more simplified drawing of the complex, its thirty tunnels, where they led, and the only four exits. It showed Sanchez's exit to his mansion, the trucking exit, the two exits for employees and visitors, and all exits also being used as entrances.

"Four days from today, team Bravo will parachute in at midnight, landing between Sanchez's exit and his mansion. They will have rocket launchers and explosives parachuted in with them. They will conceal the explosives close to Sanchez's exit to the south. The six seals will camouflage themselves in the tree-lined drive to the complex. In the morning, they can verify that Sanchez and his men are actually in the office at the labs, as they will see them drive by. The seals will be one hundred yards apart, three on each side of the drive.

"At exactly 3:05 p.m., when the 2 shifts were still in the lab, changing shifts, you guys will bomb the east, west, and north exits. We need enough bombs to seal those three exits. You need to bomb all three exits at the same time and fly away, just disappear. All the employees, approximately 120 of them, will be scrambling for 1 of the 30 spider tunnels leading to an exit. None could exit through Sanchez's exit as the office area is surrounded by steel bars, and the entrance can only be opened by remote control. The only ones who can leave by Sanchez's exit is Sanchez, his four lieutenants, and whoever else may be in the office.

"Sanchez and his men will be scrambling to their Hummers as soon as they hear the bombing. The first Hummer will be hit by two rocket launchers from each side of the drive closest to the mansion. The second Hummer will experience the same life-ending experience. The last Hummer will be destroyed by the two seals closest to the lab. The three Hummers and all personnel will be completely destroyed with no human survivors. Sanchez and his men and anyone else in the Hummers will not be able to be identified. At 3:20 p.m., you have your planes bomb the mansion. There should be eight armed guards there as they are changing shifts.

"Make sure you completely destroy the mansion. Four SEALs will gather the explosives, enter Sanchez's exit into his office, and plant enough explosives to completely level the entire lab, all the tunnels, and anyone still alive in the complex. Two SEALs will remain in the trees in case any of the armed guards escape the bombing of the mansion and head down the drive to the lab. At 3:55 p.m., you send a chopper to pick us up at the south exit. As the copter gets far enough from the lab, we will detonate the explosives, and there will be no more Moccasin, Sanchez, lab, or mansion."

One of the Feds said, "Whoa! We can't kill all those innocent civilian workers. We still have to answer to the Mexican government."

Brad said, "Bullshit. What do you mean innocent civilians? These people are manufacturing tons of heroin, opium, and cocaine. They are wearing masks and covered in drugs. Do you think that they think they are processing coffee beans? These people will be collateral damage. They have directly assisted in killing thousands of our young people in the USA, not to mention the rest of North America, including Canada. Fuck them! That's our plan, and if you can't accept it or can't do your part of the plan, then we are on the next plane out of here. We will go back to the Middle East and kill some more terrorists."

The Fed's said, "Give us some time to get approvals."

Brad said, "You have twenty-four hours. This mission is scheduled in four days. Don't come back to us with tweaks. If you can't hold up your end with accurate, pinpoint, timely bombing, you will jeopardize the lives of my men. You called us. We didn't call you. It is no sweat off our balls if you cancel this mission. I am sure the parents of all the dead teenagers who overdosed on shit that came out of this cave will be disappointed. The director of drug enforcement said we will meet right here in twenty-four hours." Brad handed him a list of explosives and rocket launchers they would need if it was a go.

Twenty-four hours later, they met. The director informed Bravo that he met with his superior and that it was a go. "My boss also told me to tell you that he knows all about SEAL team Bravo and that you will have our best men on the bombing missions. You can count on the exact times for bombing and pickup. However, you better be there for pickup as we can't stay in the area but for a few minutes."

Brad said, "We will be there."

They all shook hands, and Brad said he would like to meet with the bomber pilots and the helicopter pilot first thing in the morning. "I also want to meet the pilot and his crew that we will be using to parachute us in."

"Consider it done. You will meet them in hangar number 12 at El Paso airport at 9:00 a.m.," the director said. Before they left, the director asked, "What if some of the workers escape?"

Brad said, "They won't, but if a few of the lucky bastards get out, they won't ever want to work for another drug lord."

Team Bravo met with the pilots the next morning. Brad showed all three bomber pilots their exact target and the exact time to hit them. He told them to hit the exits hard. He wanted them completely closed. All three targets must be hit at exactly the same time, 3:05 p.m. Brad then talked with the parachute pilot and his crew, who would be packing their chutes and parachuting in the explosives and weapons to land within thirty yards of them. Brad told him the exact chutes his men wanted. Brad told them that all chutes had to be black and the crates that the weapons and explosives would be in must also be black. Brad then gave him a list of all the explosives and rocket launchers and asked him to check the list twice before they left that night.

Brad said, "I don't want my men to be stuck in the middle of three hundred Mexicans with just their dick in their hands." They all laughed.

Brad then went over the landing area with the helicopter pilot with the exact times. He told him, "You make sure you count six SEALs before lifting off, and then get us out of there as quickly as possible so we can detonate the explosives." They all shook hands, and Brad said, "Our lives are in your hands."

They all said, "You can count on us."

The night of the drop was pitch-black with no moon, as planned. The drop went as planned except Hector landed in one of the trees. They had to cut him down. He had minor leg injuries. They patched him up, and he was ready to go. They buried their chutes and concealed the explosives. Each took a rocket launcher with four extra rockets. They should only need one each, but they were all going to fire two rockets just for good measure. They all concealed themselves in the trees densely covered with leaves, one hundred yards apart, three on each side of the road.

Just after 9:00 a.m., all three Hummers drove by on the way to the compound. There were three people in two of the Hummers and four in the other.

At 3:04 p.m., Bravo could hear the planes, and at 3:05 p.m., bombs were exploding to their east, west, and north. There were deafening explosions in all directions. The sky was full of smoke, fire, and granite. Within minutes, the three Hummers were speeding down the drive. When the first Hummer was between Danny and Jake, they both fired. The Hummer was completely destroyed. At the same time, the second Hummer was between Hector and Randy, and the last Hummer was between Brad and Ed. They all fired at the same time. All Hummers were completely destroyed, and what was left of them was on fire. Nobody fired the second rocket; it was unnecessary.

Hector and Randy stayed in their positions, covering the drive, while Danny, Jake, Brad, and Ed grabbed the explosives and headed to Sanchez's entrance to the compound. Before they entered the compound, they could hear the last plane bombing the mansion at 3:20 p.m. Two guards came speeding down the drive in a small jeep. They were hit by two rockets and blown to another world. Hector and Randy stayed in position for ten more minutes. No more guards came. They headed back to the entrance and helped with the explosives. You could hear screaming and yelling and people in complete chaos, yelling for help. There were three Mexicans, two men and a woman, holding onto the steel bars, watching the SEALs place the explosives.

They screamed "Please help us!" in Spanish.

Danny, being able to speak fluent Spanish, stood up and said 'Okay, amigos, I will help you" in Spanish. Danny drew out his pistol and shot all three of them in the head.

The explosives were placed, and all six of them exited the complex. It was 3:52 p.m. At 3:55 p.m., the chopper landed and picked Bravo up.

The pilot said to Brad, "I count six."

Brad said, "Good job. Let's go."

139

As soon as the chopper got out of range of the explosives, Brad detonated them. Smoke and debris were flying everywhere. The land that the compound and tunnels were under sank like it was just sucked in by quicksand. Brad asked the pilot for a flyover. There was nothing left. There were a few dead bodies outside one of the employee entrances, and all vehicles in both parking lots were destroyed. There were no survivors.

After landing back in El Paso, Brad slapped the pilot on the back, shook his hand, and said, "Mission accomplished."

Bravo team was escorted to the director's office, and he had a big smile on his face. He asked if they got Sanchez.

Brad said, "No more Sanchez, no more compound, no more lab, no more mansion, no more moccasins, and no more drugs." They all laughed.

The director of drug enforcement informed them that the Mexican director of drug enforcement who was a bagman and protector of Sanchez had been with Sanchez that day.

Brad said, "They will have to appoint a new director!" And they all laughed again. The next day, Bravo flew back to their forward base near the Afghanistan-Pakistan border.

Danny had put in for two weeks' leave for January 1 to attend Candy's graduation.

Candy was offered a job with the FBI. She would start March 15, 2002. She was so excited and wrote Danny that her starting salary would be $90,000 plus benefits. She would spend her first six months doing on-the-job training in their field office in Washington, DC. At the end of the six months, she would be assigned to a team and would become a field agent, working with drug enforcement.

Danny wrote to her and congratulated her on her acceptance to the FBI. He told her he put in for leave and would be there for her graduation. He told her how proud of her he was and how much he loved and missed her. He also told her he knew a little bit about drug enforcement himself. He would tell her all about it when he got home.

Time was passing fast, and Bravo had gone on a few recon missions. December was already here. Bravo was assigned one more mission before Danny would be on leave, starting January 1, 2002. It was scheduled for Christmas Day. The commander wanted to give about fifty Taliban terrorists that were hiding in some caves on the Pakistan border, a Christmas present. The commander called in Foxtrot to work the mission with Bravo.

At 2:00 a.m. Christmas morning, the two SEAL teams were parachuted into Pakistan's White Mountain area. Foxtrot was dropped on the west side of the mountain and Bravo to the east. The six-man teams were covering two entrances and exits of each side of White Mountain. There were an estimated fifty terrorists living inside the mountain. At exactly 7:00 a.m., White Mountain was to be bombed from both directions by the US Air Force, using megaton bombs and ear-bursting missiles. The air attack would kill many of the terrorists in the caves, with others trying to escape out the exits. Bravo and Foxtrot were to cut down the escaping terrorists.

At 7:00 a.m., the bombing started and continued for almost thirty minutes. From the SEALs' prospective, it was a sight to behold. Half the mountain seemed to be collapsing, and what was left was covered by smoke.

Shortly after the bombing stopped, insurgents began running and screaming from the exits on both sides of the mountain. They were hit by machine gun fire, AK-47s, and rocket launchers. They were falling like sheep led to the slaughter. Minutes after the slaughter began, Bravo was being attacked from their left flank by a large number of Taliban. The SEALs were greatly outnumbered and returned fire with all they had. Brad had Danny radio for an Apache attack helicopter for support immediately and to call for immediate evacuation assistance.

Jake and Hector both were shot and were severely wounded. The SEALs were continually being mortared and fired at. Bravo was doing the best they could to hold off the Taliban. Just as Brad gave the order to retreat to the rear, the Apaches showed up and were mowing down most of the Taliban.

Danny grabbed Jake and threw him over his left shoulder. Ed grabbed Hector. As they were retreating, a mortar hit next to Danny, and shrapnel covered his right side. He fell to the ground with multiple wounds. The Apache helicopters continued firing, and one was hit by a rocket and went down. Two more Apaches showed up and finished off the remaining Taliban.

A Huey immediately landed, and Bravo, with their three injured SEALs, were evacuated from the area. Two of the Apache helicopters landed near the downed Apache and recovered its four-man crew. One was dead, and three were injured. When they lifted off, the other Apache completely destroyed what was left of the downed Apache.

The mission was accomplished but not without casualties. Foxtrot evacuated from the other side of the mountain without incident.

Back at the base, there was bad news. Jake was dead, and Hector and Danny were both severely injured. Hector and Danny were immediately flown to Kuwait, where there was a hospital staffed by US military doctors.

Danny had severe injuries. They might have to amputate his right leg, and his right arm might also be in jeopardy. He also lost his right ear and his right eye. It was not a good Christmas. Danny was in the hospital in Kuwait for sixteen days and then was flown to the naval hospital in Bethesda, Maryland.

During his stay in Kuwait, he was able to talk to Candy and Happy. He spoke to Candy every day, and she wanted to come to Kuwait and be with him. Candy was graduating in less than a week on January 4, 2002. Danny told her to graduate first and then she could come. He did not want her to miss her big day, which she had been working toward for the past seven years.

Danny called Happy and told him to make sure she did not come to Kuwait or him neither, until after the graduation. On January 4, Candy graduated. Happy, Sally, and her two brothers were there. Happy had purchased first-class tickets to Kuwait City, leaving on January 6.

After graduation, Candy called Danny and filled him in on the details. She told him that she and Happy were flying to Kuwait City in two days. Danny told her not to come. He was being flown to Bethesda Naval Hospital in Bethesda, Maryland, on January 10.

Candy said, "We are coming anyway."

Danny insisted they didn't need to come just for two days, as he would be back in the States in just a few days.

Candy said, "Shut up. I am in charge this time. We are coming, and that's it."

Danny said, "Yes, ma'am."

After their short visit in Kuwait, they all flew back to the States on the tenth. Happy and Candy gave up their first-class tickets to fly back with Danny on a very uncomfortable military plane.

After spending two days in Bethesda, Happy flew home, and Candy remained in Bethesda with Danny. Candy told Danny she was going to delay the start of her new job with the FBI on March 15. Danny knew Candy wasn't going back home. She had graduated and was free until March 15.

Danny convinced Candy to go find a nice two-bedroom apartment in Arlington, Virginia, close to the FBI headquarters. "Lease it immediately, and you can stay there while I'm in Bethesda, just a short drive away." She then would have her living quarters whenever she started her new job. Candy thought that was a great idea, and so did Danny.

Danny loved Candy very much, but he didn't want her at his bedside all day long or during his rehab treatments. Danny figured she would be busy finding the right apartment or condo and then furnishing it, and that would give him a little free space. He also told her not to think about calling the FBI and delaying the start of her new job. She had more than thirty days to decide what to do about that.

Candy found a beautiful two-bedroom condo on the first floor in Arlington, Virginia. It had a small walkout porch with a small backyard and beautiful landscaping. The complex had a big clubhouse, swimming pool, and tennis courts. She signed a one-year lease and was busy buying and taking delivery on bedroom, living room, and den furniture.

Danny was doing heavy therapy every day. They were able to save his leg, and he was starting to walk on it. He had lots of scars on his right arm and leg, but at least they were able to save both of them. He had no right ear and was blind in his right eye. From January 12 through February 15, Danny made incredible inroads with his rehab. By February 15, the Army released Danny from Walter Reed after constant persistence from Danny that he could finish his therapy at home with a live-in therapist. He was walking with a limp, had a hole for an ear, and couldn't see out of his right eye. Other than that, he was good to go.

Candy had finished furnishing her new condo, and they headed for Rhinelander on February 15, 2002.

Happy hired a full-time therapist for Danny who worked with him every day for six hours. They swam with the seals two hours a day and played volleyball. That made both Hoddie and Heidi very happy. Danny was recovering fast and convinced Candy to start her FBI job on March 15. He would be joining her in Arlington soon after she left.

Danny had been wearing a patch over his right eye since the injury occurred. He had picked up the nickname Patch from his fellow SEALs. But only the SEALs could call him Patch. Everyone else still referred to him as Danny. Happy and Danny, of course, talked about correcting his vision with the magical eye developed by Happy and to have Dr. Bennett do the surgery. Danny told Happy that he wanted the multifunctional eye and that he would be the first human guinea pig for the special eye. Happy only wanted Danny to get the normal 20/20 eye, which had a 100 percent surgical success rate. Maybe later, they could do the special eye. They argued over it for two days, with Candy being on Happy's side. They all agreed to meet with Dr. Bennett and explore all the options, the good and the bad.

Dr. Bennett explained to all three of them that the operation would be the same as the normal eye, except four more connections would have to be attached to the brain at the same time the normal connection was being made. This would make the operation about two hours long rather than the normal forty-five minutes. Dr. Bennett also explained, "Anytime you operate on the brain, there are certain risks you take—loss of life, temporary or permanent brain damage, or the eye just doesn't preform and you remain blind in that eye." The doctor was asked many questions by all three of them, and he answered them as best he could.

Dr. Bennett finalized his statement by saying, "I feel comfortable preforming the operation because of the 100 percent success rate, but there are no guarantees." If they decide to go in that direction, the operation would be done at Walter Reed Hospital in DC, and he would be assisted by the two best Army surgeons whom he had personally trained and had the utmost respect for.

Happy, Candy, and Danny discussed this in detail for two days. They all knew the final decision would come down to Danny. Both Happy and Candy did not want to go with the multifunctional eye, even though years of research had proven the eye would work. It just had not been installed in a human. It had been successfully installed in both Hoddie and Heidi as well as on an otter and an eagle. However, the brain of the mammals and the bird were incapable of changing from one function to another. Only the human brain had that ability.

Danny decided he was going with the multifunctional eye. He figured he should be dead anyway after escaping the firefight in Pakistan while trying to save Jake's life.

The operation was scheduled for May 1 at Walter Reed Hospital. A new ear was being made for Danny, and an operation was scheduled for April 15, to be performed at Johns Hopkins Hospital in Baltimore, Maryland. Dr. Bennett cancelled that ear surgery and would reschedule after the eye operation.

Candy left for her new job on March 10, which would give her five days to settle in to her new condo and prepare for her first day at the FBI. Danny stayed in Rhinelander to finish his rehab until April 1. Then he would join Candy in Arlington.

When Danny arrived in Arlington, he was walking without a limp and doing great except for missing an ear and his blind eye. Danny wore a patch that covered both his eye and his ear. He actually looked like a handsome pirate.

Candy had been on her job for two weeks and loved it and the people she was working with. She was very excited to see Danny and to tell him all about her new job. Danny arrived on a Thursday night. Candy's boss was aware of her husband's situation, so he gave her Friday off, and with the weekend, she had three free days to spend with Danny.

They never got out of bed from Thursday night until noon on Friday. Danny told Candy that was the best therapy he'd had in sixty days. Candy grabbed Danny's shaft and said, "I can live without your eye or your ear, but I am not sure I could live without little Danny here."

They both laughed, and Danny said, "What do you mean little?"

Candy said, "I meant literally, not figuratively."

They went out to dinner most nights, and on the weekends, they just made love. They could not get enough of each other. They were like two peas in a pod. They were very much in love and always acted like they were newlyweds.

On April 30, Danny checked into Walter Reed Hospital for his scheduled eye surgery the next day. Danny met with Dr. Bennett and his two assistants. Both Happy and Candy were also there. Sally stayed back at the mansion to take care of Hoddie, Heidi, and Lexi.

CHAPTER SEVEN

A New Vision

The surgery was a success. They kept Danny at the hospital for observation until May 8. The eye would be kept covered for another seven days. Danny and Happy returned to the mansion along with Dr. Bennett, who was going to be with Danny through his recovery period.

Candy stayed in Arlington at her job. She would fly back to Rhinelander as time would permit, if only for two or three days. They talked every day.

On May 15, Dr. Bennett removed the patch and told Danny to expect complete darkness for between twelve and twenty-four hours. He then would experience blurry vision. They would apply special eye drops for several days, and the blurriness would turn to cloudy. Each day for a few days, the clarity of vision would increase, and finally he would achieve 20/20 vision in his blind eye. By June 1, everything would be normal, and after about a week of normality, they would start working with the magical eye.

All the functions of the magical eye was controlled by the brain. The eye was programmed to coordinate with the brain, five main categories. Within each category, the eye could have several functions. The five categories were (1) normal vision, (2) power vision, (3) heat vision, (4) nocturnal vision, (5) laser vision.

Unless given a command, the eye would be in normal 20/20 vision. Once a command was given other than normal vision, Danny would have to command the eye to return to normal vision and leave the category he just commanded. To change a category, Danny's voice and only Danny's voice would have to say "Patch 2" or "Patch 3" or "Patch 4" or "Patch 5." "Patch 1" would return it to normal vision.

The eye could only do one category at a time but could be changed from one category to another in a matter of seconds.

Patch 1 had only one function—20/20 normal vision.

Patch 2 was power vision. This function allowed him to see through anything from clothing to eight inches of solid steel or five feet of rock or granite, up to a mile in distance.

Patch 3 was heat vision. This function allowed him to burn holes through solid steel as well as any other high-density material. It could heat any objects to three hundred degrees in seconds and can start fires.

Patch 4 was nocturnal vision. This function allowed him to have day vision at night and allowed him to see through thick fog and smoke.

Patch 5 was laser vision. This function allowed him to emit a laser beam up to three thousand yards, allowing him to fire a bullet from any handheld firearm, and the bullet would follow the laser beam to its designated target with pinpoint accuracy. It could cause temporary blindness when shone into someone else's eyes.

On June 10, they began experimenting with the eye in the lab. They placed steel plates ranging in thickness from one inch up to twenty-four inches, side by side. They had huge boulders up to five feet in diameter placed right outside the lab. They placed different items all around the labs and made other situations available, like complete darkness, smoke, and fog. Danny's first command was patch 2, converting from normal vision to power vision. He immediately saw through Happy's clothing, then he started laughing. Dr. Bennett wanted to know what he was laughing at, and when Danny told them, they all laughed.

Danny then moved to the steel plates. He started with one inch and worked his way through fourteen inches of steel and was able to see through all of them. At sixteen inches, he couldn't penetrate. They were all smiles and went outside to the boulder, and Danny was able to see through all of them. Dr. Bennett told Danny to go back to normal vision, and Danny simply said, "Patch 1." He was back to normal vision.

They went to lunch. They would try patch 3 tomorrow. They talked about all the possibilities patch 2 might have. Dr. Bennett then told Danny that his magical eye would have to be covered for at least twelve hours and preferably twenty-four hours a week. He simply needed to wear a patch over his eye three or four nights a week while he was sleeping. This was simply for rest and not overworking the eye. Also the eye should always be in patch 1 phase unless being used for other functions. He should always return to patch 1 immediately after completing his task in the other functions.

Needless to say, they were all excited and pleased with the results so far and were anxious to test out the other categories, but they were only going to do one a day in the beginning.

The next day, on June 11, they entered the lab, and Danny commanded, "Patch 3." He walked over to the steel plates and burned a hole one inch in diameter through three inches of solid steel and then burned another hole through six inches of solid steel. He then went back to the three-inch steel and enlarged the original hole one inch in diameter to two inches in diameter. Danny then told Happy to hold a two-inch piece of metal pipe about a foot long in his hand. Danny then focused his eye on the pipe, and one second later, Happy dropped it like a hot potato while shaking his hand, trying to cool it off.

Danny then focused the eye on a two-by-four piece of wood. It was on fire within seconds. They went outside, and Danny set some brush on fire then set an old tree trunk ablaze. The longer Danny kept his eye on the burning object, the bigger and hotter the flame became. Danny then commanded "Patch 1," and the eye went back to normal vision. They were all excited with the results and walked back to the mansion, where they discussed the endless possibilities for patch 3 over lunch. They were like three kids on Christmas morning. They couldn't wait until the next day to try out patch 4.

The next day, they went back to the lab. They went into one of Happy's dark rooms where he developed film. It was pitch-black in there. They couldn't see one another.

Danny commanded, "Patch 4." The room lit up like a Christmas tree for Danny. It was like being on the beach on a hot sunny afternoon. Happy and Dr. Bennett couldn't see a thing and asked Danny if he could see them.

Danny said, 'Perfectly clear, as if we are standing outside in the sunlight."

Happy said, "What am I doing?"

Danny said, "Giving me the finger."

Dr. Bennett asked Danny what he was doing, and Danny said, "Scratching your balls." They all laughed and went back into the lab.

Happy turned on a fog machine that produced very heavy fog, impossible to see through. Danny easily saw through the fog. They skipped the smoke test as they didn't want to stink up the lab. Danny commanded, "Patch 1." Then he went back to normal vision.

On June 13, they went to the lab to try the fifth and final function, the laser. They set up a firing range outside the lab. They set up targets 200, 500, 750, and 1,000 yards apart. Danny commanded, "Patch 5." Using a normal .30/30 deer rifle, Danny fired a bullet at each target as the laser beam was shining on the bulls-eye. Each bullet followed exactly the laser beam and hit each target dead center. Danny then took a pistol, which had no accuracy at any distance more than 60 yards, and fired a round at each of the targets. The bullet again followed the laser all the way to the target and hit it again dead center. Danny, being a weapons expert, could not believe it. He commanded, "Patch 1." Then he went back to normal vision.

By July 1, they had run every experiment they could think of. The eye was perfect, and there were no aftereffects. Danny had perfected each individual patch and learned how to increase or decrease each particular function. He loved playing with patch 2, the power eye. He would go to the mall and sit on a bench and watch all the girls walk by. He learned how to gear it down so if he was looking through women's clothes, he could see them bare-ass naked or just in their bra and panties. He was having a blast.

The first week of July, Danny was set free to resume his normal life, whatever that might be. He headed to DC to be with Candy.

Candy had about three more months left of her on-the-job training. She worked all week, Monday through Friday, and was off on the weekends. Danny shared with Candy all his new abilities and had been thinking of ways to put them to work. He first just wanted to have some fun time experimenting with his new powers. He told Candy he would like to play Robin Hood for a while, stealing from the rich and giving to the poor.

Candy asked Danny to explain himself. Danny told Candy that he knew that his departed SEAL friend Jake left a wife and two kids behind that were not financially secure. He would like to help them, and he also wanted to help those military personnel that were wounded in battle and were now disabled.

She said, "And how do you plan on funding these projects?"

Danny said, "In part by gambling. With my power vision, I can take the upper hand by seeing the opponents or dealers' cards and have over a 90 percent win ratio. I will come up with other ideas to use my other functions to my advantage while having fun." Danny said he would like to give it a try and see how it went. "I'll be home most nights and every weekend."

Candy said, "Give it a try, Robin Hood!" They both laughed and went to bed.

In the beginning, Danny would drive from Arlington to Atlantic City, about a four-to-five-hour drive. He would drive up on Monday morning and come home Tuesday night. He would do the same thing on Thursday and Friday.

Danny started off with a $20,000 bankroll. He would play blackjack at $100 table. Minimum bet was $100, and the maximum bet was $10,000. Danny could see the dealers' down card, which meant he knew whether the dealer had to hit or stay. It would tell Danny exactly what he needed to do because he could also read the next cards to be dealt from the shoe. He would always sit at third base, so no other players could affect the outcome of his or the dealer's hand.

Danny started out slow to get familiar with the surroundings and not to become too conspicuous. He would even lose smaller bets on purpose so he wasn't winning every hand.

There were about ten different casinos in Atlantic City, and Danny would visit them all so that he would not be readily known at one particular casino. He would always take a short break to look through the clothing of the most beautiful women. He never discussed that with Candy.

The first day, he started with a $5,000 stack and built it up to $20,000. The last two hands, he played each hand for the maximum of $10,000. He won both hands and cashed in. He was up $35,000. He quit at about 4:00 p.m. and went to his room and took a shower. He ate an early dinner of a cheese burger and french fries and went to a different casino. He played blackjack from 6:00 p.m. to 10:00 p.m. and won again—this time $45,000. He was now up $80,000. The next day, he went to a third casino and played from 10:00 a.m. to 2:00 p.m. and won $55,000. He was home Tuesday night with a suitcase full of cash. He had won $135,000 in two days.

Candy met him at the door with a sheer negligee on and said, "How did it go, Robin Hood?"

He grabbed her hand and took her and the suitcase to their bedroom. He picked her up, gave her a kiss, and threw her on the bed. He then opened the suitcase and dumped about $150,000 on her in $100 bills.

She couldn't believe it; she gasped at all the cash. She looked him in the eyes and said, "Robin Hood, tonight I am a hooker, and my fee is $10,000. You can do with me whatever you wish."

Danny laughed and did just that.

When Candy went to work the next morning, she went into the women's room to freshen up, and when she opened her purse, there was $10,000 wrapped in a rubber band with a note saying, "You were worth much more than that." She just giggled and put on her lipstick.

Danny went back to Atlantic City on Thursday, stayed at a different casino, and after commanding patch 2, went back to work. This trip he returned home with winnings in excess of $300,000.

Now Candy was getting nervous, afraid Danny would get into trouble. Danny had to explain to her it was completely legal. It was just gambling. Nobody knew about his magic powers. He was just one lucky son of a bitch. He gave her another $10,000 and told her to start a little nest egg. He would give her $10,000 after each of his trips. She was to open two different bank accounts and never put more than $5,000 in a single deposit at either bank. She was to keep her regular account to deposit her paychecks while occasionally making a $5,000 deposit and pay bills. Candy was starting to like this, even when Danny said he might have to go to Vegas for longer visits. They had over one hundred casinos in Vegas, and he could make larger wagers without drawing as much attention.

Danny flew to Vegas and played in the high roller lounge, with tables that had minimum wagers of $1,000, no maximum limits. In a matter of less than a month, Danny had won $7,000,000 and was getting better and smarter. He had opened three different bank accounts but had to be careful on how much he deposited in each account. He had over $5,000,000 in cash hidden in Arlington and Rhinelander, but most of it was at the mansion in Rhinelander.

He bought a regulation roulette wheel with regulation balls to experiment with. He found out that when he went to patch 5, he could emit a tiny laser that would heat up any numbered slot he wanted. And while everyone was making their bets for the next spin, he would heat up the receiving slot and the ball at the same time, and they would always wind up together. The heat drew them together like to hogs screwing.

It took Danny a while to get it right. At first he melted the balls or overheated the receiving slot, but after much practice, he had it down perfect. He now went from cards to the roulette wheel. He always played in the high roller lounges, where betting was unlimited. Roulette wheels heavily favored the house. With no maximum betting limits and with 35 to 1 odds, you could get rich quick or go broke quick.

Danny flew to Vegas to try out his new roulette scheme. Danny established his favorite number as 6, as in SEAL Team Six. At his first casino, he would play 6 straight for $10,000. He would lose the first two spins on purpose and then heat up the number 6 slot. On the third spin, number 6—bingo!

The dealer yelled out, "Winner! Winner, 6!" That was $350,000.

Danny now bet $20,000 on 6 and lost on purpose. He now bet $50,000 on 6 and heated the slot, and bingo, 6 hits.

"Winner, winner!" the dealer yelled. That was $1,750,000 going out.

Danny started shaking and said, "I can't believe it." He shed a few tears and said, "I now can pay off all my gambling debts!" This left everyone thinking he was a habitual gambler. Hence, they did not pay much attention to him as he walked away to cash in his $2,100,000.

Danny went to four more casinos, hit one for $2.1 million, another for $1.9 million, another for $2.3 million, and the last one for $2.6 million. Danny won a total of $10,650,000 on this trip. Danny headed home with two big suitcases full of cash. Danny hired a private jet to fly him from Vegas to Arlington, not wanting to board a commercial plane with all that cash with him.

It is now early August, and Candy wanted Danny to slow down. They had cash stashed everywhere. It was Thursday night, and she wanted them to go somewhere for the weekend. Danny asked her where she wanted to go, and she said, "To the mansion and swim with the seals." Danny hired a private jet for the weekend and paid the owner/pilot in cash.

Danny took about $7,000,000 of his cash to the mansion and hid it. They swam with the seals. They had dinner with Happy and Sally the first night, and the second night, they went to dinner with eight of their friends from Rhinelander and went dancing. Danny and Candy picked up the tab for everything, including the stretch limo that they all squeezed into.

When each of the couples were dropped off, Danny handed them all a large manila envelope and told them not to open it till Monday. Inside each envelope was $100,000 in cash and a note that said, "This is for your children's education. Ask no questions. Candy and I hit the lottery. The only thing you owe us is a dinner the next time we come home. Love, Danny and Candy."

Danny also had Candy send both her brothers $100,000. Danny and Candy left Monday morning on their private jet and made love on the fold-down seats in the cabin. They were now members of the mile-high club.

Candy said, "I bet Robin Hood never got laid on a jet."

Danny said, "This Robin Hood did."

When they arrived back in Arlington, Candy didn't have to work until Tuesday. They just lay around the house and talked about things in general.

Candy said that on September 15, when she graduated from on-the-job training, she would be given two weeks off before returning to her new job as a field agent. She would be assigned to a special task force dealing with gangs, drugs, and money laundering.

She said, "Speaking of money laundering, you need to do something with all that cash rather than just giving it away." She also told Danny she would have to be doing some traveling in her new position. Candy said, "As long as we have a lot of cash, I would like to go back to Costa Rica and lease the yacht *You Must Be Dreaming* and relive our honeymoon and take Happy and Sally with us—only this time it's our treat."

Danny said, "To address the tons of cash we have, I don't have to launder it. It was obtained legally in legal gambling establishments. However, I am opening an offshore banking account in Switzerland by advice from my financial advisor. I will maintain three bank accounts in our joint names here in the states. If anything happens to me, it all goes to you, including the offshore account. I am going to visit Jake Olson's widow, who lives in Mississippi. I have their phone number. I am going to take her and her two children to dinner, and I am going to give her $2 million—$1 million to her and $500,000 each to her children that will be set up in a trust that they cannot touch until the age of twenty-five unless it is used for medical or education purposes.

"I am going to buy us a small private jet, and I am going to get my pilot's license. In the meantime, I will have a full-time pilot who will be at our beckoning call. And if we are not using him to fly us around, he will help Happy at the lab. I will make it worth his time. I will arrange the yacht vacation in Costa Rica. If I can't get *You Got to Be Dreaming*, I will get one that's similar. I am also going to start

155

working on my idea of building a complex for wounded servicemen. I have lots of ideas for that venture, but I need a lot more money, so I will have to play Robin Hood a little while longer. Any more questions?"

"Just one," says Candy. "Can you see through women's clothing?"

Danny said, "Only when I am in patch 2, power vision. I only use that power when I am cheating at cards or roulette. I do see an occasional beautiful woman at the tables, but I can't be turning on and off my eye."

Candy said, "How beautiful are they?"

Danny said, "Some are magnificent, but none of them are as beautiful as you."

They both laughed. Candy grabbed little Danny and pulled him into the bedroom.

Candy returned to work, and Danny called Happy and Sally and the captain of *You Must to Be Dreaming*. He set the cruise for September 17 through September 24.

Danny had asked the captain if he had the same crew as on their honeymoon. He replied, "All but two, and they will be very anxious to see the four of you." Danny told Happy all they had to do was pack their bags. He was taking care of the rest.

Danny then called Jake's widow and introduced himself. She said, "I feel like I know you. Jake talked so much about you, and I want to thank you for trying to save his life."

Danny said, "I also feel like I know you. All Jake talked about was you and the kids." He told her he was going to be in Mississippi on Tuesday. He said, "I will be very close to Biloxi and would like to take you and your kids to dinner. Can you all make dinner at 6:30 p.m.?"

She answered, "Yes, we would love to. Danny told her he would pick them up at 6:15 p.m. at their home. He had the address."

Danny hired a private jet and flew in on Monday. He went to a local bank and set up two $500,000 trust funds in her name, with the children being the beneficiaries of the money. He had his attorney draw up all the legal paperwork.

On Tuesday night, he had a limo drive to their home. He had a bouquet of roses for Bonnie and two large boxes for the kids. Bonnie gave Danny a big hug and a kiss, and Danny gave her the roses. He had the limo driver bring in the two big boxes. They were gift-wrapped. Bonnie introduced Danny to the kids, Bruce and Barbara. Danny told the kids they couldn't open the presents until they got back from dinner. The kids already loved Danny and had just met him, so did Bonnie.

The limo driver drove them to an upscale steak house. They were seated in very plush surroundings. The waiter came, and the kids ordered Cokes. After Danny had checked out the wine list, Danny asked Bonnie if she preferred red or white. Bonnie said red. Danny ordered a very expensive bottle of red and ordered some appetizers off the menu. He then gave the kids each a small gift-wrapped present he had in his coat pocket. They tore them open, and they got small handheld computers. They could do everything with it. They immediately gave Danny a hug and started playing games.

Bonnie said, "That's so thoughtful of you." The waiter delivered the wine, had Danny taste it, and after his approval, poured them each a glass of the best wine Bonnie had ever tasted. Danny then proposed a toast to their father. He made the kids clink their glasses with him and Bonnie. Danny then said, "This toast is in honor of your husband and your father, Jake Olson, the best SEAL the Navy ever produced. He was a man among men, the best leader of all SEAL Team 6 units. He was respected by his peers and feared by his enemies. He was my best friend, and he loved his family. Rest in peace, Jake!"

They all cried and then started telling stories about Jake. Tears turned to laughter, and before they knew it, Danny was ordering another bottle of wine. They all ordered dinner while Danny told heroic stories about their father. Danny was still wearing a patch over his ear. He was to go into surgery next week to finally have it fixed. The kids asked him about the patch, and he bluntly told them he lost his right eye and his right ear while carrying their dad from the battlefield.

Dinner came, and it was excellent. They had banana foster and cherries jubilee for dessert, with homemade vanilla ice cream. On the way home, Bonnie could not thank him enough for the lovely evening and the kids' gifts. Bonnie invited him to spend the night. They had a spare bedroom. Danny thanked her but said that he was flying out that night back to Arlington. However, he would like a cup of coffee before he departed and would like to see the kids open their presents. Danny also had a little something for Bonnie.

As he was drinking his coffee, the kids were opening their presents. They each got a desktop computer and a laptop. They were ecstatic and gave Danny a big hug and were off to play with their new computers.

Danny gave Bonnie two envelopes.

She said, "What is this?" Both envelopes were blank and had no writing on them.

Danny said, "Open them."

Bonnie opened the first envelop, and there were two sets of paperwork for $500,000 trusts inside, one in each child's name. Bonnie's jaw dropped; she turned white and looked at Danny.

She said, "This can't be true." She then opened the second envelope, which was a certified check made out to Bonnie Olson in the amount of $1,000,000.

"I don't know what to say" was the only thing Bonnie could muster. "Where did it come from?"

Danny said, "It came from Jake. That's all you need to know. Be wise with your money. There is no more where that came from. The trusts are for the kids' education. They cannot access the funds until they are twenty-five unless the money is used for education or medical purposes. The funds are invested in a safe interest-bearing account."

Danny stood up gave Bonnie a big hug and kiss and said, "I can see why Jake loved you so much." He gave her his card with his address and phone number. "If you have any complications with any of this, just give me a call." He called for the kids and gave them a hug and told them to take care of their mother. He walked to the limo, waving goodbye, and they all yelled to him, "Thank you!"

Danny returned to Arlington and told Candy all about his visit with Jake's family, and he now felt like Jake knew his family was taken care of. Danny was satisfied.

On September 1, Danny got his new ear. It looked just like his other ear but had the cartilage of a chimpanzee. The operation took less than four hours, and Danny stayed home for a week. Danny had a CNA come over daily and swab his ear with a special cream. The stitches, 170 of them, were taken out a week before the cruise.

While Danny was home for the week, he was searching for large tracks of land in the US that was isolated but had plenty of access to water. He was looking for a minimum of five hundred acres but would like one thousand acres or more. He found large tracks of available land in Maine, Idaho, Montana, and New Mexico. He would visit the land upon returning from the cruise.

Danny's vision was to start a small town or village that would house and employ disabled veterans and their families. He wanted to give them all a parcel of land and to let them build houses and open stores, restaurants, gas stations, repair shops, and small businesses of any kind. He wanted them to start a new life with a bright future in a town they could call their own that they built. The wounded helping the wounded—it sounded like a big dream. But with plenty of money and a little help from General Smith, Danny felt like he could make this dream come true. He was going to call it Jake's Place, in memory of his fallen friend Jake Olson!

On September 15, Candy finished her on-the-job training. They had a big party at FBI headquarters. Danny, Happy, and Sally all attended. Danny had purchased a ten-seat Lear jet and hired a full-time pilot. Their maiden flight was to be to Costa Rica on September 17.

The name of Danny's new pilot was Vince Manchino. Vince was going to join them on the cruise. They landed in Costa Rica late that afternoon. They put the jet in a hangar and took a limo to the yacht. Danny had named his Lear jet *Bravo*.

When they arrived at the marina, the captain, Rusty Miller, greeted the girls with a big hug and shook Happy's and Danny's hands and said, "Welcome back." He then looked at their pilot and said, "You must be Vince." He shook his hand. Eight of the original crew was there, including Ingrid, the spa manager from Sweden, and the chef Cookie.

They had a wonderful cruise, and the weather and sea conditions were perfect. The girls were as brown as berries from all the sun. They had been pampered all week by Ingrid, and Cookie had fattened them all up. Everyone needed the rest and relaxation, and Danny got to show off his new ear.

Vince, the pilot, was in heaven. He had never been on such a cruise on such a fancy yacht. He and Ingrid, the spa manager, were seen together every night with big smiles on their faces.

Happy and Danny talked a lot about his eye, Robin Hood, Jake's Place, and what he might do in the future. Happy had become a billionaire, thanks to his invention. The general now had access to both eyes, and Happy was retiring. Happy and Sally were going to buy an ocean home on the island of St. Thomas, where they could spend the winters. They would keep the mansion in Rhinelander and travel around the world.

Happy handed Danny the paperwork to his trust fund. It now had over $500 million dollars in it. Happy said, "It's all yours, son. Do what you want with it. I am very proud of you."

Danny hugged his dad, thanked him, and told Happy how much he loved him.

Happy said, "Danny, I am one lucky son of a bitch. I could have spent the rest of my life in jail for murder. Instead I became a multibillionaire and raised a son who has been successful at everything he has done and is a war hero about to help out his fellow disabled veterans. I am married to the most wonderful woman in the world. As Louie Armstrong sings, 'it's a wonderful world.'"

As they departed the ship for their flight home, Danny handed each crew member an envelope and thanked them for all the fine service and attention they had provided. Danny winked at the captain and said, "We will be back."

They arrived at the mansion late on the twenty-fourth. Happy had an airstrip built at the mansion several years ago so that the general could fly his jet straight to Happy's home and lab. Danny would now be using it more often.

Candy started her new job with her new crew on October 1. Now that Danny had his own jet, he would be flying around the country, looking for the right tract of land for Jake's Place, and of course, more trips to Vegas, Tahoe, Reno, Biloxi, and Atlantic City, where he had hundreds of casinos that were going to help him build Jake's Place. Danny had over a half billion dollars in his trust fund. He had three bank accounts in the US and one overseas in Switzerland. Danny had millions in all four accounts and would be adding to all of them. He also had about $20 million in cash at the mansion and over $5 million stashed in Arlington.

Danny flew to Montana, Idaho, Maine, and New Mexico, searching for the right tract of land. He found a beautiful tract of land in Montana. It was close to the little rocky mountain range and had the Missouri River flowing through it. It was an old cattle ranch that had been bought by a gun club and turned into an exclusive hunting lodge. It had over three thousand acres and was in the middle of nowhere. The original owners of the hunting lodge were getting older and would sell at the right price. Danny did some research and found out they paid $4,575,000 for the land fifteen years ago. The only buildings on the property was an old farmhouse, a few old barns, a few storage buildings, and a very large hunting lodge that had over thirty bedrooms, a very large kitchen, a dining area that seated more than forty people, a huge den with three big fireplaces, and trophy elk mounts hanging on all the walls.

It was located right on the river and had magnificent views of the mountains. The lodge was beautiful and in very good shape. It was built fourteen years before. They also built four large outbuildings used for storage of equipment and vehicles. One building had about thirty snowmobiles stored inside, along with some fishing boats. The owners had spent another $5 million on the hunting lodge and outbuildings.

They were asking $20 million dollars for the entire property and all the buildings and equipment. There were four huge generators that could run the entire lodge in case of a power failure. Danny fell in love with the property and lodge. He contacted one of the owners and set up a meeting with the three men in charge of selling it. They had built an airstrip on the property so they could fly their planes into the lodge. Danny met them on October 20, 2002, at the lodge.

They were all successful businessmen in their late seventies and early eighties and had all fought in the Korean War. They fell in love with Danny after discovering he was a Navy SEAL and had been wounded in battle. After he told them about his plans for Jake's Place, named after a wounded SEAL who died in his arms during battle, they thought that was a wonderful idea.

Danny, being quite the bullshitter and a terrific negotiator, offered them $10,000,000. He told them it was all he could afford but that it would be a cash transaction. One of the men said, "Do you mean real cash?"

Danny said, "Yes, or I can write you a check, if that's what you prefer."

The three men excused themselves for a private conversation.

Danny was walking through the lodge, admiring everything about it. He would be willing to pay the $20 million but was going to get it as cheap as he could. He had a big smile on his face, knowing it was his. It was just a matter of how much. The gentlemen were gone for over an hour. When they came back, they said, "We have a fair offer for you. It is the best offer we can make, as we have seven other investors in this property. We will accept $13,000,000, the $3,000,000 in the form of a check and the $10,000,000 in cash. The $3,000,000 will be the actual selling price for tax reasons, and the $10,000,000 will be a side transaction with no records. We want the use of the lodge for this hunting season, which ends December 31 of this year. We want a nonrefundable deposit of $1,000,000 now, the $2,000,000 balance at closing anytime after January 1. A time and date of the closing will be your choice. The $10,000,000 in cash will change hands one hour before closing. The closing will be here at the lodge. Bring your attorney, and we will have ours. That is our counteroffer."

Danny said, "That includes all the equipment, all the furnishings in the lodge, as well as the snowmobiles and fishing boats?" They said yes, and Danny shook their hands and said, "Sold!"

Danny set up the closing for January 3, 2003, and told them to have a great hunt. They invited Danny to join them anytime from November 1 until December 23 to hunt elk with them.

Danny said, "That sounds like fun. I will take you up on that and will call you and give you a time frame that I can make."

They said, "Try to stay at least a week. We promise you an experience of a lifetime with some very fine, influential gentlemen."

Danny wrote them a $1,000,000 check, shook their hands, and said, "I will be in touch."

Danny jumped in his plane with Vince and headed back to Arlington. Danny had been taking flying lessons and planned on having his pilot's license by February of 2003.

Danny had been in contact with his good friend Rudy Simpson, whom he had met at boot camp and went to radioman school with in Bainbridge, Maryland. Rudy had also become a SEAL six months after Danny. Rudy had been severely injured in Afghanistan and lost a leg. Danny told him about Jake's Place, and he wanted Rudy to run Jake's Place. Danny had been sending Rudy money to help him and his family out until he could get Jake's Place up and running. Rudy was only one of a handful of people who knew about the magical eye.

Rudy was currently living in Louisville, Kentucky, with his wife and two kids, two and three years old. Danny called Rudy and said he wanted Rudy, his wife, and the two kids to fly back to the mansion with him and spend three days together to talk. He would pick them up at the Louisville airport on the October 24.

They all arrived at the mansion at 2:00 p.m. Danny introduced Rudy; his wife, Becky; his son, Charlie; and his daughter, Charlotte, to Happy and Sally. The kids fell in love with the puppy, Lexi. Danny showed them to their rooms and told them to meet downstairs in half an hour. Danny showed them all through the house and the labs. They met the seals, Hoddie and Heidi. Danny made the seals do some tricks and let the kids feed them. Dinner was at seven and cocktails at six.

DANIEL GARBER

The next day, Sally was taking Becky and the kids to shop in town, have lunch, and take the kids to a movie. Danny and Rudy would have the whole day to talk in private.

Danny explained everything to Rudy, showed him pictures of the lodge in Montana that sat on three thousand acres. "This is going to be your new home. You are going to be the CEO of Jake's Place and in charge of everything. We are going to build a small town on this property, with schools, churches, businesses, etc. Your temporary home will be the lodge until I can build you and Becky your own home. You will be paid a salary of $200,000 a year. You will be given a bonus of $250,000 to settle any debts, sell your house, and move to Montana the first week in January. You and I will be instrumental in moving wounded warriors into our new town. This is going to be our baby, and I am financing the whole operation with money I have won from different casinos."

Rudy knew about Danny's magical eye, and now he knew how he was winning all the money. He really was Robin Hood.

Danny then informed Rudy that his last big hit as a gambler was to hit Powerball. Powerball was a multistate lottery that had jackpots in the hundreds of millions. He couldn't go into detail, but when the jackpot got close to $500 million, he was going to have the winning ticket. He was going to give the winning ticket to Rudy, who would pay the onetime 40 percent tax up front on the winnings. Rudy would take $5,000,000 for himself and donate the balance to Jake's Place. That would give them all the money they needed to completely build Jake's Place and have about eight hundred residences.

Danny told Rudy that none of this could ever be discussed with anyone. "If you want in, it's yours. If you don't, I will understand."

Rudy said, "Are you shitting me? Of course, I am in. We are SEAL brothers. You can trust me with your life, and no one will ever get the details from me, including my wife."

Danny went to his room and came down with a small duffel bag with $250,000 inside. He gave it to Rudy and said, "Here, this is yours."

Rudy opened it up, and a big smile came on his face. He hugged Danny and said, "Let's go to work!"

Danny flew them all back to Louisville, and the Simpsons began making arrangements to move to Montana.

Danny flew back to Arlington and spent three days with Candy. A lot was happening fast. It was now November 1, and Candy had completed her first month at the FBI as a field agent. She was involved in her first drug bust and actually had to draw her weapon. She was so excited and told Danny all about what she had done. Danny grabbed her by her butt and said, "Don't get this beautiful ass shot off." She gave him a big kiss, grabbed little Danny, and pulled him into bed.

After making love for a couple hours, Candy filled Danny in on her whole month's experiences. It was very dangerous what she was doing, but she had been properly trained and was working with some seasoned FBI agents.

Danny and Candy would go to the firing range and shoot pistols. Danny was surprised at what a good marksman she was; however, he also knew it was different when shooting at a person versus a target.

Danny told her about what he was up to. He just bought the property for Jake's Place in Montana. As soon as he got his pilot's license, he was going to fly her out there. He told her about Rudy and his involvement in Jake's Place. He told her he needed to win some more money. It was disappearing fast. She laughed and said, "You're rich. You got plenty of money."

And Danny said, "Yes, but I don't want to spend any of ours."

She loved it when he said *ours*! She said, "Have at it, Robin Hood." She knew nothing of his Powerball scheme. Only Rudy knew of that scheme and only because he was going to cash the ticket.

Danny had made his Powerball plans. The numbers were drawn once a week in Washington, DC. There were sixteen states participating in Powerball, and every week it was at least worth $100 million and usually wasn't hit for three or four weeks in a row, which would jump the jackpot up to $500 million or more. Danny had planned on hitting the Powerball number on December 20, the last drawing before Christmas; everyone would be playing Powerball before Christmas Day. He knew the pot would be a minimum of

$200 million and hoped that no one would hit it the week or two before, making it around $500 million. Whatever it was, it was going to be his last big hit, and he would get more involved in Jake's Place. He just hoped he would have the only winning ticket so he wouldn't have to share the jackpot with other people.

The drawing of the numbers was open to the general public, and the numbers were drawn at 7:00 p.m. The numbers were selected the same way a roulette wheel operated, only this wheel was much larger and had sixty numbers. The balls were bigger, and the receiving slots were bigger so that the live audience and those watching on television could see the balls falling into a particular numbered slot. Danny had been to four previous drawings to find his best elevated spot in order to control the balls.

The wheel would be spun, and the first ball would fall into a slot. That number would be posted on the board. Then the wheel would be spun again and the second number would be posted and so on. There were six numbers selected, and then the Powerball, the seventh number, was selected. You had to have all six numbers, and the Powerball number to win the grand prize. The odds were like 5 billion to 1. They paid out partial jackpots if you had three, four, or five of the numbers.

Danny found the best viewing spot in the room and would come early and stand next to the rail. He would heat up a receiving slot of his choice, then heat the ball as it was spinning, and bingo, the two heated elements would mate. He chose two numbers on each of his visits, and both the numbers hit. He then would choose the Powerball number, and it would hit. He simply had to go to patch 5, the laser, and direct the beam at the two targets—the receiver and the ball.

He would fly into Louisville on December 18 and buy a Powerball ticket at a grocery store close to Rudy's house. He would only buy one $2 ticket with the numbers 3, 17, 22, 39, 46, 59, and the Powerball number 6. He didn't even tell Rudy he was coming to Louisville.

Between November 1 and December 15, Danny was spending the majority of his time in Vegas. It was where the high rollers went with unlimited wagering. At 35 to 1, Danny basically stuck to the roulette wheel in patch 5. He could win a lot more a lot faster.

Danny won over $300,000,000 from November 5 through December 15. One day alone, he won $40,000,000 between four casinos. Danny was barred from several casinos, and at the end, he only went to casinos he had not visited yet. There were a lot to choose from. He had made four 5-day visits during this period of time, and between trips, he would stash the cash at the mansion.

On December 18, Danny flew to Louisville and bought his $2 Powerball ticket with 3, 17, 22, 39, 46, 59, and the Powerball 6. He stood in line for over an hour to get his ticket. The Powerball jackpot had grown to over $700,000,000. Everyone and their brother were buying tickets in every state. It was the largest Powerball jackpot in history. Danny had two people in front of him when the machine ran out of paper. That took fifteen minutes to repaper, and then the two guys in front of him bought several hundred tickets each. Fortunately for Danny, most of those tickets were random tickets. When Danny got to the window, he handed the clerk his punched-out ticket and gave her his $2.

She said, "Are you only buying one ticket?"

And Danny said, "How many do you need?"

The clerk laughed and said, "Good luck."

Danny stood at the machine and verified the numbers. They were correct.

On December 20, Danny arrived early at the DC Armory, and it was a good thing that he did. Because of the record payout, more people than normal were already gathering around the rail. Danny got a hot dog and a beer and took his place at the rail. He had a perfect view. At 6:55 p.m., the officials arrived inside the pit and uncovered the huge wheel.

Danny went to Patch 5, and the laser was activated. He heated up number 17, and the spinner released the ball. Danny zeroed in on the ball, and the official announced number 17. Then 17 was posted on the board. Danny had already heated up 59, and 59 was posted on the board. And so it went with 3, 39, 22, and 46. Then came the Powerball. Danny heated up 6, and a guy jumped in front of Danny.

Danny knocked the guy to the floor and lasered in on the ball. "Six!" the official yelled. "Your Powerball is 6."

Danny walked away with the guy still on the floor. Danny had a smile on his face with the winning ticket in his pocket. He would now have to wait until tomorrow to see how many winners there were besides him. Hundreds of millions of tickets were sold, so in all likelihood, there could be a few more winners, thereby reducing the pot. With only one more winner, it was still $350,000,000. Danny felt a tap on his shoulder and knew what was coming. It was the guy he shoved to the floor. As Danny turned around, he grabbed the guy's fist, which was directed at Danny's jaw, then grabbed the guy's balls and put them in a viselike grip. The guy's eyes were bugging out of his head, and he was squealing like a pig.

Danny said, "Is there something I can help you with?"

The guy meekly said, "No, sir."

Danny let go of his nuts, and he jabbed two of his right fingers into the guy's eye sockets. The guy hit the floor, and Danny said, "Have a nice day."

Danny went to the parking lot to get in his car, but someone had parked so close to him he couldn't open the driver's door. He had to enter through the passenger side. As he was pulling out of the parking space, he rolled down his window and said, "Patch 3." He burned a whole in all four of his neighbor's tires. The car was sitting on the rims. Danny said, "Have a nice day."

Danny drove home to Candy, and they went out for a nice dinner in Georgetown. The next day, Danny saw that he had the only winning ticket worth $730,000,000. He couldn't help himself. He called Rudy.

Rudy answered the phone, and Danny said, "You are a winner!"

Rudy screamed, "Out, you son of a bitch! You pulled it off!"

Danny asked Rudy what he was doing for dinner, and Rudy said, "Nothing."

Danny told Rudy to meet him alone at Bernie's Steak House on Hycliffe Avenue, two miles from his house, at 7:00 p.m. "We will celebrate. Come alone. I have to be back in Arlington by midnight." They met at 7:00 p.m., slapped each other on the back, and laughed their asses off. They each had a martini and ordered a bottle of champagne.

Danny told Rudy they had six months to claim the money. They would claim the money in February after they incorporate Jake's Place as a wounded warrior's facility. He told Rudy he bought the ticket at a Kroger grocery store two blocks from his house on the eighteenth. "I didn't tell you I was in town, as I didn't want anyone to know. When you claim the ticket, you will be asked all kinds of questions. They will ask how you picked the numbers. You tell them a combination of birthdays and social security and service numbers. And the number 6 Powerball was selected because you were a member of SEAL Team Six. They will ask you what you are going to do with all the money. Tell them you are keeping a small amount for your family and donating the rest to a new facility that is just being built for disabled veterans who lost their limbs defending America. It's called Jake's Place and is located in Montana and is named after a Navy SEAL by the name of Jake Olson, who paid the ultimate price in defending our great country."

Rudy said, "You have thought of it all." He told Danny that with a wounded vet donating all this money to Jake's Place, the US Congress would be under pressure to help fund the project or at least make some special exemptions to certain taxes and other requests made by Jake's Place."

Danny said, "It's all in the plan. After the first of the year and you and the family have moved to Montana, you and I will sit down and start some planning. We are going to think this thing through before making any decisions. We will come up with a master plan."

Rudy said, "How much do you think we will clear after taxes on the Powerball ticket?"

Danny said, "Exactly $458,000,000. Less $10,000,000 for you, and that leaves us $448,000,000."

Rudy said, "I thought I was getting $5,000,000."

Danny said, "I changed my mind, and they both laughed."

Danny told him about the $300,000,000 he took from the casinos in the last month or so and that most of that was going to Jake's Place. Danny said to Rudy, "We are going to make a lot of wounded warriors very happy and give them a purpose in life." They shook hands and hugged.

Danny said, "I will see you the first week of January in Montana." Danny flew off to be with Candy.

On one of Danny's trips to Vegas in early December, he took the old gentlemen up on their offer to visit the lodge during the elk hunt. He informed them that he only had three days and would not be hunting. He just wanted to spend time with them and get to know them better and to learn more about the history of the property.

They welcomed him with open arms. They were all old enough to be his grandfather. Danny asked them many questions about the property. He asked them how they had all come to know one another and what they had all done for a living. There were fifteen of them. Ten of them fought in the Korean War. There were doctors, attorneys, two retired congressmen, and a retired senator, and the rest were successful businessmen. Only ten of them were financially invested in the property.

They then asked Danny about his tours with the seals. They wanted to know what medals he had received and how he was wounded, and he wanted to know about his family. They were very interested in his plans for Jake's Place.

Danny told them about his entire life and his football, swimming, and wrestling accomplishments. He told them about Happy, the murder of his wife's lover, and Happy's accomplishments as an inventor for the Army. Danny talked about his SEALs, his fiancée's tragic death in a car accident, his marriage to her sister, and her career with the FBI. But mostly Danny talked about Jake's Place and that he wanted to build a city around wounded warriors. Danny told them that he was glad that he had chosen their property to begin his dream.

Early the next morning, before Danny was going to leave, there was a big royal elk standing about a thousand yards from the kitchen door. The elk was standing at the edge of some woods. You could hardly see him. He was so far away in the distance.

One of the old men handed Danny a .300 Magnum rifle and said, "You received a marksman metal. Show us your stuff." He knew it was an impossible shot.

Danny took the rifle, said, "Patch 5," and took aim. He fired, and the bullet followed the laser beam right to the elk's heart, and the big royal dropped right in his tracks. Two of the old men had binoculars on the elk and couldn't believe their eyes. Two of them jumped on snowmobiles and drove to the elk.

They came back and said, "It's a beautiful royal shot right in the heart."

The old man took his rifle back and said, "I will be a son of a bitch. I have never seen a shot like that."

They all fell in love with Danny and gave him their names and addresses and told Danny to write or call them when Jake's Place was up and running. They might want to make some donations.

They also told Danny that they were going to mount that elk and have a plaque on it, describing the shot. They would ship it to the lodge in about six months.

Danny shook hands with all of them and told the three he would see them at the closing on the third. He and Vince were off into the beautiful blue Montana sky.

Candy had Christmas week off and took an additional week's vacation and didn't have to be back until January 10. Danny and Candy were going to spend Christmas at the mansion and were going to have a big New Year's Eve party for all their friends who still lived in Rhinelander. Then on January 2, Danny and Candy were flying to the lodge in Montana so Candy could see what Danny had bought and meet Rudy and Becky Simpson and their kids as they would be moving into the lodge.

It was a great Christmas holiday. The mansion was decorated to the hilt, both inside and outside. Sally had hired a company who specialized in Christmas decorations. There was a singing Santa on top of the chimney and a life-size Santa and sleigh with all nine reindeer standing in the snow on the front lawn. There was a twenty-foot tree decorated in the den with many presents underneath.

On Christmas morning, they all gathered for a big breakfast. They then went into the den to open presents. Candy got a solid gold watch, a beautiful diamond necklace, and a panty of the month club, where she would receive a very sexy pair of panties every month for the entire year. The first pair was in the box. They were see-through, red and white, and had white fur around the waistband and little bells around the crotch. Everyone laughed and stared at Danny. Out in the driveway was a black Ashton Martin with a big red ribbon wrapped around it.

Sally got a diamond necklace, a beautiful mink coat, and diamond earrings. Happy got a new hunting rifle, a Honda four-wheeler, and a new snowmobile. Danny got a video of their last yacht vacation sent by the crew of *You Must Be Dreaming*, a Rolex watch, a new snowmobile, and season tickets to the Green Bay Packers sent to Candy by Brett Favre. There were many other gifts—computers, laptops, sweaters, slippers, boots, etc.

It was a fun Christmas. Danny surprised Candy by flying in her two brothers and their wives on Christmas afternoon, and they stayed for three days. Danny had gotten all four of the women a whole day at the Magic Fingers Spa. He had bought out the whole spa for that day, and they had the whole place to themselves from 9:00 a.m. until 5:00 p.m. with a staff of eight to do massages of all kinds, pedicures, manicures, facials, hair, and makeup. That gave the four guys a day of snowmobiling and barhopping.

Danny and Candy flew out to Montana on January 2. Happy and Sally decided to come along as they were excited to see what Danny was up to.

They arrived around 3:00 p.m., and Dr. John Grandstone, one of the sellers, met them and showed them to their rooms. Dinner would be at seven, and cocktails would be at six in the den.

Candy, Sally, and Happy couldn't believe the view of the river and the mountains. The whole lodge was nothing but windows, allowing you to enjoy the view in all directions. The lodge was stunning, and the furnishings were exquisite. The girls couldn't believe that fifteen old men decorated this lodge. Danny told them they didn't, that their wives did and they had an unlimited budget.

They all met for cocktails, including Vince. Danny introduced everyone to Dr. Grandstone; Harry Swiggs, a retired congressman; and Benjamin Otto, the president of a large engineering firm. Harry Swiggs started the conversation by saying, "Danny had already told us some things about all of you, but he never mentioned what good taste he and his dad had in women. I must say you both are beautiful."

"Happy, we love your son, and you must be very proud of him. He has accomplished an awful lot at such a young age. Let me ask you, Happy, are you a hunter?"

"Yes, I am," replied Happy.

"Harry said you will love it here. Some of the best elk hunting in Montana is right here on this property. Did you teach Danny how to hunt?"

"Yes, I did, as a young twelve-year-old boy, he shot his first buck."

Harry asked Happy if Danny told him about the elk he shot here on his last visit. "No," Happy replied. Harry told the story and said to Happy, "You must be a hell of a shot yourself."

Happy looked at Danny and laughed. "Not as good as him."

They all enjoyed a great meal prepared by the lodge's chef. They retired to the beautiful den with all three fireplaces roaring with fire. All the royal elk mounts hung on the walls. Portraits of all ten owners scattered around the lodge. They talked into the early hours of the morning and then went to bed.

Danny's attorney was flying in at 10:00 a.m. The closing was to be at 11:00 a.m. They had some snow last night, but it shouldn't delay the attorney's arrival.

Danny met with John, Harry, and Ben at 10:00 am. Danny had two leather bags, with $5,000,000 in each bag neatly placed inside. They opened the leather bags. Each picked up a stack of hundreds and fanned them to their ear. They all laughed.

Danny said, "Go ahead and count it."

They said, "Did you count it?"

Danny said, "Twice."

They said, "That's good enough for us."

Danny could hear his attorney's plane landing; it was 10:00 am. The three gentlemen said, "We will meet you in the dining area at eleven sharp. We will use the big table in there as a conference table."

At 11:00 a.m., they all signed a lot of papers. Danny handed them a $2,000,000 check and ten small gift-wrapped boxes, with each owner's name on a box.

Harry said, "What is this?"

Danny said, "A small gift from Jake's Place—a token of our appreciation to the ten of you gentlemen."

Harry said, "Can we open them?"

Danny said, "Only the one with your name on it." They all laughed.

When they opened them, it was a solid gold pocket watch with a solid gold chain. Engraved on the front of the watch, when it was closed, was their name and a diamond studded SEAL emblem below their name. On the back was engraved Jake's Place, and below Jake's Place was engraved Honorary Seal.

Danny had them specially made by Rolex, and it cost him $18,000 each. They were beautiful. Harry, Ben, and John were stunned.

Ben said, "This is the nicest gift I have ever received." The other two followed with the same response. They all had tears in their eyes and gave Danny a big hug and said, "Good luck."

As the three men and their attorney boarded their jet and waved goodbye, Danny laughed and knew the $180,000 he spent on the watches would come back tenfold in donations to Jake's Place. Danny knew how to play the crowd. Rudy and his family would not be there for two days. Danny told everybody to dress warm. They were going snowmobiling and check these three thousand acres out. He told the chef to have some hot soup ready for them around 5:30 p.m. and plan dinner for 7:00 p.m.

They all met Danny in the snowmobile barn. They gassed up five sleds and headed out. Danny said, "Follow me." He first went to where he shot the elk. Happy looked back one thousand yards to the kitchen door and said, "Impossible."

Danny said, "Not with patch 5!" And they both laughed.

Danny took them to the river and drove along the river for several miles. They came to a bridge and crossed to the other side then drove through the woods on a snowmobile trail toward the mountains.

It was absolutely beautiful. They saw a herd of elk, a lone wolf, a few foxes, and some snowshoe rabbits. They saw a few mule deer and some other wildlife.

Danny stopped on the other side of the woods at the base of a mountain covered in snow. He got off his snowmobile and shut it off. The others did the same. Candy and Sally were taking pictures; it was breathtaking. Danny reached in his glove box and pulled out a bottle of Peppermint Schnapps. He brought out five shot glasses and poured everyone a shot. He then said, "Here's to Jake's Place. Bottoms up!" They drank their schnapps.

Candy said, "Pour another one. I want to make a toast. Here's to Happy. Without him, none of our lives would be the same, and here's to my wonderful husband, who made all this happen. And here's to God, who made this beautiful country. Bottoms up!"

They then rode for two more hours, exploring their new property.

At 5:00 p.m., it was starting to get dark, and they were getting cold. They just arrived back at the ranch. They put the snowmobiles away and walked to the lodge. The chef had two fireplaces going in the den. He told everyone to have a seat by the fireplace and warm up. "I will bring you some hot homemade stew." It was hot and delicious. They all had seconds.

Candy said, "I believe that this is the best stew I have ever eaten. What's in it?"

The chef said, "Just fresh vegetables and elk."

Candy said, "Elk! You have got to be kidding me."

The chef said, "Honey, properly cooked elk tastes better than beef."

Candy hesitated, smiled, and said, "I agree."

The chef had been at the lodge for fifteen years and had a permanent room upstairs, one of the more than thirty rooms. Danny told the chef that he could stay on at the same compensation and benefits that he was making before the old men sold to Danny.

Danny told him it would be slow for a while but he would be cooking for a small family until they could bring more people aboard. The chef's name was Slim, but he weighed about 250 pounds. Slim told Danny he kept busy doing other chores when he was not cooking—keeping the place clean, chopping wood, working on equipment, maintaining all the snowmobiles, etc. That fit Danny just fine. Danny liked Slim, and Slim liked Danny.

The next day, the Simpsons arrived. Most of their belongings were put into storage until they could figure out exactly what was going to happen. They all had met before at the mansion. The kids loved both Candy and Sally. Rudy and Becky were awestruck at the size and beauty of the place.

The Simpsons were introduced to Slim as their new chef. Becky said, "You mean I don't have to cook?"

Slim said, "Not if you don't want to, but if you enjoy cooking, you can share the kitchen with me."

Becky winked at him and said, "I am sure I can learn some Montana cooking from you."

Slim said, "You bet, ma'am."

Becky said, "Just for the record, I'm Becky. You don't have to call me ma'am or Mrs. Simpson—just Becky." Becky then pointed at Rudy and said, "That's Rudy, that is Charlie, and this is Charlotte."

Slim said, "I like you all already."

Everybody laughed. Charlie said to Slim, "Why do they call you Slim?"

Slim said, "Because I am so skinny." They all laughed again.

The next day, everyone went snowmobiling again, except for Sally. She stayed at the lodge and played with the kids. Danny took the same scenic tour as before, with a few extra twists. Rudy and Becky were in complete disbelief at the natural beauty of the property. They loved everything they saw. They returned to the lodge again at 5:00 p.m. to hot stew and a crackling fire. They had a lovely dinner and retired early. Everyone was tired.

The next day, they left for Rhinelander. Danny told Rudy he would be back in a week and spend three or four days together. He told Rudy there was a brand-new four-wheel-drive Land Rover in the first shed that was his, compliments of Jake's Place.

Rudy hugged him and said, "Man, you're too much."

"See you in a week," Danny said, and they were off again in the beautiful Montana sky.

Danny had Vince make a couple of flyovers so everyone could get a bird's eye view of the property and lodge from the air.

When they left, Danny had told Charlie to look out the window, and they would tip their wings at him, which meant goodbye. Vince flew low over the lodge and tipped his wings.

When they arrived back at the mansion, they stayed one day and headed back to Arlington. Danny was having Candy's new Ashton Martin shipped to Candy's condo by carrier.

Danny told Candy he had amassed enough money, thanks to the generosity of the casinos, to build Jake's Place. He told her he would not be doing any more gambling but devoting most of his time establishing how to make Jake's Place work and grow into its own town with Rudy. He wanted disabled vets to run the town, schools, churches, banks, small businesses, restaurants, etc.

He told Candy that Jake's Place was going to have its own police department and will need a chief of police. He asked Candy if she wanted the job. She asked when she would start if she was interested. Danny said, "By the end of the year. Things will be slow in the beginning, but you would be staffing your own department and running it like a business. You would be head honcho, lead detective, lead investigator, chief of police, and head of all law enforcement. As the town grew, your responsibilities would grow with it. You would grow with the town. I don't want an answer right now, just want you to think about it. I know you have a career job with the FBI, and I want you to be happy."

Candy gave him a big hug and a kiss and said, "You are the best thing that ever happened in my life." She grabbed little Danny and pulled him into the bedroom.

Danny flew out to Jake's Place for four days to talk with Rudy. Rudy and Becky had fallen in love with the place. Becky had met a few women in the small town of Bison about twenty minutes away. They had children the same age of Charlie and Charlotte. So now she had someone to coffee-clutch with.

Danny told Rudy they had meetings the next two days with two attorney firms from Elk City, a town about 60 miles away with a population of 60,000 and one firm from Bison a town 20 miles away with a population of 8,600. They would be interviewing 3 large developers. One was from Billings, Montana; one from Denver, Colorado; and one from Cheyenne, Wyoming.

Today they were having a meeting with the county commissioner. Everyone was told in advance what their plans were for Jake's Place. They were going to build a town from scratch to fill the needs of wounded veterans.

Over the three days, their time was completely consumed with meetings. The county commissioner was very accommodating and spent four hours with them. He thought it was fantastic what they were trying to do and that he and the county would do everything in their power to help. Once they selected a developer, they would work together to get through the normal regulations and permitting.

After meeting with the attorneys and developers, Danny and Rudy told them they would be getting back to them with more questions, but they would be hiring someone soon. They all loved the idea of Jake's Place, and all put forth their best sales pitch.

They had one more meeting with a lady by the name of Beatrice Ford. She was a friend of Harry Swiggs, who had called her and told her about Jake's Place. She called Danny a week ago and told him that she spoke to Harry and she had five thousand acres adjoining their property and she would like to talk to Danny. They met on Danny's last day there, and she asked a million questions. Danny and Rudy told her their life stories and what they wanted to accomplish. At the end of the meeting, she asked them if they were interested in her property.

Danny said, "Of course, we would love to have your property, but I am not sure we can afford it. How much do you want for the property?"

Beatrice said, "Boys, I am eighty-two years old, very wealthy, and live in Billings. I haven't set foot on that property for ten years. I let my friend Harry and his buddies hunt the land each elk season. I think what you boys are doing for our wounded warriors is heartwarming. I would like to participate by donating the five thousand acres to Jake's Place. I will have my attorney draw up the papers. Your attorney can get with him and finalize the transaction.

Danny and Rudy jumped up and gave her a big kiss and hug. Beatrice said, "Oh, my, I wish I were sixty years younger." And they all laughed.

Danny told her, "You have just allowed us to help another thousand wounded warriors."

A tear came to her eye and she said, "I always wanted to do something special for our armed forces."

Danny hugged her and said, "You just did."

Beatrice flew off on her small jet, and Danny and Rudy were beside themselves. They didn't know what to think. Danny called Candy that night and told her what happened and now he needed to stay with Rudy a few more days and make some decisions. Candy told Danny to take his time; she had to go to North Carolina on assignment for three days.

Danny took Rudy, Becky, and the kids to Bison for dinner to celebrate. Danny had a million thoughts going through his head. He pushed his thoughts aside and enjoyed dinner. At the end of dinner, Danny said to Becky, "I want you to start thinking about your dream home. Lay it out on paper as a starting point and go from there."

She said, "You are getting me excited."

Danny said, "Good!"

The next morning, Slim cooked a big breakfast, and Danny and Rudy went to the den to talk. Danny told Rudy that this new five thousand acres expanded his plans.

He then said, "I am going to throw out some ideas. I see the lodge as a temporary housing quarter for the first people we hire. After the developer we hire comes up with a master plan for both residential and commercial buildings—including streets, sewage, power, and other necessities—we will have him start building some homes and apartments for our first residents. I see the residential areas as gated communities. I see our city open to the public, but all businesses are owned by vets. Only vets can reside on the property, and all residential areas will be gated. We will have a village that consists of all rental apartments. We will have villages that are all condos and villages that are townhouses. We then will have villages of single-family homes on one-acre lots and have a village area with larger homes on three-acre lots. We will expand the size of Jake's Place to house more restaurants and a large hotel to handle overflow of guests who may be visiting.

"On the five thousand acres, I want to build a ski resort and a class A golf course. I want hotels, ski villas, and spas. I want all this to be open to the public for vacations. People will come in the winter to ski and snowmobile. They will come in the summer to play golf, tennis, and fish. We will have an amusement park for kids.

"All these people will use the downtown area of Jake's Place to eat, drink, grocery shop, gift shop, haircuts, etc. etc. etc., thereby producing people flow twelve months a year and allowing our business owners to prosper. We would use some of the five thousand acres for more residential homes and chop off maybe two hundred acres for a Navy SEAL base housing one SEAL Team Six elite group to fight gangs, drugs, and terrorism in the United States. They would have their own runway, barracks, training area, copter pads, and housing for their families. When they were not on a mission, they would be home with their families. This may sound farfetched to you, but it's not. I know Admiral Matthews personally. In fact, I have a meeting with him in three days to talk about Jake's Place and to get names, address, and phone numbers of every SEAL that has died or been wounded in action. There are no SEAL units based in the states except for those in training. Why not have a team working with the CIA and FBI here in the states, combating terror and drugs? I know I kept rambling, but things keep popping up in my head. You think about my suggestions, and tomorrow I will listen to yours. Right now, let's talk about attorneys and developers. Write your choice for attorney on a piece of paper and fold it up and lay it on the table.

"I will do the same."

They opened both papers, and they both said, "Bryce Cannon." They laughed and asked each other what they liked about him.

Rudy said, "They are a small firm with five attorneys. They represent the town of Bison Harry Williams highly recommended him. The attorney we hire has to work with the county. The other two firms are much larger and are located in a different county."

Danny said, "I agree with all your thoughts. Plus I asked him, 'What if Jake's Place grows larger and faster than we expect?' He said, 'I will hire additional attorneys, and I will work Jake's Place as my private account.'"

"Then do we both agree? That Bruce is our guy?"

Rudy said yes.

Danny told Rudy to call him right now and see if he would drive out to the lodge and have dinner with us tonight. Rudy made the call, and Bryce said he would be there at 7:00 p.m.

Danny told Slim to cook them a special dinner, set up a table in front of one of the fireplaces, and that Becky and the kids would be eating separately.

Danny and Rudy then resumed their conversation about the developers. They again wrote the name of the developer who most impressed them. They both wrote Richard Appleby from Rosselett and Maglio. Richard was the operating partner of the firm and would be the one in charge of this project if they hired his firm. They were out of Denver and were a 5A1-rated developer. They had developed many communities in Colorado, Tennessee, Maryland, and Florida.

Danny said he would call Appleby and ask for a meeting at the lodge. He would ask Richard to spend several days at the lodge with them. Danny would have a helicopter at the lodge for him and anyone else he wanted to bring to make aerial surveys. Richard could bring as many people with him as he felt necessary, and they would put them all up at the lodge. Danny wanted the meeting next week and told Rudy he would make him aware of the dates.

Bryce showed up at six thirty. They sat in front of the fireplace and had a bourbon on the rocks, Bryce's choice. Danny laid out the massive possibilities and the possible extensive legal work that it would require. Bryce told them that he had a land's contract and realty specialist on his staff. He had been the town of Bison's attorney for many years and was well versed in all the town and state legal matters.

Danny asked what their fee was. Bryce said, "My legal staff charges $150 per hour, and my paralegals are $60 per hour and my fee is $250 per hour and we require a retainer of $25,000. In your case, it would be more like $50,000."

Danny asked, "What options do we have?"

Bryce said, "I will give you one option. You give us a $400,000 retainer for twelve months at normal billing. If you exceed the $400,000 the first twelve months, your account will be credited $75,000, and your billing for the remainder of the year will be at 65 percent of normal billing. We are a no bullshit, no padding-hours company. We are honest and prompt. You can have your auditors check all our billing. In fact, we recommend it. If you have any problems, you will deal directly with me."

They had another bourbon and talked some more. Danny said to Slim, "How does dinner in twenty minutes sound?"

Slim said, "That's fine."

Danny looked at Rudy. Rudy looked back and nodded. Danny said, "Excuse me a minute, Bryce." And he went upstairs. Danny returned with a small briefcase with $400,000 cash and a note with two names on it and some instructions.

He handed the briefcase to Bryce and said, "Congratulations. You are hired." He told Bryce to open the case. Inside were four stacks of $100 bills, $100,000 in each stack.

Bryce said, "What's this?"

Danny said, "That's your retainer, and that note is your first job. We would like you to take care of it in the morning."

Bryce said, "This is a first for me." He laughed. He read the note and said he knew the attorney in Billings personally and also knew Beatrice Ford. He said, "What is this in reference to?"

Danny told him that Beatrice had just donated five thousand acres of adjoining property to Jake's Place. "She asked us to have our attorney call her attorney and get the matter taken care of."

Bryce, who was about fifty years old, said, "Jesus Christ, that's fantastic! I am looking forward to working with both of you and helping you make Jake's Place a reality."

Dinner was served—fillet and lobster tail. At dinner, Danny talked about building a ski resort, golf course, and lodging facilities on the five thousand acres. They would soon be hiring a developer whom he obviously would be working with. They then talked about their families, hobbies, etc. Rudy called Becky and the kids into the den and introduced them to Bryce.

They had an after-dinner drink, and Danny introduced Bryce to Slim. Bryce said, "My compliments, Slim. Dinner was fantastic." And he shook his hand. Bryce took his $400,000 and went home. Danny and Rudy were very happy and had their attorney.

The next day, Rudy had his turn to throw out his ideas. Many were similar to Danny's. Rudy wanted to add a large rehab building with an Olympic-size pool, workout rooms, basketball courts, a kitchen with a health bar, and a small theatre. A lot of disabled vets would have ongoing therapy for their injuries, and this building would give them a place to continue their individual therapy. Rudy also wanted to build a separate drug rehab facility for those veterans who had developed addictions to drugs while serving overseas.

Danny was leaving the next day and told Rudy to write everything down so they could discuss it with the developer. He also told him to look at some property along the river where Danny imagined the three-acre building lots would be. He and Becky should pick out their favorite spot because one of the first tasks he was giving the developer was to build both Rudy and him a new home.

When Danny returned to Arlington, it was the end of January, and Candy had just gotten back from her assignment in North Carolina. Candy told Danny about her four days in North Carolina with her three-man team—Roy Mercer, Bill Jackson, and her. They broke up a small drug-distributing center in Charlotte. There was gunfire exchanged. Three of the drug dealers were shot, one was killed, and two were injured. They interrogated two others that were arrested but not shot. They got a lot of information about the drug ring. Candy fired six rounds. None of the agents were hit. She said her adrenaline was high, but she remained calm and focused under the circumstances. The three of them were congratulated by their superior.

Danny told Candy about his trip to the lodge and the additional five thousand acres they acquired from Beatrice Ford. They now owned eight thousand acres or 12.5 square miles of property. That was twice the size of the city of Rhinelander. They talked about each of their upcoming schedules, and they would spend three days together at the mansion from February 20 to 23.

On February 2, Danny flew to Camp Lejeune to meet with Admiral Matthews. The admiral had heard about Jake's Place but had no idea of the size and scope of the undertaking.

Danny explained in detail the wounded-warrior project. The admiral was excited and thought it was a great idea. He asked Danny a million questions. He asked Danny what he could do to help. Danny gave him a long list of things he would like to have, starting with a list of dead and injured SEALs who had been discharged. He needed their names, addresses, phone numbers, disabilities, complete profiles, including wives and children's names and ages. He needed to know their educational data, past employment data, and the background of their families. Then he would like the same information separately on naval personnel, excluding SEALs. He then would like the same list of all military personnel. He explained to the admiral that they wanted to help as many military personnel as possible but they were putting the SEAL family first, then the navy, and then all other military personnel.

Danny then told the admiral about his idea of having a six-man SEAL team based at Jake's Place to fight drugs and terrorism within the US. He would like to put the team together either as SEALs or civilians working for the Navy, FBI, CIA, or a combination of the three.

His team would consist of himself and the five other SEALs that Danny graduated with at Coronado. He gave the list to the admiral. The admiral had met them at the SEALs-versus-seals event, and he explained to him that he had spoken to all of them at length about Jake's Place and the special unit. The Seals all said they were in, if the

Navy could put it together. Danny told the admiral that he would be the team leader. The admiral would assign an officer in charge of this special unit that they would take their orders from.

Danny told the admiral not to make an immediate response, to think about it for a while and just chew on the idea. He then explained to the admiral about his magical eye and told him there were only a handful of people who knew about this and that his friend General Smith was one of them.

They spent the next three hours outside, where Danny demonstrated the many powers of his eye.

The admiral was in complete disbelief. He said, "You have got to be shitting me. So you know what we could accomplish with these powers you have?"

And Danny simply said, "Yes, that's why I want you to chew on my proposal."

Danny said, "I know you will need some time to think about my proposal, but I need that profile information pronto, as we need to hire some qualified veterans right away to begin at Jake's Place. Most employees and residents of Jake's Place will come off this list that you will hopefully supply me with."

The admiral said he would get him the information. It would be classified, and he would have to pick it up himself from the admiral, as Danny had a top secret clearance.

The admiral said, "I will call you when I have the information."

They shook hands, and Danny said, "The sooner, the better." He then flew off with Vince to meet with the general.

On February 4, Danny flew back to the lodge to meet with Rudy. They now had 12.5 square miles of property and over $1 billion in cash, including the power ball money still unclaimed. Danny and Rudy never left the lodge for two days. They worked twelve hours each day, outlying their plans. They would start hiring some key personnel as soon as they received the profiles from the admiral.

Rudy would call the power ball offices and claim the $730,000,000 prize. He would set up a meeting with them to get his check of approximately $460,000,000 after taxes. The date was set for February 9 at 1:00 p.m. in Washington, DC.

Danny and Rudy set up meetings with the presidents of all three banks in Bison on February 6. They visited all three banks: Bison Bank, Elk City Bank, and United Bank. They chose Bison Bank. It was a local bank and would only be a temporary bank until Jake's Place had its own bank. It was a place to park the over $450,000,000 lotto winnings. They would start writing their checks out of Bison Bank. They still had over $650,000,000 in cash.

The president of Bison Bank was Hugh McFarland. He had a son on active duty in the Navy. Hugh was given a million dollars in cash to open the account. Hugh was told they would be depositing around $450,000,000 in his bank within the week. There would be two authorized signatures on the account—Danny's and Rudy's. The account would be set up under Jake's Place with the same address of the lodge. Hugh went white when they told him about the big deposit; he almost fainted. He was informed that it was only temporary because at some point, Jake's Place would have its own bank.

Danny and Rudy spent the next two days drawing up a footprint of how they saw Jake's Place so they would have something to hand Richard Appleby when he arrived on the twelfth. They hand-sketched a downtown area, housing areas, ski area and golf course. They made a long list of shops, courthouse, police station, SEAL base, hospital, etc. It was rough but a starting point for Rosselett and Maglio developers.

Before Rudy married Becky, she had gone to interior-decorating school and was working for a firm in Louisville. They gave Becky the task of converting seven of the lodge's bedrooms into offices. She was to have them all in the same area and would start now. They were to finish off two offices as soon as possible—one for Rudy and one for Danny.

Danny, Rudy, and Vince flew to DC on the eighth and stayed in Danny's condo. Rudy met with the Powerball Commission at 1:00 p.m. on the ninth. The press and newspeople were there to take pictures, and Rudy would hold an hour-long press conference for them and answer questions. They had two checks for Rudy: one large fake check that was three foot by two foot with his name and the amount so people could take pictures of it and then the real check. The amount was $472,000,000. The place was jammed with reporters from many different states.

Rudy read a written statement in hopes of answering most of their questions before they were asked. He closed by telling them all about Jake's Place in Montana, a city being built for wounded military personnel and their families. "All the money is being donated to Jake's Place, so all you charities out there, save your breath." Jake's Place was getting it all, with a small portion being kept for a new house, two new cars, paying off his debt, a nice vacation, college and trust funds for his kids, and a little cash for him and his wife, Becky.

Pictures of Rudy and the big check were in all the papers. More importantly, there were big write-ups about Jake's Place and where and how to make donations.

Danny, Rudy, and Vince all met with Candy and her two partners, Roy Mercer and Bill Jackson. They had a great dinner, and the next day, Danny passed his pilot's test and got his license.

The following day, on their flight back to the lodge, Danny told Vince that he wanted him to stay with him and Rudy and become Jake's Place's pilot. Rudy was going to also get his pilot's license, and they were going to keep this jet and buy a new bigger jet. They would have two jets. Vince would be flying different people to different places and would be Jake's Place's official pilot. Vince's first task was to do some research on their new purchase of a larger jet with more range and more seating capacity.

When they arrived at the lodge, Danny drove into Bison, met with Hugh, and gave him the check. Hugh was told to deposit it all into Jake's Place's account except for $10,000,000, which was to be deposited in Rudy's personal account that Rudy had just opened up. Hugh thanked Danny and said this was beyond his wildest dreams and he would personally oversee all their accounts until they had their own bank. He gave Danny the new checkbook in Jake's Place's name that had just arrived. Hugh told him he could write checks for any amount starting today.

When Danny arrived back at the lodge, he gave Rudy the new checkbook and also gave him a deposit slip; he had deposited $10,000,000 in Rudy's personal account.

Danny got a call from the admiral telling him he had all his pro-files ready. Danny said, "Great," and asked him if he could send his pilot to get them as he would be in meetings the next three days with the developer. The admiral said he couldn't do that but he would fly them out himself on the thirteenth because they were classified and he wanted to see Jake's place anyway. Danny asked him if he could spend a couple of days, and he would show him around. Danny offered to send Vince to pick him up. The admiral said, "No, but thanks for the offer. I have my own plane. Just give me the coordinates, and I will see you on the thirteenth."

Richard Appleby flew in the morning of the twelfth. They had breakfast and then took a helicopter ride on the chopper Danny had rented for three days with its own pilot. They flew around for two hours, so Richard could get a lay of the land. Richard had his right-hand man with him by the name of Barney Quigley. Barney had been with the firm for twenty-five years and would likely be the on-site project manager. He also had a photographer with him to take some aerial shots. Danny told Richard and Barney that they would spend the rest of the day together, discussing ideas. The next day, Richard and Barney and the photographer would have the chopper and Rudy's Land Rover and access to snow mobiles to do whatever surveying they needed to do. That Danny and Rudy may need the chopper for an hour tomorrow afternoon.

After Slim made them all lunch, the photographer was given a snowmobile and told to ride wherever he wanted and take pictures. He could use the Land Rover, but it wouldn't take him places the snowmobile would. Danny, Rudy, Richard, and Barney sat in the den and talked all day. Danny told Slim dinner would be at seven thirty.

Danny gave them the sketches and said, "At least it's a starting point. You can arrange it however it best suits our need. You are the experts in this field. We are building a city from the ground floor. We are going to need roads, sewers, water, power, and residential areas. We want custom home sites with three-acre lots along the river. We want single-family home sites with one-acre lots. We want town-homes and condos. We want two large apartment complexes. We want all residential areas to be gated. We want a hospital, school, police department, city office building, and all the other stuff a city needs. We want the downtown area, residential area, school, hospital, churches, etc., all located on the original three thousand acres. We would like the ski resort, golf course, ski lodges and villas, hotels, and SEAL complex located on the five thousand acres, along with some more residential areas. We want the tourist to do their shopping in our downtown area of Jake's Place, thereby supporting our veterans who have stores there. So other than a ski shop, pro shop, a few necessity stores, several hotels with spas, some ski villas and lodges, we want everything else built in our downtown area in order to support our veterans who will own all the businesses in Jake's Place."

"Only military personnel and their families will be able to live in phase 1, the three thousand acres. And phase 2 can be for any nonmilitary families. We want single-family sites to be on one acre. The different residential villages will be named after fallen heroes. We don't want any more than one hundred single-family homes per village. We want to keep some natural beauty in phase 1 and want a large playground and park in both phase 1 and phase 2. We want a rehab building in phase 1 that is large enough to house an Olympic-size swimming pool, hot tubs, basketball courts, volleyball courts, workout rooms large enough to have fifty pieces of physical fitness machines, steam rooms, and saunas. We want a separate building for drug rehabilitation. We want the apartment complex, condos, townhouses, and single-family homes to each have their own villages." Danny and Rudy rambled on and on, adding a number of additions.

All this was being recorded in their meeting, and Barney was taking notes. After Danny and Rudy were finished, Richard asked them many questions and more specifics. Then Barney asked another hundred questions.

Danny yelled to Slim to bring them some chips and cold beer. They talked some more. It was now 5:00 p.m., and Jim, the photographer, came in and was cold. He stood by the fireplace, rubbing his hands, and said, "What a magnificent piece of property." Danny asked Slim to get Jim a hot cup of coffee, and Jim said, "I'd rather have one of them cold beers."

Now Richard took over the conversation and said, "Okay, let's talk finances. How do you plan on financing the project?" Danny said they have over a billion in cash to start with. Richard said, "That's all I need to know. Some of the concerns a developer has is how he is going to be paid and if he can sell all the homes, condos, townhomes, etc. that he will be building."

Danny told Richard that the developer would not be selling property in Jake's Place. Jake's Place would pay his firm a fair price for each dwelling built. They would not need sales people, marketing, or advertising. Jake's Place would own everything and dispose of it to the veterans as they saw fit. All Rosselett and Maglio had to do was build it, meeting all local, county, and state criteria. Jake's Place would have their own city manager, bankers, attorneys, and managers. They would own their own sewer and water plants.

Danny told Richard he wanted them to come back with their survey crews. "Let us know how many residential units can be built in phase 1. Show us your model homes, condos, and apartments; cost for infrastructure, etc. We will want to know our discounted price on homes and how much a square foot other building will cost us. We will supply you with information you need to build the SEAL complex. What will a ski resort cost us? Golf course and the other amenities that we requested? Give us a time frame for completion of the entire project and approximate cost. We assume the first phase will be roads, sewers, water, power, etc. The first things to be built will be a few custom homes and two apartment complexes to house our initial residents. One village of single-family homes and one village of condos and townhomes—the others to follow. We will want our town built at the same time you are building the first residential villages. We know there is so much to cover, but this is a start. That's why we want to hire you. You are the experts, and we also know there will be suggestions and changes made along the way. What do you want in upfront money?"

Richard said, "Give us $5,000,000 for startup. We will discuss each stage of the development and approximate cost of that stage, and upon agreement, you can cut us a check for that phase. I know you will have a comptroller, and he can audit all the invoices. We can get started next week by sending in our survey crew. A month after that, we will have the first blueprints of your city, housing, infrastructure, etc., along with ball park pricing."

It was now seven thirty and time for dinner. After dinner, they sat in the den and talked further. Barney was a real character. He was an ex-Green Beret and was a great storyteller. Both Danny and Rudy took an immediate liking to him. They met the next morning for breakfast. Richard, Barney, and Jim headed for the copter. That afternoon, they wanted to travel the property by snowmobile. They would leave the next morning. Danny told them that Slim would fix them some lunch before they took out the snowmobiles. Dinner would be at seven thirty, and they would meet their guest, Admiral Matthews.

Admiral Matthews arrived at 1:30 p.m. with his pilot. They showed them around the lodge; introduced them to Slim, Becky, and the kids; and showed them to their rooms.

The four of them got in the chopper and flew all around the area then flew over Bison and Elk City and the mountains. They got back around 4:00 p.m. and went into the den for a cold beer and a warm fireplace. The admiral was dressed in civvies with an old baseball cap. He was very impressed with the whole operation and what they were trying to accomplish. He sent his pilot to his plane with Slim to retrieve all the files.

Danny told the admiral and his pilot that tomorrow morning, they would take a snowmobile ride around the property and he could see it from another prospective. The developer was leaving in the morning, and they could have a few hours of private time after they left.

The developers came in and ran to the fireplace. They were all laughing. Everyone was introduced to the admiral and had some cocktails, and Barney was telling the admiral of all the elk and deer they saw and what a magnificent piece of property this was. Slim cooked them a nice dinner. They had a glass of wine, and everyone went to bed. Breakfast was at 7:00 a.m.

After breakfast, Danny gave Richard a $5,000,000 check and said, "Let's go to work. Timing is of the essence." The developers flew out, and the admiral headed for the snowmobiles. Danny took them everywhere, but Danny was most interested in showing the admiral where he envisioned the SEAL compound. It was about two hundred acres along the Missouri River and at the base of the mountains. The admiral spent two hours riding around that sight. They didn't get back to the lodge until after four o'clock. The admiral called his base office and told them he would be a day late.

They warmed up by the fire had a nice dinner and went to the den to talk. The admiral told Danny and Rudy that he had spoken to several of his peers and General Smith and that there was a lot of interest in Danny's proposal; however, more discussions would have to take place. He needed to speak to a few senators and the directors of the FBI and CIA. The admiral said he was bushed and needed some sleep. They would continue their discussions in the morning.

After breakfast, they went back to the den to finish up their discussions. The admiral told them that if the SEAL operation was a go, Congress would pass an appropriations bill to fund the project. He wanted Danny to send him the developers' blueprints and estimated cost on just that phase and they would expand on it. He also told Danny the reason he hand-delivered the profiles; it was that his peers wanted him to fly out there and scope things out. That was why his pilot was taking so many pictures. The admiral flew out around noon.

Becky had already begun converting the seven bedrooms into office space. She told Rudy and Danny their offices would be ready in ten days. Danny told Becky to find them a local printer in Bison or Elk City that could put together an eight-page full-color brochure in a short period of time. They would need about twenty thousand copies and to set up a meeting with the printer at the lodge in two days.

Danny and Rudy started with the profiles. They were separating the vets and their families' backgrounds into categories, such as engineering, finance, politics, construction, management hospitality, groceries, banking, builders, developers, architects, medical, and so on.

They spent two days separating all the profiles. They met with the printer and laid out the brochure. It would explain what Jake's Place was all about, the size, and the landscape. It showed the city with schools, hospitals, rehab centers, restaurants, retail shops, ski lodge, golf course, housing areas, etc. They gave the printer pictures, etchings, drawings, and details. He was to lay it out and bring it back for approval.

Danny's first objective was to find someone who could be the city manager and work with the developer in design of the city. Second was to find someone with a banking/finance background. They wanted their own bank so they could unload a bunch of cash, almost half a billion, in their own bank. Then they wanted a comptroller.

They found a disabled SEAL who had a civil engineering degree, and his father was the city administrator for a town in Idaho with a population of sixty thousand. They also located a SEAL with a finance degree, and his family owned a private bank in Topeka, Kansas. They found another seal who had been working the last five years as the comptroller of a very large manufacturing company. They found a qualified hospital administrator, school superintendent, and a postmaster.

They flew them all into Jake's Place, gave them the tour, and offered them jobs. They all accepted and would move into the lodge and start within thirty days. They would do whatever Jake's Place asked them to do while they were organizing their departments. Each of them would work with the developer in designing the city, schools, hospitals, etc.

The ball was rolling. Danny left for Arlington to meet Candy on February 19, 2004. They spent the weekend at the mansion.

Over the weekend, Candy told Danny that she had given a lot of thought to the chief of police position at Jake's Place. She wanted the job. She could be her own boss and spend more time with Danny and start a family. Danny gave her a big hug and said, "Terrific. When do you want to start?"

Candy said, "I will give the FBI a thirty-day notice in April and start on May 15."

Danny said, "That's great timing. They decided to plan a four-day vacation in Disney World on April 1, before she gave her notice."

Candy was spending a lot of time away from DC with her team, and Danny was very busy with Jake's Place, so their together time had been very limited. On February 24, they both went back to work.

The brochures had been printed and looked terrific. Jake's Place was being bombarded with people and companies wanting to give donations. All the new employees were living at the lodge. Rudy had leased ten large construction trailers and had them turned into temporary offices. Each new employee had his own trailer for their offices and was given temporary employees for secretaries. Two trailers were set up as phone banks just to receive incoming calls and donations. An ex-SEAL was hired just to oversee and train temporary personnel. Things were happening every day.

Richard Appleby was told to immediately build a large office building that would be incorporated into city offices later. The new city manager was working with Richard on that project as well as tweaking the first edition of the city's blueprints. Richard was also to build a bank, a post office, and a restaurant. He was to build a large apartment complex and one hundred single-family homes. He was also to build two custom homes for Danny and Rudy on three-acre tracts on the river.

The admiral made a return visit with General Smith and two US senators. They were given the grand tour and taken for snowmobile rides around the property. Slim cooked them a great meal and got them drunk in the den by the fireplaces. They stayed two days and had a great time and were very impressed with Jake's Place. The admiral asked Danny's permission to tell the senators about his magical eye before they came to Jake's Place. He told Danny that if he would share that with the senators, it would virtually lock up the appropriation bill they would need to build the SEAL complex. Danny had agreed.

Before they left, the senators asked Danny if he could demonstrate some of the powers that his eye had. Danny performed a function in each category and explained some of the uses it could be used for. They were amazed, shook his hand, and told him they would do whatever they could to help him accomplish his goal. Danny thanked them for coming and told them he would hold them to their offer. They all laughed.

Beatrice Ford asked for a meeting with Danny. She was brought up to speed on how fast Jake's Place was moving. Beatrice offered to pay for the entire new apartment complex that was underway, no matter what the cost. Danny thanked her and told her that when the apartment complex was completed, they were going to invite her back to Jake's Place to cut the ribbon, and they were going to name the apartment complex Beatrice's Place. She started crying and gave Danny a big hug. She said that if she were just a few years younger, she would chase Danny all around the eight thousand acres. They both laughed.

The next thing Danny knew, it was April 1, and he and Candy were at Disney World. They spent one day at Epcot, one day at Universal, and two days in bed, making love. Danny and Candy had grown so close to each other that it was hard being apart for any period of time. They both were looking forward to living at Jake's Place and starting a family of their own.

Candy was going to Miami with her team to investigate a notorious gang and their drug dealings. She would be gone from April 5 to 9 and would then give her thirty-day notice to the FBI.

On the fifth, Candy left for Miami, and Danny and Vince picked up their new customized sixteen-passenger Lear jet. Vince flew the new plane, and Danny flew the old plane back to Montana.

Candy's team did not report in to headquarters for two days. They did not answer calls from their supervisor. It was customary for every team to call in once a day and give reports. The FBI sent an agent to Miami to locate them. They were investigating a gang called the Lobos. When the agent arrived in Miami, headquarters called him and told him to report to the Miami Beach Police Department immediately.

When he arrived, a detective took him to a crime scene, where they had discovered three bodies. It was Roy Mercer, Bill Jackson, and Candy. All three of them had been tortured and murdered. Candy had been gang-raped. Her breasts and hands had been cut off.

The two men had been castrated and beheaded. One of the agents' scrotum was stuffed in Candy's mouth. There was a note at the scene that read, "Don't fuck with us." The remains of the bodies were flown back to the FBI's morgue for a detailed autopsy.

On April 10, the director of the FBI got in touch with the agents' families and explained the circumstances.

Danny was devastated. All he could do was cry and vomit. Becky and Rudy tried to comfort him, and he simply asked to be left alone. Danny was told he could pick Candy's remains up on the twelfth. On the eleventh, he called General Smith and explained what happened. He wanted to know if the general could set up a meeting with him and the director on the twelfth so he could get the full details of what happened.

The general set up the meeting at 2:00 p.m. on the twelfth between Danny, the General, the director, the assistant director, and Candy's supervisor.

Danny asked the director to tell him all he knew and not to spare any details, that he was a seasoned combat veteran with SEAL Team Six and had seen it all. They brought out all the gruesome, graphic photos: Candy with her breasts and hands cut off and a scrotum stuck in her mouth; pictures of the castrated, beheaded male agents; many pictures of the bloody crime scene; the note that read, "Don't fuck with us."

Candy's supervisor told Danny all he knew about the gang, that they were suspected in the murders. They were called the Lobos. They had about three hundred members and were located in Miami, in an area called Little Pecos. There were six other chapters of the gang located in Los Angeles, Houston, Atlanta, New York City, Chicago, and Detroit. The gang had been established about twenty-five years ago in Los Angeles. They were of mixed backgrounds but were mainly Mexicans, Cubans, and Haitians. The leader of the Miami's gang was Pueblo Martinez. His three lieutenants were Manny Sanchez, Jose Fents, and Jorge Benitez

The gang was ruthless and well organized. They were heavily involved in human smuggling, prostitution, drugs, and money laundering. They were responsible for many rapes and murders. All vested members had a tattoo of a two-headed dragon on their left forearm. Over one hundred Lobos from Miami were currently behind bars, serving sentences for various crimes, including murder, rape, extortion, human trafficking, and drug distribution.

Danny was shown pictures of the four leaders and a dozen gang members all having the double-headed dragon tattooed on their left forearm. He was shown the blood-stained note that read, "Don't fuck with us." Their motto was kill or be killed.

Pueblo Martinez had a girlfriend by the name of Maria Fluentez. She was beautiful, and they had lived together for six years but were not married.

Candy's supervisor was Joe Jacobson. He was a senior FBI agent. Joe showed Danny a picture of one of the gang members leaving the crime scene approximately twelve hours after the murders. It was taken from a video camera on a store across the street. The video did not capture any other picture of anyone entering or leaving the crime scene twenty-four hours before or after the crime. Danny asked if he could have a copy of the picture, and the director said no!

The crime scene, an old abandoned warehouse, was still secure as the investigation was ongoing. Danny was told that it was very rare for any of the gang members to travel alone. They usually traveled in packs of at least three and were always heavily armed.

Joe told Danny that they would find out who was responsible and prosecute them. In fact, he was going to the crime scene tomorrow and would be there with several other agents for two days.

Danny looked at the FBI director and asked if he could meet Joe there to examine the crime scene himself. The director told Danny that was against FBI policy. The director looked at the general, and the general nodded. The director told Danny they would make an exception for him, but he would have to be with Joe at all times while on the crime scene.

Danny asked them if they found any personal belongings that was removed from Candy's body. They said no—nothing but some tattered clothing. Danny thanked the director, the deputy director, the general, and Joe. He shook their hands and asked for a few minutes with Joe. Both the director and the general told Danny not to get involved in the investigation and by no means be a vigilante and try to exact revenge on any of the gang members.

Danny met with Joe for half an hour. Joe was leaving in the morning for Miami and planned on being at the crime scene around 2:00 p.m. He gave Danny the address.

Joe told Danny what an exceptional FBI agent Candy was, how well she got along with all her fellow agents. They had big plans for her. Joe told Danny that she had told him all about her husband. "Every time she would talk about you, her eyes would light up, and a big smile would break out on her face. She was deeply in love with you. You were her hero."

Danny told Joe he was taking her remains back to Wisconsin today. He had his own plane and would meet him tomorrow around 2:00 p.m. at the crime scene. He was going to have his dad start the funeral arrangements, and the funeral would be on the eighteenth.

Joe said that he would like to attend the funeral and knew there were other agents who would also like to attend, if Danny didn't have a problem with it.

Danny said, "I am sure Candy would want that. You and any of her coworkers are welcome. I will give you the details later." They exchanged cell numbers, and Danny said, "Thanks, Joe. I will see you tomorrow."

Joe shook his hand, gave him a big hug, and said, "I am so sorry!"

Danny took the remains and flew back to Rhinelander. Happy and Sally were going to make the funeral arrangements. Sally had already called Candy's brothers, who in turn notified other friends and relatives.

The funeral would be at the mansion. It would be a closed casket. Sally would see that the appropriate pictures of Candy would be properly placed around the room and that plenty of chairs and food would be there. They would make all the arrangements. Danny said he wanted four bagpipers there playing religious music. He wanted "Amazing Grace" and "Danny Boy," her favorite songs, played numerous times. The funeral would be schedule for the eighteenth.

That gave them five days to make all the arrangements. Danny would write her obituary before he left for Miami tomorrow morning.

Danny and Candy had agreed that when they died, they would be cremated. Half of their ashes would be buried with their family, and the other half would be buried together at Jake's Place.

The next morning, Danny called Rudy and filled him in with his schedule. He told him the funeral date and to have Vince fly him, Becky, and the kids to Rhinelander.

Danny said, "Is there anything I need to know?"

Rudy said, "Nothing that can't wait, but the admiral called. He had heard about Candy. He said he had some news but it could wait. He didn't want to bother you in your time of mourning. He sends his condolences and prayers."

Danny then flew to Miami to meet Joe. He rented a van at the airport and arrived at the crime scene an hour early. The cops would not let him past the yellow tape. He told them he was to meet Joe Jacobson from the FBI.

They said, "I think he's in the warehouse. Let me go get him."

Joe was early also and came outside to let Danny in. He gave him a big badge to hang around his neck with his name on it that said FBI.

Joe explained to Danny the crime scene, where each body was found, and the position they were found, which were shown by the chalked outlines. He showed him the entrances and exits to the warehouse. The local detectives and the FBI had covered the whole warehouse, fingerprinting and gathering clues.

Joe introduced Danny to the lead detective from Miami Vice. His name was Dean Hercules. He was 6 feet, 3 inches and weighed about 270 pounds, and he was solid muscle. When he shook Danny's hand, it was like placing it in a vise. Dean's hands were twice the size of Danny's. His nickname was Herc. He said, "Just call me Herc."

Herc was told that Danny was the husband of the female victim. Herc put his huge arm around Danny and said, "Man, I'm so sorry." Herc reminded Danny of Sergeant Rock, only bigger.

Danny asked Joe if he could take some pictures and Joe said, "Go ahead." After Danny took a bunch of pictures, he walked outside at the rear of the warehouse. There were several alleys going in different directions, leading to other old buildings. Danny turned on patch 2 power vision and was looking inside adjacent buildings. There was one building about two blocks away that had a heavy steel door with no handles or locks. As he looked inside the door, it was locked and bolted from the inside. There was a cache of arms, pistols, rifles, explosives, and thousands of rounds of ammo. There were five gang members with double-headed dragons tattooed on their forearms. They were drinking beer, smoking pot, and playing poker.

Just then Joe yelled at him to come back. Joe said, "Don't wander off like that alone. You might be the next victim."

Danny and Joe were staying at the same hotel and agreed to have dinner that night at seven thirty in the hotel restaurant. They had a famous steak restaurant inside called the Prime Cow; it was supposed to be great. They had dinner, and Joe gave him a large brown envelope that weighed a couple of pounds. Joe said, "Don't open it until you are in your hotel room, and for Christ's sake, don't lose it. You don't know where it came from. I could lose my job over this. I know more about you than you might think. After all, I am a senior FBI agent, and I have my sources. I feel somewhat responsible for the loss of my three field agents. I am the one who sent them down here to gather recon. I am doing this for Candy. So please keep this to yourself. If I can do anything else for you, call me. Don't discuss any of this or any other confidential matters over the phone. We will set up a meeting where there is only the two of us." Joe shook Danny's hand. "I will see you at Candy's funeral."

When Danny got back to his hotel room, he opened the envelope. There were pictures of all four leaders of the Miami Lobos, a picture of Pueblo's girlfriend and the guy caught on video. There were other pictures of known gang members and their names. There were questionable addresses where some of them might live. They rotated addresses a lot. The name and address of a marina where the Lobos docked a large boat that they used in smuggling humans and drugs. Two Lobos lived on the boat, and the boat's name was *High Times*. Every Thursday, around 10:00 a.m., *High Times* would leave the marina with six Lobos, and they would go fishing in the ocean.

There were names of bars, restaurants, and clubs where they hung out. There also was an address to their main clubhouse. They owned many old warehouses, titled in many fake corporation names.

The envelope was stuffed full of this kind of information. The Lobos were very organized and ruthless. They had cops and judges on their payroll. They had the best criminal attorneys on retainers. They had banks laundering money, and they had their own comptroller.

Tomorrow was Wednesday, and Danny had to leave on Friday, as the funeral was on Saturday. Happy knew Danny would not be home until Friday afternoon. Wednesday morning Danny spent in the Little Pecos area, checking out some of the addresses he was given. He set his eye on patch 2 power vision and scoped out a lot of the places. He saw a lot of Lobos and took many notes. He actually saw Pueblo and his girlfriend in one of the bars.

Danny went to a hardware store and bought some tools and a toolbox. He bought a propane blowtorch, some duct tape, ten large black Magic Markers, rope, and a chainsaw. He also bought some painter's canvas cloth. He then went to a marine store and bought a fishing rod and reel and a large strong fish gaff with a sharp pointed edge. He also bought a bait casting net.

Danny then went to a different marina and leased a forty-foot fishing boat with twin 300 outboards. He leased the boat for three days. It was $1,000 a day plus fuel and cleaning with a $3,000 deposit. He gave the owner $7,000 in cash and a fake driver's license. The owner was all smiles and went over a few of the features. Danny said he would pick the boat up at 7:00 a.m. Thursday morning. Danny made sure the boat had a ladder that he could hook up to the rear transom and use to climb in and out of the boat. Then Danny went back to another hotel just in case Joe was still in the area.

Thursday morning, Danny was up at 5:00 a.m. He had already spread the painter's canvas cloth on the floor of the van. He stopped at a coffee shop, got some coffee and donuts, and headed to the marina to pick up his fishing boat. The owner took him for a trial run yesterday and gave him the keys. The boat was full of gas, and the owner told Danny to have the boat back by Saturday night.

Danny got one of the marina's pull boys with wheels and loaded all the gear from the van. He covered everything up with extra painter cloths, so the only thing you could see was the fishing pole.

Danny covered the deck of the boat with six large painter cloths and laid out all his equipment and headed to the marina where the *High Times* was berthed. Danny was about forty minutes away. When he arrived near the marina, he stayed about eight hundred yards out. Danny was throwing out a casting net like he was trying to catch bait fish. He turned his eye to patch 2 power vision and scoped out *High Times*. There were two gang members on the boat, placing fishing poles in all the rod holders and doing various fishing chores. In about fifteen minutes, four more gang members came, wheeling in three cases of beer and lots of ice and boxes of fried chicken.

They unloaded all the goods and were laughing and high-fiving one another. In twenty minutes, they cast off the lines and were on their way to go ocean fishing. As they drove by Danny throwing out his bait catching net, they gave him the finger and said "You dumb bastard, we bought our bait fish!" and laughed. Danny let them get quite a bit away from him as his boat was twice as fast as theirs and much smaller. Once *High Times* was well into open waters, with no other boats around, Danny opened up the throttles and closed the gap. He followed them another forty minutes, and now they could barely see the distant shore. There were no other boats in the area, so now was the time. Danny opened up to full throttle, and when he got within fifty yards, he put his eye into patch 3 heat mode. He burned six gaping holes in *High Times*, all right below the water line. The boat sank within five minutes, and the only thing left were the six Lobos flailing in the water, screaming for help. Danny now put his eye in patch 5 laser mode. He drove the boat right into the middle of the screaming Lobos.

Danny hollered at them, "The only way you can get on this boat is by climbing up this ladder, one at a time!" Danny showed them the ladder and placed it on the rear transom. The first Lobo climbed into the boat, and Danny clocked him on the back of his head with the butt of his pistol. He hit the deck and was out cold. The second Lobo was about to get on the boat, and Danny shot him right between the eyes. Danny then put the laser on the remaining four and shot them in the head. All five were dead and floating in the water.

Danny dragged the live one down below and tied him up and secured him to a table with the rope he had brought. He blindfolded him and wrapped six layers of duct tape around his head and mouth. He was still unconscious.

Danny went back upstairs and grabbed the fishing gaff. He gaffed the floating Lobos and dragged them aboard. It was hard work, a lot of dead weight, but Danny was up to the task. He piled them all on the painter's cloth. Danny looked all around and still saw no boats in the area.

He started up the chainsaw and cut the left forearm off each Lobo at the elbow. All had the double-headed dragon. He pushed each body through the transom hatch door and into the ocean. They were all bleeding like slaughtered hogs. Shark bait. Danny started the boat and moved several miles away, leaving the Lobos for the sharks.

Danny went down below, where the surviving Lobo was now conscious and scared shitless. He must've heard the chainsaw. Danny said to the Lobo, "We are in the middle of the ocean, and no one is around, so no one can hear us." He then opened up his toolbox and took out a large pair of very sharp wire cutters and the propane blowtorch.

Before Danny tied him up, he stripped him naked. He had his hand and arms stretched over the table and tied own. His waist and legs were secured to the chair and table. The table itself was secured to the bulkhead, so neither the table or the Lobo could move.

Danny told the Lobo he was going to remove the duct tape and ask him some questions. "If I think you are lying, I will cut off one of your fingers and heat up your balls with this blowtorch." Danny lit the blowtorch and grinned. He then removed the duct tape. This guy was scared shitless, and he should be.

Danny pulled out the picture of Pueblo and asked him if he knew who he was. The Lobo said, "No!"

Danny took the wire cutters and cut his little finger off at the knuckle and put the blowtorch to his balls. The Lobo was screaming at the top of his lungs. Blood was gushing all over the place, and his balls were on fire.

Danny then took a picture of Manny Sanchez and asked him if he knew who he was, and the Lobo again said, "No!"

Danny cut another finger off and held the blowtorch to his balls a little longer. The Lobo was about to pass out in pain. He was screaming and crying at the same time. There was now blood squirting all over Danny and the boat. The guy's balls were blue, and he was in pure agony.

Danny said, "We are going to try again, and if you lie, I will cut the rest of your fingers off and set your cock and balls on fire. If you cooperate with me, I will let you live. If you don't, I will torture you unmercifully until you die in pain."

The Lobo said, "No more please. I will tell you anything you want to know." Danny pulled out the picture of Pueblo, and he identified him as Pueblo Martinez, leader of the Lobos. Danny then pulled Manny's picture, and he identifies him as Manny Sanchez. And so it went.

The Lobo identified the picture Danny had of the guy they got on video. He was Pueblo's brother. He identified everyone Danny had pictures of. He gave Danny addresses—or at least street names of where most lived.

Then Danny said, "This is your last question, and if you want to live, you will give me the correct answer. We have already been given the names, so if your answer doesn't jive with what we already have, you are a dead man. Give me the names of the Lobos who killed the three FBI agents last week."

He couldn't get it out fast enough. "Pueblo Martinez, Jorge Benitez Felipe Caracas and a guy simply known as Rocco."

Danny said, "And what is your name?"

He said, "Michael Mendez."

"How many members are in your gang in Miami?"

Michael said, "Approximately three hundred, but I don't know them all."

"Where do most of them hang out?"

He gave Danny the name of two bars, a nightclub, and the address of their clubhouse headquarters. Danny then asked for each member's name that was on this fishing trip. Michael Mendez gave him all their names. Danny was writing all the information down as well as recording it.

Danny said, "Two more questions, and I will let you live and drop you off at a hospital before you bleed to death. First question: when is your next big drug shipment and where?"

Michael said, "It is Wednesday, the twenty-second, at some marina in Key Largo. It's coming from Mexico, and it's big. That's all I know."

"Last question. What's the Lobos' motto?"

Michael said, "Kill or be killed."

Danny said, "If you insist." And he shot him between the eyes." Danny untied him and took him up top and started up the chainsaw. He cut his left forearm off and stacked it with the rest. Then he said, "What the hell. I am going to need the practice." He then cut his other arm off then both his legs at the knees. Then he cut his head off and said, "That was for Candy." He then threw his arms, legs, head, and torso into the ocean and said, "Come and get it, boys."

Danny laid all the forearms in a row on the painter's cloth, hosed them down, and dried them off. Danny let them bake in the hot sun for an hour while driving back to the marina. Danny threw all the tools and drop cloths full of blood overboard. He had two drop cloths left and a burlap bag.

Before turning the boat back in early, he took out the large Magic Markers and wrote different sayings on each forearm: "You fucked with the wrong guy," "I will be back," "Kill or be killed," "Pueblo, you're next," "Your boys sleep with the fishes," "Candy sends her love."

Danny wrapped the forearms in a drop cloth and put them in a burlap sack. Danny hosed the boat down, cleaned up the blood, and wrote the owner a note: "Fishing was great, got seasick, and decided to go home early. Thanks. The keys are where you told me to leave them. Keep the deposit."

It was now 5:00 p.m. It took Danny all day to do his job. He now drove the van to the address of the Lobos' main headquarters and threw each forearm out of the van's front window, one at a time, scattering them all over that block. Danny went back to his hotel, had some supper and two stiff drinks at the bar, and went to bed. He was up at 5:00 a.m. Friday morning. He took the van to a car wash, cleaned it up, threw all the drop cloths and burlap bag away, dropped the rental van off, and was in the air by 7:00 a.m. and was home by 11:00 a.m.

All the funeral arrangements had been made. Rudy, Becky, Candy's brothers, and the general were already at the mansion. Paying respects and remembrance of life was from 10:00 a.m. to 2:00 p.m. The service was from 2:30 to 3:30 p.m. At 3:45 p.m. there would be a thirteen-gun salute by the five Navy SEALs. Food and cocktails were served from 4:00 to 7:00 p.m.

At 10:00 a.m. the mansion was packed and stayed packed all through the day until 7:00 p.m. The line to pay last respects at the closed casket was a hundred people deep all day long. They had put folding chairs all along the line so some of the older people could sit. Some of the special guests were brought directly to the casket to pay their respects as they couldn't stay for the service.

In attendance were the governors of Wisconsin and Montana, Admiral Matthews, General Smith, the director of the FBI, Joe Jacobson and ten other FBI agents (who all flew in on an FBI jet), two senators, Harry Swigs, Beatrice Ford, the five SEALs whom Danny graduated with (Dave Matthews, Tom Akins, Billy Kennedy, Bones O'Hara, and Hank Armstrong), Captain Rusty Miller from the yacht, Bryce Cannon, their attorney, and Hugh McFarland (their banker). Both were from Bison. Richard Appleby, the developer of Jake's Place, flew in from Denver. Dr. Bennett, Barry Wise, and Bonnie Olson, Jake's widow also came. All of Candy's and Danny's friends were there. Candy's brothers from Milwaukee and what seemed to be half the town of Rhinelander were also there.

Four bagpipers and an organist played music all day. When the service ended at 3:30 p.m., everyone went outside to witness the five SEALs dressed in their dress blues with all their medals, preforming a thirteen-gun salute. With the admiral barking the commands and the bagpipers playing "Amazing Grace," the salute began. The admiral commanded, "Order, arms." The SEALs aimed their rifles to the sky. The admiral ordered, "Fire," and all rifles fired. The order was given by the admiral twelve more times, honoring Candy with a thirteen-gun SEAL salute. The FBI agents, along with the director and General Smith, stood at attention while saluting as the SEALs fired their weapons.

The admiral then ordered, "Arms, rest." The rifles went silent. Everyone saluted the heavens as the bagpipers continued to play "Amazing Grace" and finished up with "Danny Boy," Candy's favorite song. Everyone mingled for the next three hours, talking, eating, and drinking.

Danny took Joe Jacobson to his study for a private talk. Danny said, "Joe, do not ask me any questions. I stayed until Friday morning. Sorry I lied to you, but I didn't want anybody in my way. Thank you for all the information you gave me. It was very helpful. There is a really big drug deal taking place at a marina in Key Largo on Wednesday, the twenty-second. Drugs are coming from Mexico. Cash will change hands, and the drugs will be delivered to the Lobos. Here are the names of the unidentified gang members you had pictures of but no names for. I have the names of the four members who murdered and butchered Candy and the two FBI agents. You cannot have their names at this time. I have plenty more information, but that's all I can tell you at this time. Six of the Lobos swim with the fishes."

Joe opened his mouth, and Danny said, "No questions. I will explain later." They shook hands and returned to the wake.

Joe told Danny he knew he was seeking revenge and told Danny the director also knew it. The director knew more about Danny than he might think. The director was very close to Admiral Matthews and General Smith. "I think you should take him into your confidence, explain to him what has taken place, and don't withhold any details. I think you will gain a friend with much power and influence. He can give you much more information than I can. He can help you gain your revenge and could be of great assistance with Jake's Place.

He really liked Candy and had big plans for her. He envisioned her becoming the first female assistant FBI director."

Danny thanked Joe and asked him if he thought the director would support him or limit him. Joe said, "He would definitely support you, especially if he trusted you. He has the same goal as you. He wants to destroy the Lobos, but his hands are tied in how he can go about it. You should meet with him and discuss what you have done in detail. He will not try to stop you but will give you some confidential advice."

The director's name was James Buchannan, and he was one of the most powerful people in America. His nickname with his close associates was JB. Danny thought about it. He trusted Joe and figured JB already knew about his powers and abilities, so why not take him into his confidence and create another powerful ally?

Danny found the director and invited him into his study for a confidential talk. Danny told JB about the upcoming drug deal between a Mexican cartel and the Lobos. He then in graphic detail told the director everything he had done the past four days. He told him about his magical eye and what he could do with it, what his goal was at Jake's Place, and how he was trying to convince Admiral Matthews to establish a US-based SEAL unit at Jake's Place to fight terrorism and drugs within the United States.

The director listened intensely, and a small grin broke out on his face. "I will deny hearing any of this. You have my support. I would like to have a meeting with you within the next ten days." The director gave Danny a piece of paper with his private cell number and said, "Call me if you get in any trouble before our meeting. If you by any chance run into or are arrested by local officials, you tell them that you are an undercover agent for the FBI and have them call me directly. I also can help you with Jake's Place and should be able to influence the admiral's decision about your special SEAL unit."

Danny said, "Mr. Director, I am glad I talked with you. Thank you for your support."

The director said, "From now on, call me JB."

At 7:00 p.m. the crowd disappeared, and all those staying at the mansion went to bed. On Sunday, the admiral, the five SEALs, Rudy, and Danny met all day long. The admiral controlled the meeting and thanked all the seals for their dedicated service. He told them that they were a special lot and he was working on their proposal and was making some great headway. If they could put this unit together, only a handful of people would know of their existence. He asked each one of them if they were sure they wanted to be attached to this very special unit. They could not share any information about any of their missions with anyone, including family members. "And yes, that includes your wives."

Their missions would be authorized by a panel of five people: himself, General Smith, the director of the FBI, the director of the CIA, and the Homeland Security chief. They would be given unlimited support and pretty much a free hand to accomplish their missions.

The admiral then asked each SEAL their thoughts and suggestions. After each SEAL spoke, the admiral asked, "Are there any more questions?" He then told the SEALs they were on thirty days' leave, starting tomorrow. He had spoken to each unit commander and cleared the way.

They were to gather up their families and go to Jake's Place. While there, they were to spend time at the proposed SEAL complex and come up with suggestions of the design and construction of the complex: buildings, training facilities, airstrips, helicopter pads, hangars, outbuildings, new homes to be constructed in the complex, barracks, security, and anything else they could think of. They would have a thirty-day access to a naval plane and helicopter and their pilots. He wanted them to learn the whole terrain of Jake's Place and the entire vicinity of two hundred miles surrounding Jake's Place.

The admiral told them to keep all receipts for any money they spent on anything for the next thirty days and they would be reimbursed by the Navy. The admiral scheduled a meeting for May 15, 2003 at Jake's Place for everyone in this room.

The admiral then dismissed the meeting and told everyone to enjoy their thirty days' leave. He said, "By the way, I am proud of each and every one of you. America owes you a great deal of respect and gratitude."

The admiral and Danny then had an hour-long private meeting with just the two of them.

By Monday morning, everyone had left the mansion, except for Rudy, Becky, and the kids. Danny and Rudy met all day Monday. Danny filled him in on the Lobos, not holding back any of the details. He told Rudy he was going back to Miami tomorrow to finish his business with the Lobos. Should anything happen to him, he showed Rudy where the half billion in cash was hidden, and he made Rudy promise that he would see that Jake's Place became a reality.

Rudy tried to talk him out of going back to Miami, but Danny said, "It's something I have to do—for both Candy and me."

On Tuesday, April 21, 2003, Rudy went back to Jake's Place, and Danny flew back to Miami with lots of hardware to visit his friends the Lobos.

About the Author

Daniel John Garber was born in Louisville, Kentucky, on December 9, 1945. After spending his young adult life in Northern Wisconsin, he joined the US Navy and served two tours of duty in Vietnam. Shortly after being honorably discharged from the Navy, he started a very successful plastics company. At the age of fifty, he sold his business, retired, and traveled the world. Later in life, he became a licensed auctioneer and started an auction company. At age seventy, he decided to become an author. His first book was his autobiography, titled *Garber's Bench*. *The Eye of the Seal* is his second book, and he is currently working on his third book, titled *Jake's Place*.

Dan's philosophy in life has always been "The harder you work, the luckier you get." He is currently married to his third wife, Barbara. He has three daughters, Brandi, Mandy, and Lindsay. He has two grandchildren, Lily and Luke.

CPSIA information can be obtained
at www.ICGtesting.com
Printed in the USA
BVHW01s1025260818
525628BV00005B/68/P

9 781642 987546